By the same author

Fiction

Bunco

Empress

All Visible Things

The Dance We Danced

A Cold Dish & Other Tales *(Short stories)*

Non-fiction

Words For the Wise *(Quotations for students)*

The 50 Wealthiest People of All Time

Books to Inspire Young People Series:

   100 Amazing Lives, *Volume I: From Pharaohs to Shakespeare*

   100 Amazing Lives, *Volume II: From Newton to Malala*

   An Amazing ABC of People, Places & History That Make Great Britain Great

   The Amazing Worlds of Myth and Imagination

All available from Amazon:

   France: https://tinyurl.com/BMPFrance

   UK: https://tinyurl.com/BMPUnitedKingdom

   USA: https://tinyurl.com/BMPUSA

See endpapers for information about each of these titles.

MURDER
IN
MONPAZIER

Brian McPhee

EP

Published by Entente Publishing

www.ententepublishing.com

hello@ententepublishing

CONTENTS

FOREWORD

A Reminder of a Strange Time

This story opens in the picturesque village of Monpazier in southwest France, on March 5, 2022, during what would turn out to be the final convulsions of the COVID pandemic. On January 24 the official digital health pass (required for entry to bars, restaurants and much else) had been upgraded to require a recent vaccination. Anyone failing a COVID test was required to isolate. Masks were required in most settings.

A Word on French Officials

The senior elected official in a French village, the mayor, is properly, when a woman, *'Madame le maire'*. She works in a building called *'la mairie'*. Even a small village of around 500 people, like Monpazier, has a Mairie. For the convenience of English-speaking readers, I have chosen to capitalise the Mairie.

French towns and cities have their own police forces. Rural areas and villages (like Monpazier) are cared for by *gendarmes* who work for a semi-military uniformed national force called the *Gendarmerie*, out of a building with the same name. UK/US equivalents to Gendarmerie ranks are shown in this table:

FRANCE	UK	USA
Capitaine	Inspector or Chief Inspector	Captain
Adjudant	Sargeant	Sargeant
Gendarme	Constable	Police / Patrol Officer

While the *Gendarmerie* does distinguish between detective and general duty roles, there is no distinction in titles (i.e. there is no equivalent to Sargeant / Detective Sargeant).

A *Capitaine* in charge of investigating a case will work in a *Brigade de recherches* (BR), an investigative unit or a *Section de recherches* (SR), a major crime unit. He or she initially operates under the direction of a *Procureur* (prosecutor) unless and until the case is handed to a *Juge d'instruction* (judge) at which point both are involved – in addition to senior officers in the Gendarmerie of course.

A *Notaire* is a form of public service lawyer who handles non-contentious legal matters like conveyancing, preparing straightforward wills, drawing up rental agreements and so on. *Notaires* commonly act for both parties involved, seeking to achieve a fair outcome for both parties.

MONPAZIER

In the plan below, you can see the alleyways, called *carreyrous,* running behind many of the village streets.

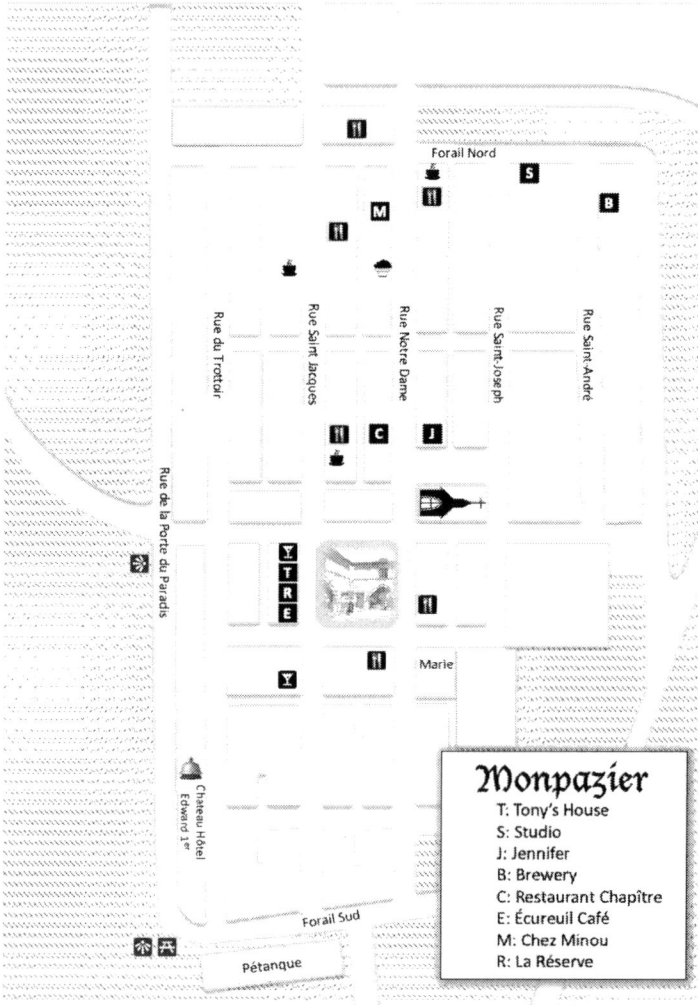

Monpazier
T: Tony's House
S: Studio
J: Jennifer
B: Brewery
C: Restaurant Chapître
E: Écureuil Café
M: Chez Minou
R: La Réserve

Saturday, March 5, 2022

In the cool, silent house, rigor mortis set in quickly, and the flies slowly. The scene would not have been out of place in a graphic novel. It had everything. Handsome corpse. Check. Macabre pool of blood. Check. Contorted limbs. Check. Crime scene bathed in a haunting glow. Ominous, foreboding shadows. A death scene lifted from film noire. Check. Check. Check.

But the final tragedy of Tony Grant's life in art was that he was no longer around to capture the singular scene of his own demise.

The old-fashioned streetlamp mounted outside the window bathed the room in otherworldly orange-yellow hues. Not one of the locals who passed by in the night had been sufficiently nosey to peer in through the street-level windows, although one or two did notice the cat perched on the window ledge. The cat had been at first perplexed, then irate, when Tony failed to respond to her appeals for her food. The cat didn't belong to Tony, even in the laughable sense that people who pay vet bills like to think they own a cat; but he was in the habit of feeding this one a late supper each evening when he was home. Not tonight though.

Nor any other night ever again.

* * *

1985 – Glasgow

"How much does it cost?"

The young librarian's head snapped up, a caustic response primed on her lips; she had been concentrating on an essential, but interminably tedious task; until this second, she had been oblivious to the unwelcome arrival. Her instant impression of the woman at the counter was of exhaustion; the careworn intruder stood in silent apology; a fading petal poised to fall at the slightest disturbance. She didn't seem terribly old; forty something, Amy supposed, but she looked unimaginably tired. Amy's irritation dissolved instantly and in a gentle tone the young librarian responded.

"I'm sorry; how much does what cost?"

The petitioner's eyes flickered uncertainly around the cavernous room.

"This, the library, the books. How much does it cost?"

"The library doesn't cost anything; it's free."

Amy waved an arm to encompass her domain, savouring once again that glow of pride that never failed to envelope her as she announced, "Every one of these books is already yours; they belong to all of us."

But the woman was clearly suspicious, unconvinced; so Amy persisted, determined to secure another convert.

"I promise; you don't need a penny. You can take out four books at a time, any books you want. You only pay if you keep the books longer than you should. If you bring them back in two weeks, it won't cost you anything at all."

As she said this, the librarian was discreetly assessing the two figures on the other side of the mahogany counter, polished over the decades by a million hands and books. The little boy looked to be about six; clean and tidy with a severe parting in his slicked-down hair. The hair was jet-black, but with a small flash of white above his right eye. Later she was to learn that the boy was coming up on his eighth birthday; poor diet had stunted his growth.

Dark blue mittens, hand-knitted from coarse wool, hung loosely at his side, dangling by the connecting ribbon running through the sleeves of his thin coat. Amy could just make out a long tear running up one sleeve, carefully repaired with a line of purposeful stitches. On closer examination, Amy realised that the woman wasn't as old as she had first assumed, possibly not much older than herself. Sallow, prematurely lined skin and uncared-for lank hair aged her, as did the enormous weight bearing down on her shoulders.

"Would you like to join? I only need your name and address, that's all. We're supposed to see a rent book but," she hurried along, "I think we can forget about that if you don't have it with you."

Even now, the woman was uncertain. Suddenly, her son's urgent enthusiasm tipped her into a decision.

"It'll be OK, Mum. I won't forget to bring them back, promise. Then it'll be free, won't it?" he finished, eager eyes beseeching the librarian's support.

Amy was the shiniest person the boy had ever been this close to. Even his teachers weren't as immaculately groomed as the angel behind the desk. She looked like the ladies he saw in the out-of-date magazines that his mother devoured. And the library lady would never shout at him or hit him or call him stupid; he just knew it. And she smelled … he didn't know of what, but something fresh, clean; this is what a princess would smell like.

"Yes, it will. So, it's you who wants to join, not mum?"

His mother, now resolved, took charge.

"I want him to join, so he can get books to help him. He's a great wee drawer, he really is."

Amy didn't quite follow this but wisely decided that further enquiry should be postponed.

"Here; here's a form; let's fill it in. Now, what's your name?"

"Tony, Tony Gallagher."

"Anthony?"

"Yes, I suppose."

"And what's your address, Tony?"

"43 Campbell Street."

"Campbell Street? That's not too far then. You'll be able to come whenever you want, won't you?"

In less than five minutes, Tony was proudly examining his new library card before showing it off to his mother.

"Look, Mum. It's got my name on it. And it's brand new. Look!"

Maggie took her son's hand and, with a shy nod of thanks to Amy, led him into the library.

Pointing to her left, the librarian directed them, "The children's section is over there."

Amy watched as mother and son made their way to the colourful children's stacks, laden with picture books, story books, every classic imaginable. She could see that the pair were being overwhelmed by the choices arrayed before them. As she took a first step to go to help them, Tony's excited voice reached her, magnified by the institutional silence, as he urgently pulled his mother further into the shelves.

"Here, over here, Mum."

They hurried over to the section Amy knew held books on art and painting and, of course, on drawing. *'A great wee drawer.'*

"You look and pick your books. I'll just sit over here while you do that, alright?"

"OK, Mum."

As Amy watched from the corner of her eye, Maggie Gallagher gratefully lowered herself onto the blonde wood chair, relieved to be sitting down at last. The walk to the library had exhausted her, even though it was less than half a mile and a trip she had made a thousand times to get to the shops. It had been weeks, perhaps a couple of months, that she had been feeling this way. Maybe it was time to see the doctor.

Maggie looked around the serene wood-panelled room. Perhaps she should think about joining herself? It had been years since she read a book, before she married Joe. How much idle time she had had back in the days before housework and motherhood consumed every waking moment. Still … maybe next time.

* * *

In the years to come, that day would replay in Tony's memory more times than he could begin to count. That first visit to the library was the last time he did anything with his mother, the last time she ventured outside their tiny second-floor flat. When at last they had returned home, Tony proud

4

and excited to be carrying his four library books, his mother had been happy to leave him at the kitchen table with his new treasures.

"I'm going to have a lie down. I'll get up to make lunch before Dad gets home."

It was Saturday, so Joe, Tony's father, worked only half a day and would be home around one. But Maggie was still sound asleep when Joe swept through the door, and she stayed in bed for the rest of that day, and all of Sunday. On Monday morning, Joe announced that Tony wasn't going to school.

"I need to go to work, so here's a note you've to take to the doctor. You know where that is, don't you?"

"Aye, of course. Next to the Co-op. Is Mum still not well?"

"Och, I'm sure she'll be fine. She's just very tired. The doctor'll come and see her. I expect he'll give her a tonic. You take that note at nine sharp, right?"

The doctor came that afternoon and within ten days Maggie knew she was dying of untreatable cancer. Of course, Tony was told nothing, just that his mother was sick, and that he needed to be quiet around the house, which he always was anyway. The good news was that he was kept off school so he would be available to bring his mum drinks of water or anything else she needed, which eventually included letting her put some of her weight on his young shoulders as she dragged herself to the toilet.

Tony hated school. Hated it and feared it. He found himself constantly perplexed, often with absolutely no idea what was going on. His classmates seemed to have some mysterious insight into what the teacher wanted. She would stand there, at the front of the class and demand the answer to the sum. Tony would try to shrink, to become invisible; but all too often his name would be called, and his eyes would immediately prick in anticipation. What sum? Had he been sleeping and missed the question? Was there some other way his classmates were understanding what she wanted? He desperately wished he could be let into the secret, because he was fed up being shouted at and worse, being despised and bullied for being a *'stupid, stupid boy'*. So not having to go to school was a huge treat, although he was worried about Mum, who didn't seem to be getting better. And he was having trouble with his drawings, well, his paintings actually. He could copy some of the pictures from the library books really well, Mum said, but there were efforts he didn't show her because he knew they weren't any good, and he couldn't understand why. He'd just have to keep trying, he decided.

5

* * *

On his second, unaccompanied, visit to the library, Amy watched as the boy flipped through one book after another, clearly looking for something specific.

"Can I help you, Tony? What is it you're looking for?"

For a moment, Tony was too shy to speak, but eventually, looking determinedly at his feet, he tried to explain.

"Well, Miss, I make copies of the paintings in the books. My mum says some are quite good, but a lot are really rubbish, and I don't know why."

"Can you show me one that you were able to copy?" she asked.

Tony picked up a book that he had borrowed two weeks ago and quickly found a painting he had enjoyed copying. His mum had made him pin it on the wall of her bedroom when he showed it to her. It was a painting by Turner, of Venice at dawn.

"That's a very nice painting, Tony. Now show me one you struggled with."

After another quick search, he showed her a page with Constable's famous *Haywain*.

"That's a more complicated picture; I can see why you found the shapes more difficult."

"No, no!" he interrupted, looking straight at her now. "It isn't the shapes, Miss; I can do them no bother; it's the colours and the…the *feel* of it I can't get."

The librarian thought for a moment.

"What do you paint with, Tony?"

A huge grin spread over the boy's freckled face.

"Santa brought me a paint box!" he proudly announced. "It has forty colours, although the blue is nearly finished," he ended with a worried look.

"And are the colours little squares and do you wet your brush with water to make them soft?"

"Yes; why? Am I doing it wrong?"

We can't always know when we inadvertently do something that will be seared in the memory of another person for the rest of their life. When a seemingly simple moment becomes an epiphany and is fixed, ever vibrant, in another's life story until its final chapter. Perhaps it is these moments that flash before our eyes as finally they dim forever.

And so, it was with no awareness of how much the simple gesture would mean to the young boy, that Amy reached out and ruffled Tony's hair.

"Not at all. You're doing very well. What you have are watercolours, and this painting," she was still cradling the book with the reproduction of Constable's painting open in her other hand, "this painting was made with oil paints, which are quite different. Come over here, to the grown-up section. You're allowed, you're with me."

She led Tony to the art section of the adult library and quickly pulled out two large format books, '*Watercolours for Beginners*' and '*How to Paint Landscapes, A Guide for Watercolourists*'.

"Here you go. You'll be able to copy the colours in these books, I think."

* * *

Only a few weeks later, on another Saturday, Tony stood patiently in his trench coat and, under protest, his scratchy balaclava. He held out a mittened hand as his father pushed two tightly folded pound notes under the wool and into his palm.

"This'll get you and Jeannie your tickets and an ice-cream. You hold Jeannie's hand and do what she tells you. And be a good boy. Now go and knock the door and let Jeannie know you're ready."

Tony was being packed off to the matinée with the 14-year-old girl from next door. He resented being forced to have a babysitter, but Jeannie was nice enough, although he had no intention of holding her hand any farther than the entrance to their close. He was glad to be going out, their cramped flat was jammed with too many whispering neighbours and the intimidating doctor.

As soon as he got home, his father hurried to help Tony shrug out of his outer clothes.

"Mum wants to see you. She might be sleeping, but just lie beside her, nice and quiet."

Tony climbed onto his mother's bed and lay his head on the pillow beside her. Her eyes were indeed closed, her face younger, less lined; she must be getting better, Tony decided.

Slowly, Maggie opened her eyes and her gaze settled on the face of her son. Fighting the cotton wool fog brought on by her medication, Maggie focused intently on her only child; the best thing, the one truly good thing, in her life. Her heart broke, but her love was boundless – she would not upset him. With a huge effort she spoke, voice barely above a whisper.

"How was the film?"

"Good. Well, quite good."

"I wanted to see you."

"What is it, Mum?"

"Nothing, I just wanted to see you."

She held his gaze with her pale eyes, blinking strangely slowly.

"I love you, son; you know that don't you?"

Tony squirmed a little but didn't break eye contact with his mother.

"I love you too, Mum. Are you getting better?"

But Maggie was sleeping again, her shallow breaths barely disturbing the air between them. Tony watched his mother until, after a few minutes, his dad gently touched his shoulder.

"Come on, we'll let her rest now."

Thirty minutes later, Maggie Gallagher, 26 going on 50, died.

* * *

There are days in the west of Scotland when it seems like the rain will never stop and you almost forget there was a time before the rain had started. On such a Sunday afternoon, the sky outside the rain-steaked windows a sombre leaden eiderdown, just two months after he had buried his wife, Joe Gallagher sat his young son down at the kitchen table. They were going to have a 'talk'. Joe had told Tony this yesterday, so the boy was curious and a little fearful. Despite Joe's ineffectual efforts to protect him from reality, the youngster knew that things had been difficult since Mum had died, and he guessed that the talk was connected with these problems.

Joe Gallagher wasn't a bad man. He was simply a terminally limited man – by his genes, his experience and his culture. He had struggled and failed to keep himself and his son fed, clean and presentable in a world that paid them little attention. He was lucky in just one regard; although he was only a labourer, he worked for the council, and so, as long as he kept turning up and working as hard or as slowly as the men around him, his job was safe, and steady. The foreman had shown some sympathy for Joe's situation, but that sympathy, and tolerance for late starts, was rapidly running out. Joe grasped that the situation was untenable. He had no living relations to turn to for help. And Maggie's only family was her mother in Fife, and she was in an institution where dementia was ravaging her brain.

Joe knew that Tony would have no worries about leaving behind familiar places and friends. Even Joe had enough insight to grasp the extent of his son's hatred of school, and to see that Tony seemed to have no friends. His obvious unhappiness meant the boy had closed himself off to everyone he encountered; there was no one or nothing he would miss from school.

And Joe had a plan.

The widow in the next close had already sent unmistakable signals that she was interested. There was no attraction or desire involved, simply a mutual recognition that there were benefits from being a couple. And Joe intuited that Tony was an unwanted complication.

"I've talked with Father O'Donnell. He's already been in touch with the Sisters, and you're going to go and live with them. By the seaside; that'll be good, won't it?"

The boy looked bemused.

"What do you mean, Dad? You mean for a holiday?"

For a moment Tony looked excited.

"No, no, not for a holiday. To stay. You're going to stay with the Sisters at Girvan. They'll look after you, send you to school an' that."

"But what about you, Dad? Are you coming too?"

"No, son, I'll be staying here. I cannae look after you right. Your mum did all the cooking and cleaning an' that. It'll be better."

"OK then."

A more perceptive man than Joe might have been concerned by the seeming ease with which Tony accepted this news. With the death of his mother, any chains that bound Tony to anything or anyone had been severed.

Except for Miss Johnson. By now Tony knew Amy's name and had developed an eight-year-old's crush on the young librarian who had continued to show interest and kindness to him ever since that first encounter. Miss Johnson was the only person Tony would miss when he went to Girvan. He had occasionally comforted himself with the thought that one day he would marry Miss Johnson, especially after she had ruffled his hair. That meant she liked him too.

So it was with a heavy heart that Tony went for his final weekly visit to the library to return his last books and say goodbye to Miss Johnson.

"I made this for you," he said shyly, after he had explained where he was going. "It was in one of the books you showed me. It's of a place called Ludlow Castle, by Turner. He's my favourite."

Slowly he handed her his painting. For an eight-year-old boy it was truly outstanding. He had captured the essence of Turner's superb landscape, with its lowering sky, haunting castle and picnic group accurately rendered. Before Amy could begin to thank him, Tony explained.

"I picked this one because it was really hard. And," he continued brightly, "it doesn't have many blues. My blues are all finished. Too many skies, I suppose."

To her surprise, Amy Johnson felt her eyes welling up. She quickly turned her head to collect herself before turning back to Tony as she reassured him.

"I'm sure you'll be able to get blues in Girvan. Thank you very much for this, Tony, this will be one of my treasures."

She admired the painting once more then exclaimed, "Just a minute, you haven't signed it! Proper artists always sign their paintings."

She handed him a pen and watched as the young artist carefully signed his name at the foot of the painting.

* * *

Sunday, March 6, 2022

Procureur Lenglet's phone rarely rang before noon on a weekend with good news.

"Yes, Commandant. What can I do for you?"

"Good morning, sir. I'm sorry to disturb you on a Sunday, but we have a suspicious death, an Englishman, an artist, Anthony Grant. As he seems to be rather famous, I thought we'd better take over the case immediately."

"Tony Grant? My God, I know him. Well, I've met him a few times. When did this happen? And why is it suspicious?"

"It seems to have occurred sometime last night, or in the early hours. CIC haven't been on the scene yet; they're on their way now to Monpazier from Périgueux. We'll have a better idea of the time of death later today. According to the mobile unit who responded, he either fell or was pushed from an internal balcony onto the stone floor below. So, it's suspicious until we decide which it was."

"Very well. Who are you assigning?"

"This is why I wanted to bring the case here, to Bordeaux. I'm proposing putting Capitaine Coman on the case."

"Coman? I don't know him. Why not Lalucq or the other one, the tall one?"

"Dubois is on paternity leave and Lalucq is up to his neck. But, even if I could shuffle things, Coman would be my choice for this case. He's relatively new to this office, but he came highly recommended, from Normandy. He handled a very sensitive case up there just last year; did a terrific job. And he speaks perfect English – his mother is English, and he's certain to have to deal with lots of expatriates, so I thought, in the circumstances…"

"Well, it's your call, Commandant, but I can't see why not. Keep me posted."

"I'll come and brief you as soon as I have anything useful to report."

Procureur Lenglet thought for a moment, then placed a call to Françoise Sandral, the on-call Juge d'instruction. No one liked to be surprised by a high-profile case. Sandral wouldn't much appreciate a call on a Sunday either, but it was the lesser of two evils as far as the Procureur was concerned.

* * *

Thomas studied the young woman across the desk. Around thirty he guessed. She still looked to be somewhat in shock; but he had to press on, but gently.

"I know you've already been over this with the other gendarmes, Lucy, but I need you to tell me all over again. I'm sorry, I know it's upsetting, and you won't have to do it again. Not today anyway."

The young woman's response was indistinct, tears and hysteria not far away.

"Are you French? You don't sound French."

The detective smiled.

"Yes, I'm French, but my mother is Welsh. That's why my first name is Thomas. Lots of Thomases and Dais and Gareths in the family. I spent my childhood between Wales and France."

Captain Thomas Comas was a true Celt. The genes of his Breton father and Welsh mother had combined to produce a classic example of his race – dark, short, broad and with an open, friendly face; a significant asset in his line of work. And he brought a rich baritone voice to his choir. Even if he did miss a lot of rehearsals.

He had pretty much decided that the young woman sitting across from him in the requisitioned office in the Mairie was a witness, not a suspect. Quite apart from her obvious distress, he had never encountered anyone who could faint on demand. When the responding gendarmes had arrived at the scene, they found Lucy slumped unconscious inside the unlocked front door of the victim's house. Indeed, for a moment they took her to be the victim, until a shake of her shoulder brought her around.

"Before you tell me what happened, perhaps you could tell me why you were visiting Mr Grant this morning?"

"I work for Amazon Video. We're making a documentary about Tony, Mr Grant. We were going to drive up to Domme this morning, to do some filming against the panorama. Tony thought it would make a dramatic backdrop. I have all the gear in my car, so I was picking him up to drive us."

"Was this the first day of filming?"

"God no! I've been here for three weeks, and we had at least another day or two of filming to go. And that's just in France. We were in Scotland, then London and we're supposed to be in New York next month. I suppose now…"

Thomas waited patiently until she regained control.

"Sorry."

"No need to apologise. What time were you scheduled to pick up Mr Grant?"

"Ten o'clock. He doesn't like to get up early. I knocked on the door a few times, but he didn't answer."

She stopped talking and looked at her feet.

Once again, Thomas waited, this time deliberately.

"I knocked four or five times. But he didn't come to the door. So, I let myself in."

"The door was unlocked?"

"No, I have a key." Lucy paused, and then her words came in a rush. "He gave me a key; in case I needed it. I often left my gear in the house, if we had been filming there. Having the key meant I could get it if I needed it, even if Tony was out."

"I see."

She was lying now, for the first time. Thomas decided to let it go for the moment.

"And you saw the body immediately?"

"No, not at first. There's a big armchair. It blocked the view of…of Tony until I stepped passed it."

Her voice rose and broke. "It was horrible! Blood. His head was – his neck was all bent."

Lucy dropped her head into her hands and wept uncontrollably.

Thomas carried tissues for occasions such as this. He handed the packet to the distraught young woman. When he judged she was ready, he gently asked her, "I have to ask you, Lucy, did you touch Mr Grant's body, perhaps to check if he was alive?"

"No, I could see. I mean, I could see he was dead. Oh God! The blood was everywhere, it was dry, and his eyes were open."

"That's fine. Enough about that. So, what did you do?"

"I went back to the front door. I thought I was going to faint. I needed fresh air and to get away from ... I called 112 and then I had to sit down. I think I passed out."

The mobile gendarmes had been on the scene in minutes. Pure luck, of course, they were already in the village, giving out parking tickets to make the quota. And clock up some Sunday overtime.

There was a knock on the door.

"CIC are at the scene, sir."

"Thanks."

He turned to Lucy.

"I have to go to Mr Grant's house. I need to talk with you a little more. Please stay here. One of the officers will bring you a coffee. I'll try not to be too long."

"Captain Coman, may I ask? Has anyone called Caroline, Tony's partner. To tell her I mean. She's in Bordeaux, or maybe in the air. She's flying to London this morning."

"Do you have a number for her?"

"Yes, I do."

"Good, please write it down on this card. Thank you."

* * *

Thomas pushed his way through the crowd that had formed around the house. Inside he found the scene of crime team already at work.

"Where's the Médecin Légiste?" he asked the first technician he encountered.

"On his way, Capitaine. He'll be here in – there he is!"

"Hi, Mic. Still off the smokes?"

Thomas and the pathologist had served together early in their careers. When Thomas had been offered the posting to Bordeaux, Mic was the first person he had called to sound him out about the unit and the senior officers.

"Don't ask, it's murder."

"You need some new material, Mic."

The pathologist pointed to two gendarmes who were having a conversation near the door.

"You two, masks on. All the time."

The two friends walked over to the corpse lying twisted, face down on the stone floor. They took one look, and then simultaneously lifted their eyes to the balcony above. From the ground floor, they could see only part of the upper floor. It was protected by a wooden balustrade, topped with a well-polished handrail.

The pathologist anticipated Thomas's question.

"Before you even ask, it's unlikely I'll to be able to tell you if he fell, jumped or was pushed until I get back to the lab, if then."

"I doubt he jumped. Not high enough to be absolutely certain. Looks like he landed headfirst – hard to do that deliberately."

"I'll just go back to bed, shall I? You seem to have this under control."

"Yeah, yeah. Can you give me height and weight before you leave? And Mic, check for head wounds sustained *before* he hit the floor."

"I never would of have thought of that," replied Mic, aggrieved. "I guess that's why you get the big bucks."

Thomas climbed the stairs. A fingerprint tech was already at work, dusting the handrail and balustrade directly above the dead man.

The balcony was much, much larger than was apparent from below. It wasn't a balcony at all, rather a large room that had one completely open wall, the balustraded opening giving onto the magnificent double-height room below. It was impressive.

The mezzanine, as Thomas now thought of the imposing space, had been fitted out like a games room in a gentleman's club. There was a splendid antique snooker table and cue rack, a large glass-fronted bookcase, a darts board and a pair of long leather sofas. Upholstered dining chairs were lined up along the wall behind the snooker table, presumably for spectators. Near the front was a low circular coffee table, with two inviting club chairs positioned around it. To the right as Thomas reached the top of the stairs, a door led further into the house and there was another door on the wall facing him.

At the far end of the balustrade one of the upholstered dining chairs was lying on its back. Two long scratches on the wooden floor provided graphic clues to what had occurred. A pair of leather slippers lay neatly near the legs of the fallen chair.

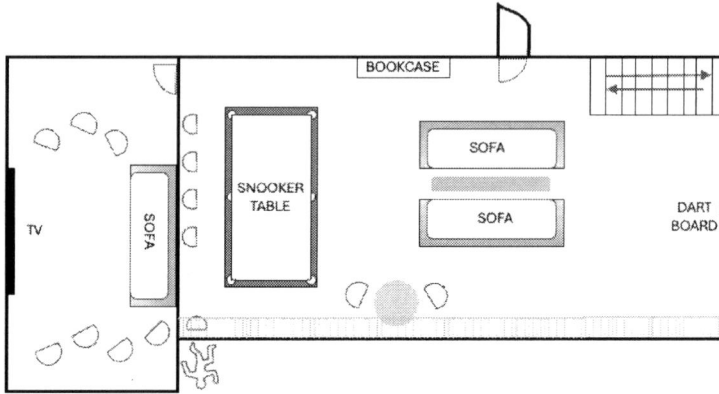

Thomas walked over to stand between the chair and the banister and looked over. The body lay directly below him.

As he approached the chair, Thomas noticed a painting hanging askew on the part of the wall that jutted out over the lounge below.

When he entered the second room, Thomas saw that it was dominated by a large TV mounted on the wall, opposite yet another leather sofa and several matching armchairs.

The other door opened onto a short corridor leading to a huge master suite. The bed was made; there was no clutter anywhere. It could have been a luxury hotel room, empty and awaiting the next guest. After a cursory look around, Thomas returned to the mezzanine and took in the expansive prospect. Everything he could see looked expensive, tasteful, curated – and spotless. There were an astonishing number of paintings on every wall, each served by a brass picture light.

His inspection was interrupted by an announcement from Mic, looking up from below. Thomas realised how high the upper floor really was, Mic must be well over four metres below him, maybe five.

"180 centimetres, around 86 kilos, maybe a little more. Fit, barely any fat."

Thomas looked around again. He was too new to this unit to recognise many of the CIC guys, even if they hadn't all been wearing masks. Soon after Thomas's arrival in Bordeaux in July, the country had gone into a new, post-lockdown phase of COVID restrictions. This time everything remained open, but passes were required pretty much everywhere, and of course, masks were still mandatory. An exception was made for the gendarmes when interviewing witnesses and suspects – it was difficult enough assessing people's veracity, without allowing them to hide behind a mask. But it had certainly interfered with the business of getting to recognise and know his new colleagues. Just like everyone else, Thomas was heartily sick of life under COVID restrictions.

"Mic, could you ask that guy over there to come up, please?"

Thomas was indicating one of the forensic team, the photographer who had just finished his work downstairs. The tech picked up his cameras and made his way upstairs.

"Before you start your work up here, could you just stand there for a moment. I'm guessing you're around 180 centimetres?"

"181, sir."

"That'll do. Stand against the balustrade, please. I'm sorry, what's your name?"

"Technician Jean-Pierre Gauvin, Capitaine."

The balustrade reached a fraction below the photographer's hip bone. People were shorter when this house was built, Thomas mused.

"What do you think, Gauvin? Think you could reach over to straighten that picture?"

"No, it's too high, sir."

Thomas slipped on a pair of evidence gloves and picked up one of the chairs standing against the wall, from the same set as the one lying toppled on the floor. He set the new chair against the balustrade and signalled to the gendarme.

"Careful now. Climb on and just reach out your hand, don't lean."

The gendarme did as he was sked.

Thamas continued, "Now don't do it, but if you *were* to lean, could you reach the painting to straighten it out?"

"Yes, I could. I wouldn't be at full stretch I reckon; the near corner is tilted away from me, so I'd have to snag it with a finger and pull it straight. But even so, it wouldn't be too hard. Want me to try, sir?"

"No thanks, Gauvin, I wouldn't want to lose you. And anyway, all that matters is that Grant *thought* he could reach it, not whether he could *actually* reach it. You can come down now, Gendarme. Thank you, I'll let you get on."

As Thomas came downstairs, he saw Mic signal to his assistants to bag up the body.

"Best guess?"

"Between nine and midnight. I'll pin it down a bit more at the lab."

"Périgueux will be all over this, Bordeaux, maybe even Paris. Can you get the lab to prioritise everything? I'll try but get Colonel Digne to place a call – it can only help."

"Will do. So, what's the verdict, Clouseau? Fall; or push?"

Thomas ignored the gibe.

"Everything points to a fall. He sees the wonky picture, can't stand it any longer – God knows it's been bugging me since I noticed it. He pulls the chair over and steps out of his slippers, because he's a neat freak. Steps up, leans over, the chair slides from under him and over he goes. Splat!"

"So why do I get the feeling you're not entirely convinced?"

"Look at this place."

Thomas swept his arm around to encompass the majestic space. "Have you ever seen a tidier room? And how many paintings are there? Fifty, sixty? And all perfectly hung, all with neat lights above. How did that one painting come to be crooked?"

"OK. So …"

But Thomas wasn't finished.

"And there's another thing that's bothering me. Look at the body. It's lying nearly a metre out from the balustrade, face down. Imagine, he's on the chair, leaning, but his centre of gravity is still inside the rail. Suddenly, the chair slides away and he's falling – straight down. His thighs, perhaps his knees, hit the balustrade and flip him, so maybe he lands more or less on his head, but with his hips still falling backwards. I think he should be lying on his back, legs pointing away from the balcony."

They both looked at the corpse, limbs straightened now by the lab assistants. It was still face down, feet pointing towards them as they stood, under the overhang.

Thomas took a quick tour of the rest of the house; he would be back for a thorough look. A corridor off the lounge led to a showroom kitchen, full of high-tech appliances, then to a small gym, a glazed conservatory, a shower room and guest cloakroom. Thomas opened another door in the corridor and discovered stairs down to a small cellar, professionally racked out and holding well over a hundred bottles of wine – fine Bordeaux for the most part. At the end of the corridor was the back door and another staircase leading up to a separate wing containing two other bedroom suites. It was an impressive house, and every room was immaculate, like a set staged for a magazine shoot. Thomas opened the back door and saw that it led out to the narrow *carreyrou* running behind the houses.

Before he left, he sought out the senior gendarme on duty, who turned out to be an athletic blonde woman.

"Adjudant, you can lock up as soon as the tech guys are done. Lock the shutters, lock and tape the doors and make sure the mobile units change their rotations, so someone passes here every hour until tomorrow morning. And make sure they check the tapes every circuit. Someone on the door full time from seven 'til seven until we're done with the scene. Understood?"

The gendarme gave him grateful smile. Most senior officers would have demanded an utterly pointless 24-hour guard on the door, Sunday or no Sunday.

"Yes, sir. Thank you, sir."

* * *

The victim's house was on the west side of the beautiful square at the heart of the almost perfectly rectangular village. The crowd of the curious and morbid had mostly dispersed of their own volition when they saw the ambulance leave with the body. Thomas left the square through one of the arches and walked down to a boulangerie where he ordered two croissants and two chocos. It was a bit late for breakfast, but he was famished.

When he arrived at the Mairie, he found the coffee machine and gave a silent prayer of thanks that it still held two cups of black coffee.

"Hello again, Lucy. I'm sorry you had to wait. I thought you might be hungry. Help yourself."

The young woman nodded her thanks and selected a chocolate croissant. Thomas followed her example and took a seat across the desk. After a few minutes silently eating and sipping coffee, he re-started their conversation.

"Just a couple of things, then you can go. You mentioned Mrs Grant?"

"She isn't Mrs Grant, they're not married, she's Miss King. Caroline went to their London flat. She was staying in Bordeaux last night, flying out this morning on BA. Caroline refuses to use Ryanair, and the BA flights from Bergerac don't operate on Sundays."

"Do you know why she went to London?".

Once again, Lucy looked down. But this time, she didn't tell a lie.

"I'd rather not say. I mean, it's none of my business."

Thomas thought about another croissant, then reached across and helped himself to a tissue from the packet Lucy had left on the desk. He wiped his fingers carefully.

"You won't know how the police work in France. It's not like England or America. Before I'm finished, it is my duty to know everything there is to know about the victim and anyone who could be a suspect. I'll talk to his friends, neighbours, clients – anyone I can find who can help me understand the man and why he died. I'll know where he went to school, where he had his hair cut, how he liked his coffee. So you see, everything is *my* business."

"They fought, Tony and Caroline."

"What about?"

There was a long silence before Lucy continued.

"Caroline found out that Tony had been having an affair and that there was going to be a baby. She had known about the affair, but the baby was the last straw apparently. Recently Caroline told Tony she was leaving, forever this time. I don't think this was Tony's first affair."

"Who had he been having the affair with?"

Another long silence ensued.

"With Camille, his model."

"I see. What's Camille's full name?"

"I don't know, but she lives in Monpazier. She works in Minou's."

"Minou's?"

"It's a restaurant and bar, in the village."

"When did Caroline find out about Camille and the baby?"

"I'm not sure, but before we started filming. It must have been early last month, or probably in January. But then she was away, on business, and then she was in London. And then Tony was in Glasgow and London with us, filming."

"Thank you. And you mentioned a plane?"

"Tony has a jet, a Cessna it's called. From here, it can reach Athens or Stockholm, he told me."

"That's useful to know, thank you, Lucy."

Thomas leaned forward and fixed his gaze on Lucy, holding her eyes with his as he continued.

"Now, as I said, I will build a very comprehensive picture of Mr Grant, his work, his life, his contacts. Everything my colleagues and I discover about him and about what happened here gets written up in a huge file. It's called the dossier. This is where the English word comes from. The dossier goes to my boss, and to the prosecutor and the judge who will decide the case. It is a very serious document. Do you understand?"

"Yes, I think so."

"Good. Once a statement is in the dossier, it can never be removed. It can be amended, but the original version will always be there. And changing statements after they have been written up is a very, very serious matter. It makes me look like a fool; and makes the witness look guilty. Now, I'm going to ask you once more, why did you have a key to Mr Grant's home?"

He watched as she fought conflicting fears. When she blushed, he knew she was about to tell him the truth.

"It was a game. It wasn't an affair; it was just a game for a few weeks. Sometimes he'd call me from the studio or a restaurant or a boring dinner party and tell me to go to the house and be in bed waiting for him. It was a bit of excitement."

Her voice became stronger, defiant, and her complexion resumed its natural colour as she continued. "I knew Caroline had left him, so what was the harm?"

"What about Camille?"

"What about her? She never came to the house; Tony wouldn't allow her. Camille's gorgeous, but she's pretty dim, and she smokes. They did their thing in Tony's studio, when he was painting her. I suppose he found it exciting – he was having sex with two young women at the same time, sometimes on the same day. I didn't care, I wasn't having an affair, I was having fun."

"Where is his studio?"

"You can't miss it. It's the grey building with huge windows on Forail Nord."

She took in his blank look.

"On the north edge of the village, opposite the war memorial, near the brewery. Ugliest house in the village."

"So just to confirm. For some time, Mr Grant has been having an affair with his model here in Monpazier. His partner finds out and announces her intention to leave him. At which point he starts having an affair, sorry, having occasional sex, with you. Is that right?"

"It does sound weird when you say it like that, but it seemed pretty harmless at the time."

"Thank you, Lucy. One last thing. I need to see all the material you have filmed so far."

* * *

February 2022: One Month Ago – Glasgow

"So, tell me again how this is going to work."

"Didn't you read the briefing document?" Lucy asked with an exasperated sigh.

They were sitting in the front row of the BA flight from London to Glasgow. Tony had the window seat, and Lucy the aisle.

"Yeah, yeah, I read it, but quickly. Anyway, tell me again."

"We've got the next two days in Glasgow, for your family and early childhood. Then two days in London, then as long as it takes in Monpazier, and then New York a bit later."

"And you'll be with me all the time?"

"Yes, I'll do all the interviews and I'll be behind the camera."

"How can you be working the camera and interviewing me at the same time? I mean, I've hardly never done TV before, but I always thought there were a million people involved."

Lucy laughed.

"This isn't drama, Tony, this is an arts programme—even if it is Amazon TV. And we're not in a studio. I'm the producer, lighting tech, sound and camera operator. I'll never be on screen. I'll ask you questions, but they'll usually be edited out. It will end up sounding as if you're just reminiscing. So, it would be good if you don't interrupt me, I'll just have to repeat the question."

Lucy was smiling as she said this, and she held his gaze as she did. She was already enjoying flirting with this handsome and interesting man.

"We'll see," he replied, daring her to break eye contact. "Who else will be involved?"

"Just Bobby, Bobby Anderson, our researcher, now and then. You'll meet him tonight. He's been checking out locations. You'll be pleased to know your old home in Glasgow is still standing."

"Cheeky pup! I'm no' that old."

Once again, Lucy chuckled.

"I see your Scottish accent is coming back, we must have crossed the border."

* * *

"OK, Tony, the camera is rolling."

"This is where I lived in Glasgow. In that flat there, on the second floor. There was no front door to the street back then, just the entrance to what's called the close, the entrance way that led to the stairs."

Tony turned slowly and pointed through the light rain, which was finally showing signs of stopping on this, the second day of filming.

"And down there is the primary school I went to."

With real venom in his voice, he continued. "God, I hated that fucking place. Hated every fucking minute of it."

He stood in silence, clearly reliving his detested childhood experience. Finally, Lucy prompted him from behind the camera.

"Why was it so awful?"

"They had no idea, none whatsoever. I was rubbish at football, that's all it took, believe it or not. I was soft. I liked to draw and I…I struggled in class. It turned out I was extremely near-sighted, so I couldn't see the blackboard. I couldn't see the questions."

His tone hardened again. "And no one took the trouble to find out. They were content to just call me fucking stupid and give up on me."

Lucy closed in to capture the raw emotion in Tony's face as he recalled the torment he suffered.

Eventually, he regained control.

"Thank God for the library."

"And Amy Johnson?" Lucy prompted.

"I don't remember mentioning her name."

"That's why we have Bobby, to find out things. You mentioned her once in a magazine article."

Lucy glanced over her shoulder, then lowered her eyes once more to the viewfinder. She watched intently as Tony followed her gaze down the street, seeing now the elegant woman walking towards him with a small smile on her handsome face. At 68 Amy still cut an elegant figure.

"Hello, Tony. It's been a long time."

Lucy had, of course, hoped for emotion, but she was horrified as Tony first stared at the woman from his past and then completely broke down in heaving, uncontrollable sobs. He quickly covered his distraught face with his hands and Lucy turned off the camera.

When Tony eventually regained control, he looked at Lucy who shook her head.

"It's OK, Tony, I wasn't filming."

She saw relief and gratitude in his eyes before he turned and held out a hand to Amy.

"I'm so sorry, you just took me by surprise. I had no idea. You must think me a complete idiot."

"Not at all. The last time I saw you, you reduced me to tears, so now we're even."

They smiled together, embraced warmly, and all was fine.

"Can I film now?" enquired Lucy. "And can you walk towards us again please, Miss Johnson?"

Tony looked at Amy, who nodded gently.

"Sure."

This time, after Amy's greeting, Tony wrapped his arms around her, even now still obviously deeply moved. He paused and then looked straight to camera, one arm holding Amy close.

"The entire shape of my life, whatever I've ever achieved, has been down to three women. My poor mum, who wanted everything for me, but didn't live to see any of it. My partner, Caroline, who kick-started my career as an artist and supported me in that endeavour, and this lovely, lovely person beside me, the first woman I fell in love with, Miss Johnson, the librarian. I was eight years old. The day I met her, was the last time my mum …"

His voiced tailed off and he gave a short cough as he brushed a single tear from his eye.

He turned to Amy and gave her wistful smile.

"I dreamt of marrying you, you know. But it wouldn't happen until I was probably fifteen or so, I imagined."

They smiled together and Tony continued to camera.

"Other than my mum, Amy was the only adult to reach out to this lost boy, to help me find myself. She showed me nothing but encouragement and kindness and she was the only person I was sorry to leave when I left Glasgow."

Amy Johnson reached into a smart leather tote bag she was carrying and pulled out a framed painting.

"I got my reward, though. I imagine this is the very first signed painting by the famous artist, Tony Grant, although he wasn't Tony Grant then.

"Maybe it's worth a lot of money," she finished with a grin as she held up the watercolour copy produced by the young artist.

Tony looked at his early work.

"I doubt it very much. But I promise, as soon as I get back to the studio, I'm sending you a painting. It's quite unlike my usual stuff, it's a landscape, with our local castle, Château Biron. It'll make a nice companion to Turner's Ludlow Castle."

He turned to Amy and wrapped his arms around her to give her another hug. As he did, he whispered in her ear, well below the level that would be picked up by Lucy's microphone, "And between you and me, that one *is* worth a fair amount of money."

* * *

Monday, March 7, 2022

"Good morning, Charlie. How is your head this morning?"

"My head is just fine, Thomas, thank you, as you well know. I can't wait for breast-feeding to be over, although Sylvie hasn't appeared for breakfast, so I suspect my sister may be hurting."

Charlotte's sister and brother-in-law had come for a visit from Grenoble on Friday and were staying with them until this afternoon.

"I'm sorry I had to abandon you, honey, really."

"I know. It's fine, they understand. We had a fabulous dinner; I wish I had married Gilbert; he's an amazing cook."

"And with the belly to go with it. How are the kids?"

"They're good. David has a follow-up assessment this afternoon, but he isn't in the slightest bothered about it, so neither am I. I really love this school, I hope he gets in, and we can stay here as long as possible."

Thomas didn't respond to his wife's implied plea. It was the only thing they ever argued about, the prospect of constant re-assignments every four or five years. In truth, it was already starting to grate with him as well. Their first two postings had felt like adventures, but now with David starting pre-school, the appeal of continuity was becoming more palpable. Of course, on his salary, they couldn't possibly have afforded to send their son to Bordeaux's International School, but Charlie's father had stepped in with his customary grace and made it clear that the subject of school fees was simply not to be discussed, now, or in future years. And that included Nathalie in due course.

Nathalie. This was the first time he had worked away from home since his daughter had been born, and he couldn't believe how much he was missing her and the rest of his family.

As if she sensed his mood, Charlotte spoke again.

"I'm sorry, I know you feel the same as me, really. We'll figure it out. Will you be home at the weekend?"

"Yes; well, unless the case is about to break and I can wrap it up. You know how it goes; either these things are cleared up in days or it can take months."

"Well, keep me posted. Love you."

"Love you. And apologise again to Sylvie and Gilbert. And tell your brother-in-law to ease off with the cordon bleu, unless he plans on moving in. I can't possibly compete!"

* * *

Thomas had taken over a large conference room in the Mairie for his temporary headquarters. It was time to get a team organised, so he placed calls to Beaumont and Bergerac, asking each to send him some gendarmes. Anne Lagache, the mayor of Monpazier, had been exceptionally co-operative. Even though yesterday had been Sunday, she had quickly arranged for him to have use of this large room in the Mairie and offered him whatever support he needed until such times as he could make other arrangements. And at least one family was happy to see him - the owners of the splendid Hôtel Edward 1er in the village. COVID had been a disaster for tourism, and the hotel owners had been delighted when he requested two rooms, with an indefinite hold on 2 more in case any of the team would be facing an unacceptably long commute home after what were bound to be long days. They had been a little less charmed when he told them to call the Bordeaux Gendarmerie to negotiate the terms.

He needed to get a handle on the expat community in the village. He called the mayor, got a name and number from her and made another call.

"Mrs MacDonald, this is Gendarmerie Captain Coman. I imagine you have heard of the death of Mr Grant? Yes, a tragedy indeed. The mayor suggested I give you a call; I wonder if I might call round for a chat. I need to build a picture of Mr Grant's relationships in the community and Madame Lagache seemed to think that you would be useful starting point. You would? Excellent. I'll be there in five minutes. Thank you."

The mayor's actual words had been to the effect that Elizabeth MacDonald was an appalling snob and an inveterate gossip, but she and her husband had lived in Monpazier for over twenty years and Elizabeth made it her business to know every foreigner who arrived in the village.

* * *

"Thank you again for taking the time to see me, Mr and Mrs MacDonald. I won't take up any more of your day than absolutely necessary."

"Not at all, Captain; take all the time you need. Paul and I are only too happy to be of assistance, aren't we, darling?"

She didn't wait for a response before adding, "I must say, Captain, you speak remarkably fluent English. I pride myself on speaking French rather well, if I may say so, but your English is, well, perfect."

"I'm half Welsh, Mrs MacDonald, I grew up in a bilingual home. Now, to Mr Grant, did you know him well?"

"Fairly well. I wouldn't say we were intimate friends, but we certainly encountered each other regularly at social events; dinner parties and the like. I must say I always found him very charming, although his political views rarely accorded with ours, would that be fair to say, Paul?"

Again, it was clear that Paul was neither expected or encouraged to react to his wife's words one way or another. She carried on, "He donated a rather nice framed sketch of the church to last year's Ladies' Charity fundraiser, which was generous I thought; he's very highly thought of in the art world I understand. We raised €4000 in the auction for the drawing."

"Very generous. Who would you say were Mr Grant's close friends?

"As far as I am aware, Tony spoke only basic French, so most of his circle would be among the English expats, excuse me, Captain, the British expats. And we have a few Americans as well, surprisingly gracious, and Australians, South Africans, Norwegians and a new couple from Ireland. Russians, even! But from London, not, you know, the other kind. And of course, there are some English-speaking French who socialise with the expatriate community from time-to-time, relocated Parisians mostly, but a few of the more sophisticated locals – the mayor, for example. You might talk with the Taylors and, well, I'm the last one to spread gossip, Captain, but you may wish to include Jennifer Oakes on your list."

"I'm sorry, Mrs MacDonald, but why did you mention gossip?"

"Mr Grant is, was, a very attractive man and, to speak plainly, he enjoyed the company of the ladies of our community, and they enjoyed his, some perhaps more than others. There, I've said too much. Not another word on that subject. Would you care for a cup of proper English tea, Captain?"

"That would be very nice, thank you, Mrs MacDonald."

As soon as his wife had left the room, Thomas turned to the hitherto silent Mr MacDonald.

"What about you, sir? Any ideas who I might approach for a complete picture of the expat community?"

"Well, Captain, you might talk to some of the groups that meet in the village"

"That sounds like excellent advice, Mr MacDonald, do you have any particular suggestions?"

"Well, there are the book clubs. I believe there are two or three different English book clubs in the village. There's the choir, which has a number of expatriate members, and the pétanque group, of course, which is made up mostly of the expat community. It's certainly the largest group of expats in the village, in the summer months especially, when they play every week. If the weather is suitable, like now, they play in the winter as well. And there are other groups: bridge, mahjong, all the usual stuff. And you might wander up to Bière de la Bastide, the brewery, it's very popular with the French and the expat community."

"Sounds like a very vibrant community you have here, Mr MacDonald. Allow me to help with that tray, Mrs MacDonald.

"I was just saying to your husband, the expatriate community in Monpazier seems very active. He's been telling me about some of the interest groups that exist."

Thomas wasn't sure that Mrs MacDonald altogether approved of her husband divulging information in her absence, but she was too late to stop him.

"We play bridge ourselves, and I occasionally lend my voice to the choir."

"And pétanque? Is that something that interests you?"

"Oh, dear no! The pétanque group; what can I say? We know quite a few of them, of course, and some are extremely good people, but as a group? Grown men in shorts, drinking wine and beer in public. Rather a lot if you ask me. Directly out of bottles!"

Thomas smiled to himself as he retraced his steps to the Mairie. Madame la maire might well be a useful guide to local characters; she'd certainly nailed Mrs MacDonald.

* * *

Thomas popped into the office to the right of the Mairie door. His temporary phone line had yet to be installed and so for the moment the Mairie secretary was taking his messages.

"Any messages?"

"No, Capitaine, but there is someone here to see you, a gendarme. I put her in your office. I hope that's okay?"

Thomas took the steps two at a time and opened the door to his temporary office. A young gendarme, who had been sitting by the window, stood to attention.

"Good morning, Capitaine, Adjudant Eloise Brunel, we met yesterday, very briefly. I hope you don't mind me coming to see you this morning, Capitaine, but I would really like to be assigned to this case. I think I could be an asset to the team. I've only recently been assigned to the Beaumont brigade, but I used to be based here in Monpazier, when the village had its own gendarmerie office. I'm just about to start my training to get into BR, and I think my local knowledge could be of assistance to you. And I speak some English, not as well as you do, I believe, but well enough, I think. And as the victim was English …"

Thomas was impressed. He admired ambition in others, if it was demonstrated appropriately.

"Well, Adjudant Brunel, I have indeed made a request to Beaumont for some assistance in this case and also to the brigade at Bergerac. Why don't I call your superior officer right now and clear matters with him? And let's test that local knowledge of yours. Where's the best coffee to be found in Monpazier? The stuff they have here is shocking."

"I'll run over to the Écureuil, they do excellent coffee. Normal coffee?"

"Noisette, please. And thanks. Here's a fifty, put the change in this jar; let me know when it runs out."

By the time Eloise had returned with their coffees, Thomas had spoken to the senior officer at Beaumont. She was happy to release her Adjudant and gave Thomas details of the two other gendarmes she had assigned to the case. They would be on their way shortly, and Thomas should expect them immediately after lunch. His call to Bergerac was just as satisfactory – they also agreed to release two gendarmes, who could be expected early in the afternoon. One, André Lefèvre, was currently living in the Mussidan barracks, so his commander suspected that he might be interested in taking up the offer of temporary accommodation in Monpazier, especially as he was single.

Thomas got to know Eloise a little better over a simple lunch, and he was confident that she would indeed be an asset.

* * *

After lunch Thomas was finally able to gather his new team for a first briefing and initial divisions of responsibility. As well as André Lefèvre, who confidently announced that yes, he could speak English quite well, Bergerac had sent Christine Le Roux who at 35 was older than the typical gendarme but also claimed to have a reasonable grasp of English. In addition to Eloise, Beaumont had sent Pierre Griset and Christophe Baye, neither of whom had any useful English skills.

Thomas addressed his team as they sat around the central table, more usually employed for council meetings. After initial introductions and a summary of events of the past 24 hours, Thomas got down to details and his biggest concern.

"Language is going to be a pain in the neck. It's going to slow us down, and, if we're not very careful, we'll be off on one wild goose chase after another caused by misunderstandings. When you interview an English-speaker, you need to be 100% certain that whoever you are talking to *really* understands your questions and that you *really* understand their answers. The honest people will want to be helpful, even if that means pretending they understand every word you are saying, while in truth, they are often guessing. Very few of the expats will be truly proficient in French, even those who initially seem fairly competent. Don't let them trip up by saying one thing in their garbled French, when they mean something quite different.

"We'll work in three teams. Team one will be myself and Le Roux; team two is Adjudant Brunel and Lefèvre. Between us, we're going to talk to every English-speaking expatriate in the immediate area – this morning's interview with the MacDonalds has given us plenty of names to start with. Griset and Baye, team three, are going to start in on the French speakers – starting with the people the MacDonalds identified as mixing with the Anglos. I also want you two also to sit down with Madame le maire and pick her brains for anyone else who might have had any kind of relationship with the victim. But before we start in on the English, Le Roux and I will track down this Camille, who was apparently having an affair with the deceased.

"And now for the bad news. Griset and Baye, for the first week, you two are responsible for coordinating the dossier and the nightly reports. I know it's a shit job, but there are a huge number of interviews to be managed with the expats. And I promise, I'll review the assignment for week two. Adjudant, I want you to keep a master list of each expat as we identify them and keep a record of who has been interviewed; share it with Griset and Baye each afternoon. Any questions?"

After a few brief discussions, Thomas was ready to close the meetings, except for one final instruction.

"Everyone back here at eighteen hundred for a debrief. Let's go."

* * *

It took no time at all to track down Camille – she still lived in the village house she had shared with her brother, Augustin, since the death of their mother some years ago. As Lucy had told Thomas, Camille was extraordinarily beautiful. She had the lovely, flawless face of a Madonna, long, glossy hair and an exceptional figure. The gendarmes soon found out, not for the first time, just how deceptive looks could be.

"No, we were not just having an affair, we were in love. Tony would have married me after Caroline left, I'm sure of it."

"Did Monsieur Grant tell you that?" asked Thomas.

"He didn't have to, it was obvious. Even before."

"Even before what?" asked Le Roux.

Camille now had a sly look on her face.

"Even before I told him I was pregnant. With his child."

Kiki continued the questioning.

"When did you discover you were pregnant, Camille?"

"At the beginning of last month; Docteur Dupuits confirmed it for me."

"I see. And when did you tell Monsieur Grant?"

"Right away. I knew he'd be excited."

Thomas changed the direction of the conversation.

"You spent time with Monsieur Grant in his studio, modelling for him. Were you often in his house?"

"I modelled for him all the time, but no, I was never in his house. That we where he spent time with Caroline. It would not have been appropriate," she added, primly.

Thomas withheld his thoughts of the appropriateness or otherwise of this relationship.

Kiki understood why Thomas had changed the subject abruptly and she followed his lead.

"And how did Monsieur Grant take your news?"

"He was surprised, naturally. Tony is a little older than me, he probably didn't expect to become a father."

"And did he tell Caroline, Madame King?"

"He didn't have to; that *sale connard*, Clémentine Martin, she told her. The bitch hardly knew Caroline, but she found an excuse to talk with her right away."

"And how did Clémentine find out?"

"Bad fucking luck. She was in the doctor's waiting room as I was leaving. She heard Docteur Dupuits's last words to me 'And remember, Camille, no more alcohol, and no more cigarettes, understand?' She guessed why he was talking like that and couldn't wait to tell Caroline."

"Why?"

"I suppose because of last year, with Theirry, who wasn't really her boyfriend anyway. Bitch!"

Thomas re-entered the conversation.

"Have you told anyone else about the baby?"

"A few people. My brother Gus of course, some friends, oh, and Monsieur Ambassadeur Taylor and his lovely wife, Gemma. Well. I didn't have to tell them, they heard through their cleaner, a friend of mine, and they have been extremely nice. They even took Gus and me to dinner, at the Privilège! It was lovely."

"Where is Gus now, Camille?"

"In Bergerac, on business."

"What kind of business?"

"Personal business."

Thomas closed his notebook and stood to leave.

"One more question, Camille. Where were you on Saturday night?"

"Working. Until a little after midnight. Then a few friends came back here to celebrate my news. We had a few drinks. I decided a few more nights smoking and drinking wouldn't hurt the baby. I'm stopping from Monday. Probably."

"I can't imagine Tony Grant was too thrilled to hear Camille's news."

The two colleagues were walking back to the Mairie.

"My God, no," Thomas replied. "She isn't even smart enough to be confused by changing the subject. Although she's certainly holding something back. I wonder what Gus is doing in Bergerac."

"Something to do with that baby, I think. She had a look about her when she told us – and she couldn't wait to tell us. All of it is odd."

"And the business with the Ambassador and his wife. Madame MacDonald mentioned them. Next call, I think."

Le Roux was thoughtful for fifty metres.

"But I still don't see her as the murderer. What would be her motive? And I have a huge problem seeing her pitching Grant over that balustrade – he must weigh two of her. Not that I'm jealous of course," she added, patting her own backside, before continuing, "I'm having trouble seeing *anyone* throwing Grant off that balcony. The man in the newspaper photographs looks as if he could take care of himself."

Thomas nodded. "I agree, and there are absolutely no signs of a struggle, no scuff marks, apart from the scratches caused by the falling chair, no damage to the railings, nothing. Even picking Grant off the floor unconscious and throwing him over would be a serious challenge for most people. It's a mystery. Maybe the autopsy results will tell us something – drink, drugs, something!"

* * *

The Taylors also provided surprises, starting from the moment Madame Taylor, Gemma, met them at the door. She was another beautiful young woman; in her mid-thirties, Thomas judged. And when she introduced her husband, Zachary, Thomas estimated that there was at least forty years between husband and wife.

Thomas moved the conversation along after the introductions.

"I understand that you are a former ambassador, Mr Taylor."

"Quite correct. Served all over the world: Nairobi, Lima, New York, Brussels and others. Finished my service as Her Majesty's Ambassador to France."

Thomas turned to Gemma.

"And where did you two meet, Mrs Taylor?"

"In Paris, of course," interjected her husband. "My wife, my first wife that is, passed away while I was there. Ambassador has to have a wife. Gemma here fit the bill. Perfect French, already vetted, as she was my secretary and, as you can see, rather beautiful."

Le Roux thought she would make another attempt to engage with Gemma.

"Did you know the deceased, Mr Grant, socially, Gemma?"

"A little, yes," she replied, hesitantly.

Her husband was quick to fill the silence that followed.

"The man was a disgrace, a menace. Absolutely no moral code whatsoever. He worked on a building site you know, carrying bricks and cement. Not even a skilled craftsman. Never in the military. The man had some facility with a paintbrush, I'll give him that, but no depth, no backbone.

"One doesn't like to speak ill of the dead," he continued, "but he was the sort who gives the British a bad name with our hosts."

* * *

"Let's have your reports. Why don't you start, Adjudant?"

Thomas looked at his team arranged around the meeting table. He always had a sense of anticipation the first time an investigation team met for a debrief, and this was no different.

"Well, Capitaine," Eloise began, "we're going to have a hard time achieving your goal of interviewing *all* the expats in the community, there are a lot of them. Apparently in the summer there can be up to fifty people just playing pétanque for example, the vast majority of whom are expatriates. Fortunately for us, there are fewer at this time of year. Still, there will be somewhere between forty and fifty people that we'd have to reach if we want to interview all of them. But we did have a very brief conversation with Jennifer Oakes. She was on her way to an appointment, in Villeréal, so we only had a few words. She confirmed that she knew the victim but didn't volunteer any details. We both think we should talk with her again, when she can give us more time, and maybe when we have some information about her."

"And what about you two, Griset, Baye, what have you been up to this afternoon?"

Pierre Griset took the lead.

"As you suggested, Capitaine, we met with Madame le maire; very helpful – and we talked with Adjudant Brunel. The dynamics of the village are complicated – there are two political camps it seems, and a lot of feuds and animosity between them. There are also four or five extended families who each own various shops, businesses and several houses in the village. However, we doubt if this has much bearing on the case as Monsieur Grant was, of course, an outsider. Many people knew the victim; that is to say, they knew who he was, they would say 'good day' when they encountered him, perhaps had a brief chat in a café, but we haven't found any of the French who really *knew* him, spent any time with him. Of course, we didn't speak with the Pichon family, or the Brouzets."

"The Brouzets, who are they?"

"Madame Brouzet has been the victim's cleaner for some years and was, by one account, unusually close to Grant. Apparently, she has a key to both his house and studio. The person who told us," Griset looked down to his notes, "a Madame Hélène Bory, implied that there was something odd in the relationship between Loulou Brouzet and Grant, but she wouldn't, or couldn't, explain what she meant. Anyway, we thought you might want to interview Madame Brouzet and her son yourself, Capitaine.

"There seems to have been a certain degree of, well, pride, in having a well-known artist living here. Everyone is genuinely sad about what happened. Baye, do you want to add anything?"

"Just that he seems to have been very generous. He regularly gave money to the fire station, sponsored a match every year for the rugby club, paid for a new set of kit for the women's football team – that sort of thing. He was a popular figure, for an Englishman. Or I should say, a Scotsman. Every year, on St Andrew's Day in November and Robert Burn's Night in January, he bought two bottles of whisky at Minou's and left them on the bar for people to help themselves. No wonder he was popular."

Christophe Baye looked around, "Robert Burns was a famous Scottish poet apparently," he explained.

Thomas smiled as the others nodded at this new information.

"Le Roux, why don't you fill the others in on our interviews today."

Kiki gave a quick summary of their interview and finished by observing, "I want to interview Madame Taylor again, but away from her husband."

"Agreed," said Thomas. "I think you'll have to bring her in formally. We have enough justification, given her affair with the victim."

* * *

Thomas took his time making his way back to his hotel. He detoured through a couple of the quaint *carreyrous* and stopped to examine the windows of some of the village shops. He was particularly enchanted by a window where the artisan had fused ceramics and wood to create innovative objects. He noticed that, while a couple of the restaurants were still closed, those that were open were already filling up for the evening.

He decided that, if the case did drag on, he'd suggest that Charlie bring the kids here for a weekend. He knew that she would be going stir-crazy after a week alone with just the little ones for company, and he was sure she'd enjoy exploring the village, not to mention staying in a lovely hotel with no cleaning up responsibilities. And, although he wouldn't be dining there without her, she would surely appreciate eating in the fabulous restaurant, even if they would have the baby monitors on the table.

Eventually he reached his suite in the hotel and threw off his uniform jacket and belt before calling home.

"Hi. How was your day?"

"It was great. David got on really well at the school; he wants to tell you all about it himself. And Thomas," he heard his wife's excitement, "he'll get in, for certain. The headteacher as much as told me. They liked David, think he's developing really well, and they love the idea of a gendarme parent! Apparently, they've never had one and think it would be a great addition to the school. I think you'll be getting asked to do lots of talks for the pupils. Oh, Thomas, it's really a lovely place, you must come and see it yourself."

"I will, promise, as soon as poss."

"How's the case?"

"Just getting started."

He told her about the team and added, "I'm never going to be teased by any of my Welsh family every again about over-sexed Frenchmen. The Scottish victim was involved with at least three women at the time of his death – and quite possibly more, so no more randy Frenchmen stories. Is David there, let me talk to him."

"Papa, Papa! Did you know, there's a country called Costa Mica, no, Costa...Maman! Where is Riccardo from? Costa Rica, Papa. Did you know?"

"Who is Riccardo?"

"He's at the school. Maybe I'll be going there, Maman says. Bye!"

And with that the phone went dead. Thomas smiled. His son had inexhaustible energy, far too much to stand still for more than a minute talking with his father on the phone.

Thomas was already beginning to really appreciate the fact that he had been assigned a two-room suite in the hotel. Having a proper desk and space to spread out his papers was making completing his nightly reports a lot easier. After a light dinner, he was reading the draft dossier prepared by Griset and Baye when the hotel phone on his desk rang.

"Good evening, Capitaine, there is an English lady here to see you. Shall I send her up?"

Thomas looked at the paperwork spread all over the desk and side tables.

"No, ask her to wait in the bar, please. I'll be down in a moment."

There was only one person in the small bar area, a woman, mid- to late-thirties Thomas guessed; slim, smartly dressed and rising to greet him, hand extended.

She addressed him in perfect French, "Good evening, Capitaine. My apologies for disturbing you so late in the evening, I came as quickly as I could. Detective Sergeant Susan Howard, London Metropolitan police, I've been asked to assist you on the Grant case, I hope someone told you to expect me?"

"Yes, I was told to expect someone, although perhaps not so quickly. But welcome to Monpazier, Sergeant." All this was said in English.

Susan laughed.

"Touché! Perhaps English would be better."

Thomas smiled back at her.

"Your French is excellent, please don't think I was suggesting otherwise."

"I know. I also know I'm the last thing you need right now, I'm sure you're up to your eyeballs with this case. I'll stay out of your way, promise. But if you do need anything from the UK – background material, criminal records, financial data, whatever, my job is to see that you get what you need, and as quickly as possible."

"Well, I'm impressed that London sent a fluent French speaker, that will help. "

"I'm a hybrid, like you, Captain. My father is French, and my parents have a holiday home in France, in Provence."

"What do you work on normally?" asked Thomas

"I'm with the Diplomatic Protection Unit, but I think I was selected for this role because of my French connections."

"Have you arranged somewhere to stay while you're in Monpazier?"

"I should receive a text any moment I hope, there wasn't time to arrange anything before I left."

"I have rooms booked here, and to be honest, I don't think there are many options in the village at this time of year. Why don't you let your admin people know that you can stay here? We'll let them sort out the billing issues with Bordeaux. I'm staying here, one of the other gendarmes on the case will be from tomorrow and I expect that the partner of the victim will have to stay here, as we'll need access to the scene for several days more."

"That sounds great, thank you."

"Let's go to reception and get you signed in. You can call your office, then, if you wish, come up to my suite."

He saw the look on her face and grinned.

"No, Detective; I'm only half-French, remember? Reception has received a memory stick with the first tranche of video on the victim. He is, he was, the subject of a documentary being made at the time of his death."

By the time Susan knocked on his door, Thomas had set his laptop on the coffee table, and he indicated a seat beside him on the sofa.

"The producer, a young English woman called Lucy, explained that she uploads all her footage daily, and when she has confirmation of its safe arrival and backup, her camera storage is wiped clean for another day. Such is the speed of Monpazier's internet, she could only download about one day's filming at a time onto the USB stick I gave her, which isn't really a problem, because even at one terabyte, one day's filming was all the memory stick could handle.

"And, by the way, Lucy was having a casual affair with the victim. But I've pretty much ruled her out as a suspect."

He found the file and they sat back to watch the video footage. It was odd to be watching scenes of a man whose dead body he had seen just yesterday.

1986 – Girvan, Scotland

It was the green jumper that caught Lorna's eye. She'd been watching the black car coming up the driveway, a taxi she realised. She had read about taxis, seen pictures of them in some of the picture books when she was younger, but this was the first time she had seen one up close in real life. The taxi was OK; it looked just like the ones in the books. But the driver was a major disappointment. For one thing, he didn't get out and open the door for his passenger, he just sat there staring at nothing special as far as the girl could see. Even more disappointing was the fact that the driver wasn't wearing a hat or a cap, or whatever they called the things the drivers in the books wore.

Sister Mary Joseph had appeared, and the girl watched as the fearsome nun strode up to the driver's door and rapped on his window. Lorna focused as hard as she could, but she couldn't hear what Sister was saying. She did see the driver pointing over his shoulder, at which point Sister Mary Joseph marched swiftly round to the other side of the taxi, the side facing Lorna, and snatched open the door to the passenger compartment.

"Out!" she ordered. "Come on boy, get out here."

And that was when the lurid green jumper appeared, enclosing a skinny boy with wild hair with a distinctive flash of white on one side. The boy hesitantly slid his way completely out of the taxi.

The nun had barely closed the door before a crunch of flying gravel ushered the vehicle back down the long driveway.

Sister Mary Joseph watched the cab for a moment then whipped her head around to the boy, who hadn't moved.

"Your things! Has that awful man driven away with your things?"

"What things?" replied the boy, clearly bemused.

"Your things; your clothes, your shoes. Your things!" she snapped, cuffing his head.

The boy looked completely at a loss.

"I'm wearing my clothes and look; here are my shoes."

He lifted a thin leg to demonstrate the obvious truth of his statement. Lorna could see a large scab on the boy's bony knee.

"I can see that, you stupid boy. I mean your other clothes, your coat or jacket, your wellingtons. Did you leave your case in that taxi?"

With her vast experience Lorna could clearly detect the signs that Sister Mary Joseph was about to have one of her rages. These were a regular occurrence and interesting to watch so long as you weren't the target of her wrath. She felt sorry for the boy.

"What case? They didn't give me other clothes. These are my clothes."

For three or four seconds the nun paused, perhaps realising that she had made a wrong assumption, but she recovered quickly and smacked the boy's head again.

"These are my clothes, *Sister*."

Leaving the boy standing on the spot where he had descended from the taxi, the austere nun turned to climb the five stone steps leading to the Children's Home's front door, steps worn smooth by over a century of hurrying feet. Immediately she spotted Lorna before the girl could duck behind the curtain in the open window.

"What are you doing there, Lorna Cruikshank? Never mind; take this boy to Sister Bernadette and tell her that he's the arrival from St Peter's. Can you remember that?"

"Yes, Sister Mary Joseph," Lorna assured her.

"Very well. Go now and don't take all day about it."

Lorna listened as the nun's heavy black shoes clacked their way across the flagstones of the entrance hall then heard the sound change to a series of heavy, dull thuds as they mounted the worn wooden staircase to the first floor. She closed the door to the small waiting room behind her and went out to get the boy.

"You did well not to cry when she hit you. When she knows someone cries, she hits them more often, I think."

"I've been hit a lot harder than that," he boasted, and Lorna thought he was probably telling the truth.

"Where are you from?"

"St Peter's."

"What's St Peter's?"

"A Home."

"Why have you come here?"

"Dunno. They just told me yesterday. Said I was to come here for everyone's good."

The boy had looked away as he answered her last question. 'Probably lying.' she thought.

"What's your name, then?"

"Tony. Tony Gallagher. What's yours?"

"Lorna. Let's go and find Sister Bernadette. She's OK; at least she's not as bad as the others anyway."

* * *

From that first meeting, Tony and Lorna were inseparable. They ate together at mealtimes, sat together at playtimes and had little to do with the other children in the Home. Lorna became Tony's guide, mentor and guardian. She intuitively knew how to avoid getting into trouble with the nuns, even the really horrible ones like Sister Mary Joseph. Time after time, she made excuses for her friend until, under her example and guidance, he too learned to placate the austere women who held unquestioned authority over every aspect of their lives.

It was Lorna who suggested to Sister Bernadette that Tony could paint the backdrop to baby Jesus's crib for the Nativity Play. She had seen Tony painting in their art class and even an eleven-year-old could grasp that the boy was far more talented than their classmates. The object of the task was to secure Tony status as 'not a troublemaker' in Sister Mary Joseph's ever-changing inventory of her charges, but before then, it would change his life in a far more important way.

"Why did you tell her that?" Tony demanded. "I might make a mess of it, and then what? I'll be in trouble."

"But you won't, you're really good, and you can just copy that picture." Lorna was pointing to a cheap print of the nativity scene hanging on the wall of the dining hall.

"How? I can't make it out enough."

Lorna looked again at the picture. It was really big, and she could clearly...

"What can you see?" she asked.

"Well, I can see something, but I need to climb on a chair underneath."

Tony had had a mother and a father, neighbours, teachers, a family doctor; but it took an eleven-year-old girl to understand that Tony had a major problem, and to work out what to do about it. She went to see Sister after choir practice.

"Sister Bernadette, can I show you something?"

"Of course, Lorna. What do you want to show me, dear?"

"Well, can you see that picture, on the wall, of Our Lady?"

"Of course, what about it?"

Lorna turned and called across the room. "Tony, come here a minute."

She turned Tony to face the wall with the framed image.

"Tony, what's that a picture of? That one there," she said, pointing.

Tony trotted over to the wall opposite and dragged a chair from behind the nearest desk to climb on.

"It's Our Lady," he called over his shoulder.

Two weeks later, Tony proudly wore his new NHS glasses for the first time. His life would never be quite the same.

As usual, the two friends were sitting on their low wall at playtime. Tony was still bemused by his new-found secret power.

"Look at that bird away up there, Lorna! And all the leaves on that big tree! I bet there's a million leaves. A million billion."

Although, of course, nothing had been said, Lorna knew Tony was really grateful for what she had done. She sensed the opportunity to clear up something that had been bothering her since that first day when they had met.

"Tony, what happened at St Peter's?"

Immediately Tony's face closed, all excitement gone.

"I don't ever want to talk about that, Lorna. Not never."

She put her hand over his.

"Sure."

* * *

Lucy was so wrapped up in Tony's account of his early years that she left the camera running long after he had stopped talking, stopped even looking at her and the lens.

Eventually she gave herself a shake.

"So, what happened to Lorna?"

Tony gave her an enigmatic smile.

"That's a tale for another day. Now, I need a drink."

He gave her an entirely different smile.

"Then I need to be distracted."

* * *

Tuesday, March 8, 2022

Early on Tuesday morning, Thomas let himself into Tony Grant's house. The body had long since been removed, and someone had made a cursory attempt to mop up the blood, although the extensive dark patch was still clearly visible. It would take a professional to get it thoroughly clean, Thomas thought.

He had spotted the keyring hanging by the front door during his first visit. No matter how often people were warned not to do this, millions persisted in hanging their keys in the most convenient spot for an opportunist burglar or crooked delivery man to pick them up. The keys included one high-security key, which Thomas surmised, correctly as it turned out, to be the key to the studio.

Gendarme Le Roux and Susan Howard were waiting for him when he arrived at the studio on the north edge of the village. Selecting the security key, Thomas turned it smoothly in the lock and opened the door. Immediately there was the ear-splitting sound of an alarm going off.

"Merde!"

Thomas quickly located the alarm keypad inside the door and noted the supplier. He pulled out his phone and called a number in Bordeaux. He had to walk away to be heard over the sound of the alarm, even after they had closed the door once again.

"Solange, it's Thomas Coman, I need a favour, immediately."

Five noisy minutes later, the alarm company remotely stopped the alarm and called Thomas and talked him through setting a new code of his own choosing.

"I'm not used to French formality," said Susan as they waited for Thomas's call to be returned, "what do your colleagues call you? Please don't tell me they call you Gendarme Le Roux"

"On duty, of course!"

She paused to register Susan's dismay.

"Of course not," she chuckled, "my name is Christine, but I go by Kiki. I know, I sound like a stripper, don't I? And now, let's hear it for the one and only, Kiki Le Roux!"

"I love it!" exclaimed Susan, "Maybe I should think of an improvement on Susan — so boring!"

Even though the cold winter sun wasn't directly visible through the north-facing window, its refracted light flooded the large room they entered directly from the street. It was obvious why an artist would love this space.

"It's nothing like how I imagined an artist's studio would look," observed Thomas.

"This is cleaner than my house," agreed Susan. "In fact, this is cleaner than any house I've ever been in. I feel like I'm soiling it just by standing here."

The studio was truly immaculate, it looked like the place had *never* been used, which they knew was far from the truth.

Thomas turned to Kiki, "Gendarme Le Roux, can you go and track down Grant's cleaner and bring her here? We need to better understand how this place worked."

Susan and Thomas began their examination of the surreally clean and tidy studio. It didn't take long to grasp the essence of the place. There was an easel holding a partially painted canvas — a scene set in an urban street; Susan thought it was probably somewhere in London, maybe south London. The easel sat on a strip of paper unrolled from a large spool held on a revolving rail behind it. The paper projected about one metre in front of the easel, and it was, like everything else, spotless. Under the pegs that held the canvas on the easel was a grooved ledge, resting place for a stick with one padded end. They later learned it was called a mahl stick, used to steady the artist's hand as he painted fine details.

On the wall next to the easel stood a large custom wooden storage unit, standing about one and a half metres tall and roughly the same in width and depth. On the front were fifteen vertical slots, each about ten centimetres wide. Each slot was finished with green baize at the bottom and sides, to protect canvases as they were inserted and removed. Three slots were in use, each holding what turned out to be a finished painting. Above the slots were two drawers.

The unit was clad in vertical tongue-and-grooved panelling on each side and the top was made of black granite. The top held a large box of tissues and two rows of pots, one row red and one blue, eight in each. Most of the pots held a dozen or so artist's brushes of varying sizes, with the last of the blue pots holding a set of palette knives. The last red pot held an array of well-sharpened pencils. There was also a solitary white pot, which was empty.

Susan picked up the empty pot in her gloved hand.

"These are Le Creuset pots, sold for kitchen utensils. Pretty."

The left-hand drawer was full of neatly folded white cotton squares. The other drawer had a plastic liner divided into sections of varying sizes holding charcoal sticks, dividers, a pencil sharpener, a pocketknife, a cylinder of waxed string and other assorted bits and pieces, presumably useful to a busy artist.

On the other side of the room stood what looked like a kitchen unit, with a seamless sink set in a stainless-steel worktop such as might be found in a professional kitchen. A large drawer to the side of the sink held a vast array of neatly arranged artists' oil paints and the cupboard below was used to hold turpentine, white spirit and yet more liquid art supplies. From a series of hooks on one side of the unit hung various sizes of palettes, the first objects they had seen that showed any sign of use. There were patches of colour all over the distinctively shaped palettes, but no bumps or ridges of paint residues, they had all been cleaned before being hung up.

On the wall opposite the huge windows, there were two shelves, each about two metres long. Both held black Moleskine artists' sketchbooks. Those on the top shelf were pocket-sized, while the lower shelf held larger books. Every book on both shelves had been neatly numbered with a small white label affixed to the spine. When Susan and Thomas picked up a couple, they quickly established they were all fully used – hundreds of sketches of every subject under the sun.

"I think you had better get this lot inventoried and secured, Capitaine, I suspect they are worth a lot of money."

"I was just thinking that myself. And, sadly, now that Grant is dead, everything in here will go up in value, especially those three paintings. Let's see what's through here."

Thomas led the way through the only interior door in the room. It opened into a pitch-black space. When he hit the light switch, strips of fluorescent tubes cast a harsh light on what was a very well-stocked storeroom. Running along the back wall of the studio and perhaps three metres wide, the room had no windows. Each long wall had been expertly fitted with varying height shelves holding an Aladdin's cave of artists' materials: canvases of various sizes, stacked unopened boxes of brushes, pencils, oil paints and watercolours, wrapped bags of cotton squares, more new palettes, charcoal sticks, turpentine – every conceivable thing a busy painter could possibly require. A clean white lab coat hung on a hook on the inside of the storeroom door.

"I need to get an expert in here, we could be overlooking something important, and I would have no idea," Thomas observed.

At the far end of the room another door opened into a compact toilet with a small washbasin holding a liquid soap dispenser and a solitary window high up on the wall opposite the door. The lower half of the walls and the floor were tiled in functional white squares, and a clean hand towel hung from a solitary hook.

As they returned to the main room, Kiki was entering with a petite white-haired woman whose erect bearing and steely gaze instantly dispelled any notions of her being 'a little old lady'.

"This is Madame Loulou Brouzet, Capitaine. Madame Brouzet was having a coffee in the tabac, I promised we would buy her another when you are finished."

"Certainly. Good day, Madame. I would like to ask you a few questions about Monsieur Grant. How long have you worked for him?"

"Monsieur Tony, what a wonderful man! I shall have a Mass said for him next week. A kind man, a generous man, a man with very particular requirements, but a man who had total respect for cleaning, unlike most of my former clients who saw it as an unfortunate necessity. Monsieur Tony was different. Oh yes! Knowledgeable too! We would often discuss various products, different approaches to cleaning particular items."

She stopped, obviously finished.

"And how long, Madame?" Thomas prompted her.

"Ah yes! Eight years." she announced proudly. "He had tried others, of course. Hélène Bory, for one." she almost spat out the name, such was her obvious contempt. "But he fired them all, none were adequate for the particular needs of a man such as Monsieur Thomas."

"And what were those particular needs, Madame?"

"Where to begin? So. His brushes. He telephoned me every evening, around six. He would tell me if he had been working here that day, and if he was planning to work the following morning, in which case I would arrive here at seven, to have everything ready for him. He would also tell me if he would be having guests at home that evening and if so, which rooms in the house would require special attention."

"Special attention?"

"For example, if he was providing dinner, I would know next day to polish the table and dining chairs. If he had his friends over for drinks, next morning I would wipe down the snooker table and cues, and so on. He did not permit smoking in the house, but there was a small table with an ashtray on the rear balcony, so I would check that. Just in case. Of course I would clean the rooms every day anyway, but these were particular tasks."

"Thank you. You were saying about his brushes?"

"Ah yes. He used new brushes every day. If he had been working, he would wrap his used brushes in a cloth soaked with turpentine and leave them in that white pot, along with any knives that he had used. I would clean the knives, as well as his palette, of course, and take away the used brushes. He used to put them in the waste, but I explained that my granddaughter's school could make good use of them. So that is when he started wrapping them so they would not dry out. He gave me a huge bottle of turpentine to take home, so I could clean them properly before Emilia took them to school. And do you know, Capitaine?"

She paused to dab her eyes at this point.

"After I mentioned the school, every year he delivered to the head teacher, huge boxes of coloured pencils and dozens of paper pads and boxes of oils and watercolours and boxes and boxes of brushes for the children. He said that administrators always thought it was fine for children to use inferior materials, but no, he said, 'Children deserve nothing but the best.'"

Madame Brouzet had to pause at this point, to compose herself. Susan fetched one of several odd chairs ranged along the wall below the bookshelves and held it for her to sit down.

"No thank you, my dear, I am fine. You know, I used to have nine clients, one each morning and afternoon except for market on Thursday morning. Soon after I started work for Monsieur Tony, I had to give them all up, just so I could be available when he required. He paid me almost double what I had been making before. And can you believe, he paid me even when he travelled, sometimes for two months! The man was a saint!"

"Perhaps Monsieur Grant had other requirements, Madame?" prompted Thomas.

"Many. For example, this paper. This was my idea, you know. I had been to see Docteur Dupuits, about my feet, and noticed that he had a large paper dispenser above his couch, so he could provide a fresh surface to examine every patient. I suggested to Monsieur Thomas that he have a special dispenser made to rest on the floor. He loved my idea! So now, if he has been working, I move the easel to the side, roll out fresh paper and dispose of the old, which will have drips of paint perhaps. And his coat, fresh every day. He has some in the store, and I collect used coats and take them to wash and fold for him. We had such an understanding! I felt I was truly contributing to his work as an artist. He gave me a sketch of the church you know, in a beautiful frame. Yes, last Christmas that was. He explained to me once, 'I don't mind getting dirty if required, Madame, but I hate *being* dirty. So long as I can wash up soon after, it's fine. The same with my home and this studio. Things are spilled; things fall on the floor. This is natural, and nothing to get upset about. But there is no excuse for leaving things untidy or unclean.' Of course, I could not have agreed more."

"Of course," agreed Thomas. "Now, Madame, please tell me when exactly you last spoke with Monsieur Grant, when you last cleaned both here and in the house, and when he last worked here or entertained at home."

"You have a lot of questions, Capitaine! Let me see. As for the studio, he last painted on Thursday. He had to go to Périgueux on Friday on some business matter and returned to entertain some friends in the evening. So, I was able to come here on Friday to clean before going to the house. On Friday evening Monsieur Grant and his friends watched rugby in the TV room and played some snooker upstairs. On Saturday morning I went to the house to make sure everything was completely tidied and cleaned after the visitors the previous evening. I must say, his friends are quite reasonable. I think they have learned how Monsieur hates dirt and mess. But I dust and polish everything anyway, of course."

"And you saw Monsieur Grant on Saturday morning?"

"I did, but only briefly. He left soon after I arrived. He told me he was going to Domme, to check out camera angles, I think he said. I confess, I had no idea what he meant, but after all, he is an artist, so one could not expect to understand him all the time, eh?"

"Well, that explains a lot," Susan observed as Madame Brouzet left with three euros for coffee to replace the cup she had left behind. She replaced the chair exactly where she had found it, and as she did, she exclaimed,

"Of course, for models! Different chairs for different poses. I wondered why they were all odd."

Thomas added his own takeaway from Loulou Brouzet's meanderings, "It also confirms how meticulous he is. He and Lucy Morrison were scheduled to go to Domme on Sunday to film. On Saturday he took the trouble to reconnoitre the best places to stand. A very diligent man."

Kiki Le Roux spoke up.

"If you give me his car key, when we're done here, I'll check Grant's GPS for trips in the last couple of weeks, and in particular see if he entered a destination for his trip to Périgueux on Friday. It would be good to know exactly what he was doing."

"Good idea."

"Should we have a look at these three paintings? You never know," Susan asked, before adding, "And there's something odd here. Everything in this room is fanatically tidy and ordered, but these paintings seem to have been stuck in any old slot. I would have expected them all to be in the first three slots on the left, or the right."

In fact, the paintings were in slots three, six and eleven, counting from the left.

"That is curious." agreed Thomas, "Let's take a look."

Carefully, Thomas lifted the unfinished painting from the easel and rested it gently across two of the empty chairs. Kiki slid out the first painting from slot three. It was of a man and a woman sitting opposite each other at a small round table in a street café. They seemed to be arguing. Another woman, seen only from the rear, was walking away from them. She wore a strapless sheath dress. Had the couple been arguing about the other woman? A lover, ex-wife, a call girl?"

The second painting showed a group of children playing rounders in a cobbled city street. A boy watched disconsolately from an open window in a tenement building. From their clothes and the occasional parked car, Susan immediately thought it was a remembered image from Grant's childhood in Glasgow.

The final picture was much larger, showing a dramatic sunset with a solitary figure looking out from a rugged headland and taking in the expansive view of manicured farmland and an ancient village stretching below him. Was it France? Was the figure enjoying the view? Contemplating suicide? Then Susan noticed a tiny detail; in the village churchyard far below the figure there was a fresh grave, the newly dug soil still proud of the surrounding earth. Was this figure the spirit of the recently deceased, taking one last look at the world he was leaving? Or a bereaved husband, lover, brother?

The three police officers studied the mysterious scene for many minutes before Kiki went to put the painting back in its slot, commenting,

"He was an interesting artist, wasn't he? He really makes you think about the stories in his paintings."

As she was saying this, the gendarme was carefully sliding the intriguing painting back into its slot. But it wouldn't quite go all the way in. She was inserting it as it had come off the easel, but now she had to bring it back out, turn it on its side, and slide it back in in a vertical position. She recalled that this is how she had found it.

"This is odd," she murmured. "It should fit either way, the unit is easily deep enough."

Thomas and Susan joined her at the storage unit. Kiki was quite right. Even the long edge of the painting was barely one metre long, and the unit was half as deep again.

Susan bent down and peered into a slot.

"They don't go all the way to the back. There must be a void behind the slots, in front of the wall."

Thomas thought for a moment.

"Maybe he wanted a larger top for his pots of brushes? But that makes no sense. Why not just have the slots made deeper?"

The three of them examined the unit more carefully. Thomas rapped his knuckles on the side wall in front of the supposed void. Susan knelt down at the other side and carefully felt all over the grooved panelling, feeling for a latch or hidden handle. She found nothing until she put out a hand to steady herself as she prepared to stand up. One strip of panelling gave way by a tiny fraction, and she then realised that the top ten centimetres or so one of the vertical tongue and grooved strips was actually on an invisible hinge. She used a fingernail to ease the strip open, revealing a hidden lock.

After an hour of looking in every possible hiding place, it was Kiki Le Roux who discovered the key, hiding more or less in plain sight in the studio.

"Capitaine! Here, I found it, the key."

Tony had devised a simple and completely effective hiding place for the key. He had cut a large paint brush in half and then, using glue and electrical tape, had attached the key to the brush head, with its bristles and metal ferrule intact. Then, he simply dropped it into the pot with the other brushes of the same size. They had looked at it twenty times, but only when Kiki had grabbed the entire bunch of brushes to empty the pot, did she inadvertently lift the key out and, of course, immediately spot the imposter.

Thomas gave an operatic sweep of his hand to indicate that Kiki should have the honour of opening the mysterious hidden lock.

"Look at this,' she exclaimed as she turned the key and opened the door to its limit to reveal a tall green safe. "That's a gun safe, and an impressive one at that."

The front of the safe had the manufacturer's name, HEINRICH HÖRMANN GmbH and the safe brand, HÖRMANN Tresore. There was a large dial for inputting a combination and a brass handle to open the door.

"It's high time I called Bordeaux," said Thomas. "I need an art expert and now I need a safe expert as well. This afternoon we'll go over the house, this studio and Monsieur Grant's effects to look for the combination of this safe, but in the end, I suspect we won't find it."

* * *

At the precise moment that Thomas was opening the front door of Tony's studio, Adjudant Eloise Brunel and Gendarme André Lefèvre were watching as an elegant Cessna jet rolled to a stop in front of a hangar at Bergerac airport. They accompanied the Border Security officer to the foot of the steps which smoothly emerged from the plane's fuselage. A very chic woman appeared and stood motionless for a heartbeat, before gracefully descending the airstairs. The Border officer quickly ran through the formalities of registering Caroline's arrival in France and handed her over to the gendarmes.

"Madame King, our condolences on your loss. I am Adjudant Brunel and this is Gendarme Lefèvre. We will escort you to Monpazier. Now, I understand that your car may be at Bordeaux airport, is that correct?"

"Yes, it's in long term parking."

"Very well, if you let me have the keys and the registration details and roughly where it is parked, we'll have it brought to Monpazier for you, if you wish."

Caroline reached out a manicured hand and laid it gently on Eloise's forearm, "That would be wonderful. I've been wondering what to do about that."

Eloise had arranged that André would drive them back to Monpazier, so she could make discreet notes in the front passenger seat as she talked with Caroline.

"Do you mind if I ask you some questions as we drive, Madame King? It will speed things up when we get to Monpazier."

"Of course."

"Please understand that there are certain questions we must ask everyone who knew the vic... Monsieur Grant. Do not be offended. Can you tell me what you have been doing since Saturday morning."

"Of course, I understand completely. On Saturday morning I washed my hair. After lunch I drove to Bordeaux and did a little shopping. Oh, first I checked into my hotel, *then* did some shopping. I bought a handbag and went for dinner in a small restaurant. Then I returned to my hotel and the next morning I drove out to the airport to catch my flight to London."

"You arrived by a private plane this morning, did you use it to go to London as well?

"No. Look, I should tell you that Tony and I, Mr Grant and I, were not getting on, we had decided to go our own ways some weeks ago. In the circumstances, I didn't feel like asking him to use his plane. But on Monday morning I got a call from Gerald, Tony's pilot, saying he would be happy to bring me here. I assume he knows what he's doing, I guess he figures it's appropriate in light of the circumstances. Tony's company will be paying the bills, but I have no idea who is making those decisions at this point – lawyers I assume. Gerald told me he will fly to Scotland in a day or two, to fetch Lorna and her husband for the funeral whenever we get a date."

"Lorna? That would be Lorna Cruikshank?"

"Lorna Hamilton is her name now. She is devastated. I called her on Monday to tell her. And I called Lorenzo, Tony's art dealer. He'll tell all the art people, and the media. I didn't know who else to notify. Tony has no family, and his friends are mostly here, in France, and I assume they all know. Well, that isn't perhaps quite correct. For all I know, for all Tony knew, his father may be alive, but they have had no contact since Tony was a young boy."

Her voice turned harsh and bitter, Eloise thought.

"I don't even know if I can arrange his funeral. You bloody French, you're so damn formal and stiff about everything. Tony and I lived together for twenty years, and your government treats me as if we were total bloody strangers, just because we never married."

She was clearly angry but collected herself.

"I'm sorry, I shouldn't be angry at you. But really, who will arrange Tony's funeral? I don't think anyone will talk to me, I'm not his wife."

"Don't worry, Madame, the Mairie are arranging everything, and I am sure they will be very happy to seek your advice on every detail. Please, do not be concerned; I'll make sure you see Madame le maire this afternoon. Now, can you let me have, for our records you understand, the name of the hotel and restaurant you used in Bordeaux? And perhaps your flight details on Sunday?"

"Of course. Here, I'll get my French bank record for the last few days, you can get all the details from there, I'm sure."

A few moments later, Caroline leaned forward and handed Eloise her iPhone, open at her Credit Agricole debit card transactions. Sure enough, there were toll records, a shopping bill from Galleries Lafayette and hotel and restaurant details. Eloise took a photo of the phone using her own. It certainly looked like Caroline was in the clear.

As she passed the phone back, Caroline added, "I was on BA 349 from Bordeaux on Sunday morning."

"Thank you," replied Eloise.

"Where should we drop you, Madame?" André asked, "We understand you have been staying in the Maison Anglaise, but we thought you may have moved out. We are holding a room for you at Edward Premier. Unfortunately, you cannot stay in Monsieur Grant's house until further notice. I'm sure you understand. If there is anything you need urgently from the house, just let one of us know and we will escort you to retrieve whatever you need."

"Thank you. Ed Prem, please. I moved most of my things out of the house in the past month, but now that Tony's gone, there are a few bits and pieces of mine I need to arrange to move, paintings mostly."

Eloise's promise regarding the funeral turned out to be empty, but not because of Caroline's lack of standing.

* * *

At 2 p.m. Thomas assembled the team in their conference room.

"Griset and Baye, a break from paperwork. Griset, Lefèvre, Le Roux and you, Adjudant, you four take the house. Baye, you'll be with me in the studio. Susan, please feel free to move around as you prefer. You may want to start in the house as you haven't seen the crime scene yet. But come to the studio when you wish. The professor from the art school and the safe expert from Bordeaux should be there late this afternoon. And remember everyone, gloves and masks at all times."

Neither search turned up anything resembling the combination of the safe.

The bright spot in the day was the early arrival of the safe expert who, luckily, had been on a job in Bergerac when he got the call.

"Good day, Capitaine, where is this safe?"

He was led to the storage unit and shown how the secret door opened.

"A Hörmann Tresore! Among the best. And without the combination, virtually impossible to open. Until the correct sequence of numbers is entered, the handle cannot turn. And there are many ingenious precautions built into the safe's mechanism to thwart would-be thieves. In short, this safe cannot be beaten by any normal means. In fact, I've never heard of a Hörmann Tresore being cracked without tools or explosives. What's behind it?"

"What do you mean, behind it?"

"A Hörmann Tresore is only about 45 centimetres deep. What else is in this space? There must be another metre at least surely?"

"Oh my God, how stupid am I? Of course there is."

Thomas went round to the other side of the unit and closely examined the same spot, and once again the secret hinged panel was opened. This time, when they used the same key to open the door, they saw another three lined storage slots for canvases, but all were empty. Another mystery. Why would an artist hide his own paintings? It made no sense.

A while after the safe expert started his work, the professor from the art school in Bordeaux arrived, looking none too happy to be here. He had been driven in a gendarmerie vehicle at high speed, lights on.

"I do not appreciate being dragged here, Capitaine, I am a busy man. If it was for anything but Tony Grant, I would have refused. But he was a great artist and a good man. So, what exactly do you want from me?"

"I need you to look around. If something in this studio relates to Monsieur Grant's death, I hope you can spot it. There is nothing obvious, at least to a lay person. That is why I requested an expert. Take your time. There are only two rooms: this one and a storeroom behind that wall. You are looking for anything at all that shouldn't be here, or anything missing that *should* be here."

"Well, I'm sure you don't need me to tell you how strange it is to see a working studio in this condition."

Thomas shared what they had learned from the cleaner about Tony's obsessive requirements and his need for order and cleanliness.

The professor walked over to the two shelves and picked up one of the larger sketchbooks.

"My goodness, these are amazing. Capitaine, you need to…"

"I know. They will be removed this evening and stored securely in the Gendarmerie until matters are resolved. As will the three canvases and the unfinished piece on the easel."

"Very well. Now this is strange. He has almost as many watercolour brushes as oils. But I've never seen a Tony Grant watercolour."

The man continued walking, talking as he did.

"What's in here? Oh yes, the storeroom. My God! I've seen art shops with fewer supplies. Rosemary & Co brushes, very English, but excellent. Michael Harding oils, Daniel Smith watercolours. Well, I suppose it is understandable. He formed his habits in England long ago and so now he orders in quantity. Most artists are creatures of habit. And again, all these watercolour brushes and paints. Very strange. I wonder where all the watercolour works are. Any ideas, Capitaine? Have you found any watercolour paintings, or sketch books? Anything?"

"All we have is what you see here, there is nothing in the house."

It took the safe expert nearly an hour to drill out the lock. He had used the heaviest equipment he had; it had taken three of them to carry the drill stand in from his van. But eventually it was done, and he opened the safe door. Although sold primarily for storing shotguns and rifles, this particular safe had been customised with a series of shelves. He stepped aside and allowed Eloise to lift out about a dozen folders. She laid them out on top of the storage unit. The top folder was neatly labelled.

FRANCESCO GUARDI

Veduta del Bacino di San Marco con la Dogana al Tramonto.

Eloise opened the folder. There were several sheets of paper. The top sheet held a photograph of a painting:

CATALOGUE ENTRY

Francesco Guardi (Venice, 1712–1793)

Veduta del Bacino di San Marco con la Dogana al Tramonto

Oil on canvas, 54 × 83 cm | c. 1770

An elegant rendering of the Bacino di San Marco at sunset, this work shows the Venetian waterfront bathed in warm ochres and fading pinks. The Dogana di Mare is prominently featured to the right, with sailboats and gondolas drifting towards the Riva degli Schiavoni. The treatment of the water – a signature Guardi flourish – shimmers with brisk, feathery brushwork, while the atmospheric perspective suggests a mature hand from the Guardi workshop or more likely, Guardi himself.

The composition echoes elements of known works at the Ca' Rezzonico and the National Gallery, London, yet contains enough variation to suggest it was a studio variant or private commission.

Notably, the absence of a signature is consistent with documented works from Guardi's late period, and pigment testing confirms the use of 18th-century materials consistent with Guardi's palette.

Provenance includes reputed ties to the Fagnano family estate near Lake Como, and subsequent residence in Swiss and Belgian private collections.

Offered with:

- Full conservation report (Fratelli Aversa, Rome)

- Authentication opinion (Prof. Lorenzo Bruni, Padua, 2016)

- Italian export licence (Protocol 1281/VEN/2017)

Price on request.

GPM ART CONSULTANTS

INVOICE

Buyer: Mr Henry L. Kemble, 238 Kensington Court Circle, London W14 5DN, United Kingdom

Date: 9 October 2021

Invoice No.: GS-INV-2271-R

Item Description:

Artist: Francesco Guardi (attrib.)   **Date**: Circa 1770

Title: *Veduta del Bacino di San Marco con la Dogana al Tramonto*

Medium: Oil on canvas   **Dimensions**: 54 × 83 cm

Condition: Very good; cleaned and revarnished (2016)

Provenance: See attached documentation (Fagnano family, Dr Heydel, Galerie Mirano)

Includes:

- Full conservation report (Fratelli Aversa, Rome)
- Authentication opinion (Prof. Lorenzo Bruni, Padua)
- Italian export licence (Protocol 1281/VEN/2017)

Sale Price: €290,000.00

VAT Status: Art object under resale regime (Margine IVA)

Payment Method: Wire transfer – Banque Julius Baer, Geneva, Switzerland

Notes: Sale executed under Italian law DL 42/2004. Work sold as "attribuito a Francesco Guardi" with no express guarantee of authorship. Buyer has acknowledged inspection and accepts historical uncertainties as detailed in catalogue.

The professor was the first to react.

"I think you have a major problem on your hands, Capitaine. I wish you well."

"Professor, you will not mention a word regarding this matter until you are cleared to do so by my superiors. Do you understand? This is a murder enquiry, and this information could be extremely relevant. So, not a word to anyone. Please treat this conversation as a formal instruction, *not* a request. We will ensure that someone contacts you as soon as you may discuss your role today. The officers will drive you back to Bordeaux. Thank you for your assistance."

During this exchange, Eloise brought out the rest of the folders and, from another shelf, a series of small, cheap red notebooks. Each had once again been neatly labelled, on the front this time, with years going back to 2004.

She picked out the book for 2023.

"Perhaps you should take a look, Capitaine, it's all in English of course."

It took Thomas only a minute to work out Tony's record-keeping system. At the front he apparently recorded each of the forged paintings he had produced that year. There were details of the artwork, its description, with many corrections and edits and details of the selling prices with, in each case, a deduction of 20% marked GPM.

The final page of that section contained a summary.

Egon Schiele	D	*Mädchen mit Blick zurück*	£250
Odilon Redon	W	*Papillon au clair de lune*	£300
Lovis Corinth	OP	*Frau im Gartenstuhl*	£375
Modigliani	W	*Jeune homme au col blanc*	£420
Franz von Stuck	OC	*Die Priesterin der Nacht*	£380
Emil Nolde	W	*Sturm über der Küste*	£300
Gabriele Münter	OB	*Haus mit rotem Dach*	£350
Christian Rohlfs	W	*Feld in Gelb und Grau*	£280
Max Pechstein	OC	*Dorfstrasse bei Abendrot*	£400
			£2705

As soon as he realised that final column was thousands of pounds, Thomas issued a terse command.

"Get him back!"

The next section of the book appeared to be a list of charities and, he could only assume, donations, again in thousands, he suspected.

Aberlour Child Care Trust	£50
Barnardo's	£200
Children in Scotland	£200
Enable Scotland Trust	£75
Enfance et Partage	€100
L'Enfant Bleu	€50
La Voix de l'Enfant	€200
Le Rire Médecin	€75
Les Papillons	€75
Lothian Autistic Society Trust	£50
NSPCC	£200
Save the Children	£100
Scottish Book Trust	£75
Seescape Trust	£50

The third and final section held simply a list of months and amounts, with a second entry for July – 'Greece £550' and two final entries – 'Lease £600' and 'Gerald £250'.

The amounts totalled £1400.

When he caught up with Eloise later, Thomas realised that the third section was mostly the cost of operating Tony's Cessna jet, although 'Greece £550' would remain a mystery a little longer.

When the professor, even less happy than before, reappeared, Thomas pointed to the summary of the opening section.

"Talk to me about this," he commanded, cutting off the professor's complaint before it had left his lips.

The professor spent a while looking back through the individual pages and examing a couple of the folders before answering.

"'OP' is oil on panel, 'OB' indicates oil on board and 'OC' is oil on canvas. 'W' is watercolour, which clears up that mystery, and 'D' is drawing. The artists are all, how can I put this, all in Ligue 2. None are really high profile, although Schiele and Modigliani are candidates for promotion. All were active before, say, 1930. It is just conceivable that all these works could have been lost, or hidden, or hanging unrecognised in some bourgeoise mansion. You really need a professional valuer, perhaps from one of the auction houses, but I'd say that the works were reasonably priced, perhaps at the lower end of valuations for these artists. Of course, that is without seeing the items."

He closed the book to look at the cover and then looked at the small pile of identical notebooks now lying on top of the storage unit.

"This is a nightmare."

He picked up the volume for 2022. There were 15 works listed. 2024 the same. It appeared that 2023 may have been a light year.

"My God! This will cause uproar in the market, uproar. We are talking about maybe 300 paintings, perhaps 100 million euros worth of art! Have you any idea what this could mean? And if any buyers are public galleries? Reputations will be ruined, just watch."

"Just remember my earlier instruction, professor; not a word of this, to anyone."

* * *

"Did you have any luck with the GPS, Le Roux?" Thomas asked at their daily end-of-day briefing.

"Yes, Capitaine. The victim doesn't seem to have used his car much at all. The GPS only stores the last forty destinations, which for Grant takes us back to December. In December and January there are some random addresses in the area. We'll check them out, but I suspect they will be homes of friends he visited around the Christmas period. In December and again in February there are trips to the airport and return trips three or four days later. From the middle of January there are regular trips to supermarkets in Villeréal and Bergerac. I imagine that after Caroline King left, he had to do his own shopping.

"Last Friday, he input a destination in Périgueux, which turns out to be a small regional office of Gide Loyrette Nouel, the big Paris law firm."

"Interesting; I wonder what that was about. We'll get on that tomorrow."

Thomas realised he hadn't invited Susan to speak yet, and also that he had no idea where she had been all afternoon.

"Detective, do you wish to add anything?"

"Well," she started, "the weather today was lovely, wasn't it? Cold but beautifully sunny, so the pétanque group had arranged to play. And I decided to join them."

The French gendarmes smiled with condescension, until Susan continued.

"Everyone knows about an affair between Gemma Taylor and Grant. There was a summer party last year, at the Hawksbys, an English couple who live on the edge of the village. The Ambassador had two or three drinks too many and started going on about his first wife. 'Magnificent hostess, charming, refined, elegant, managed the embassy like clockwork.' On and on and on. Eventually Gemma couldn't take any more of this and ran, sobbing, to the bottom of the garden, out of range of the party lights. The Hawksby's have a treehouse down there, apparently. Next thing, she's missing and so is Tony Grant. Zachary Taylor was too far gone to notice, but plenty of others could see what happened. It became a regular, if bizarre, ritual. They'd all appear at a party somewhere; Taylor would get drunk, and Gemma and Grant would go off somewhere. The consensus is that, since it only happened when Caroline was in England, she didn't seem to mind too much. However, it may be that the Ambassador wasn't always quite as drunk as he appeared; at least some of the time."

"Wow!" exclaimed Eloise. "You got all this playing pétanque?"

"I suspect not much happens in the expat community that someone in that group doesn't find out, one way or another. And they do like to gossip; 'just chatting' they call it.

"Oh, and Gus Pichon, Camille's brother, is usually mixed up in anything unsavoury going on in the village, including drugs, soft and hard, both of which are readily available apparently."

The gendarmes looked at Susan with considerably more respect than before.

"I'm having a drink with Lucy Morrison at La Réserve wine bar tonight, Capitaine. She had lots of access to the studio and I have a few questions for her. I'll call later this evening and give you my report."

Thomas had brought his laptop to the Mairie so they could all see the emerging video material. He and Susan watched the earlier sections again along with everyone else, then paid rather more attention when Thomas opened up the latest file.

* * *

Tuesday, March 8, 2022

1991 – Girvan, Scotland

In later years, Tony would have trouble remembering much about the next few years of his young life. With his vision problem finally resolved, he made rapid progress in his schoolwork, so that within a year or so, he had caught up with his peers and was now a solidly average student – a far cry from languishing as the class dunce for so many years.

The one area where he continued to excel, was art. By age twelve he could produce instantly recognisable portraits of the nuns and his classmates. At thirteen he began experimenting, creating his own art, rather than simply copying paintings from books. He still copied, but now it was styles, rather than images. He went through phases, producing pastiches of artists as far apart as Tintoretto and Picasso. He didn't know it, but all the while he was seeking his own artistic personality.

In his own, quiet way, Tony was happy, or at least content. The rare, brief, misspelled letters from his father soon dried up – Joe never once came to visit. This was never consciously an emotional issue for the young boy. He often missed his mother in the small hours of the night, desperately so sometimes; but his father had never been an emotionally significant figure in his life.

His true contentment and tranquillity came from his hours with Lorna. The two children had by now formed a remarkable bond, akin to close siblings, twins even. Their relationship had gradually become more one of equals, although Lorna was still the principal emotional intelligence of the pair.

Neither child could have explained the nature of their relationship. The Home was brutally austere – spotlessly clean, ordered, soulless – ironic perhaps given the avowed mission of the nuns. The children were brought up to understand that they were the product of failure – failed parents, failed people. Most were the product of unwed mothers, their original sin evident for all to see. It was entirely unlikely that they would rise above their unfortunate beginnings. The most that could be expected was for a pious, uneventful life and the hope that this would secure sufficient favour in the hereafter to balance their sinful origins.

In this bleak environment, it was perhaps the fundamental instinct to seek warmth, to be nurtured by something meaningful, that drove the two youngsters to open chinks in their emotional armour to one another. Whatever the reason, they formed a remarkable bond of deep affection, shared dependence and mutual protection in the inhospitable world they inhabited.

The clinical emptiness of the Home's interior was balanced somewhat by the untamed, expansive grounds surrounding the Victorian structure. There was a groundkeeper, two actually; but as the convent paid terrible wages, they attracted terrible staff. Between them, the two would-be gardeners just about managed to keep the narrow flower beds populated with shrubs, and they spent most of their time in a desultory, never-ending campaign of weeding the long gravel driveway and the parking area which was big enough to allow a bus to turn around. The remaining acres were by and large left for nature to take her course.

The nuns lacked the imagination to devise entertainment for the children in their leisure time, and a TV was out of the question. Instead, the children were left to entertain themselves as they saw fit, just so long as they went about it quietly and within the gym or the grounds.

Tony and Lorna came to know every inch of the property intimately. They climbed the climbable trees, threw sticks to bring down the conkers from the trees they couldn't climb. They pushed through the massed rhododendrons planted by the real gardeners of a long-ago owner when the Home was an actual home to a wealthy family who had made their money in the eighteenth century, tobacco trading in Glasgow.

They were happily diverted for a couple of weeks by the discovery of a semi-derelict brick shed once used to store a wide assortment of now rusted tools and gardening implements. Most were mundane, but a few implements were completely baffling to the children. As several had fearsome looking blades, they thrilled each other with stories of gruesome torture, meted out in failed attempts to discover the location of the hidden treasure that undoubtedly would have existed in such a grand property.

Theirs were the first eyes in twenty years to see the wildly overgrown and hidden group of statues left behind and long forgotten in a far corner of the site. As the statues were of various nude nymphs, much hilarity was derived from daring each other to touch the untouchable bits of the forlorn marble figures.

Then one day, Tony suddenly announced, pointing to an especially winsome figure, balancing a water ewer on a smooth hip, "I want to draw that one."

So, they stole small pieces of fabric from here and there and a block of hard soap. Then, with the help of a pair of rusted shears that they managed to loosen up, over a few weeks they cleared the weeds and cleaned off the moss to reveal a statue that, while far from pristine, was somewhat closer to her original condition.

Then, over two long Saturday afternoons, Tony drew the nymph in the glade. At first Lorna watched, amazed at her friend's easy facility with his pencils, but eventually she became bored and wandered off to explore on her own.

One Monday morning, Lorna opened her desk to find a carefully folded drawing inserted into her English exercise book. The finished drawing demonstrated the astonishing draughtsmanship that would characterise Tony's art in years to come, together with his sure touch for handling light and shade. Even a naïve young woman could see that this was a truly special work of a precociously talented artist. She turned the sheet over to reveal its dedication: 'To the best friend in the world. Ever.'

Even as Lorna was showing signs of her own body's budding changes, nothing altered between them. They remained what they had been since the very first day – innocent soulmates and utterly devoted to each other.

* * *

Lorna and Tony's lives should have proceeded undisturbed until first one then the other hit their sixteenth birthdays, when they would be unceremoniously ejected from the Home. But the regimented pattern of their lives was to be shredded by the arrival of Father Casey.

To avoid the trouble and expense of transporting the children to the nearest Catholic church for Mass, at some point in the past, two large rooms in the main building had been knocked together and consecrated as a church.

As with everything the nuns touched, the space was functional and spartan, the only decoration being the gruesomely realistic figure of the crucified Christ above the altar; saccharine representations of St Teresa and the Virgin Mary flanking it on each side, and various mismatched framed prints of saints, virgins and martyrs around the walls. Every Sunday, each religious holiday and on the first Friday of each month, the children would troop in to take communion and listen to a sermon that invariably focussed on the evils and wickedness of the world, with particular emphasis on wicked children generally, recalcitrant orphans in particular, and the dreadful wages of lust and sinfulness, as exemplified by themselves.

One Sunday, a new priest appeared, a replacement for the ancient Irishman who had finally been forced into retirement when his drinking became both unmanageable and highly visible. The new curate's first sermon was mercifully brief, largely consisting of a few words explaining how much he loved forward to 'getting to know each and every one of you'.

It happened that the new priest had arrived in the week that Tony turned fourteen. Lorna was, of course, the only person who knew or cared about this fact and certainly the only person who gave him a present. As the children had no access to money, presents were necessarily limited in their scope. This year, Lorna presented Tony with an enthusiastically knitted brown scarf, long enough to wrap around his neck and hang to his waist front and back. He loved it and immediately took to wearing his new fashion accessory every time they went outside.

The moment the new priest had stepped onto the altar, Lorna had felt her friend stiffen and remain rigid throughout the forty minutes of Mass. As soon as they filed out and into the gym, where the children milled about waiting to be called back into the same room, hastily rearranged to serve its normal function as the dining hall.

"What's the matter?" she whispered.

"Nothing," Tony replied.

"Come on, something's bothering you. Did you know that priest before?"

For the first time in their years of friendship, Tony snapped at his friend.

"Just shut up, Lorna, why don't you?" he hissed. "Shut up and leave me alone."

And with that he turned his back on her and eased his way through the crowd of pupils until she saw him slip through an open door. She knew he wouldn't be back for lunch.

For the next month, Tony was a completely unrecognisable boy. Silent and morose, he talked to no-one, not even Lorna. It was impossible for him to avoid her completely, but he tried his best. Even though they continued to sit next to each other in class, (moving around was not permitted), he let her know he was not interested in talking with her, playing with her, being with her, unless it was unavoidable. The young girl was at first wounded, but as ever, wise beyond her years. She understood that the change in her friend was not about her but somehow connected to the arrival of the new priest.

True to his word, Father Casey spent considerable time in the Home and set up a schedule to interview each pupil one-on-one, starting with the youngest class. Initially each student was grilled after their interview, but as the answers fell into a boring pattern: either a refusal to discuss the subject at all, or a repetitive 'nothing much', 'asked if I knew my family', 'asked if had ever thought of becoming a nun (or, for the boys, a priest)', interest soon waned and the notes being handed into class asking this or that pupil to come to Father Casey's office became routine and unremarkable.

Eventually, the priest's schedule worked its way up to Lorna and Tony's class and, in alphabetical order, one by one the pupils were asked to report for their interview with the curate. Lorna Cruikshank was soon summoned and afterwards, for the first time in nearly a month, Tony sought her out at the first break after her return.

With no apology or explanation for his previous behaviour, he immediately grilled her.

"What did he do?"

"Nothing. Asked some questions, asked if I thought I could be a nun, I said no. Asked what I would do next year when I left, that sort of thing. The usual. Why do you care anyway?"

Tony ignored her question. His eyes were bright she noticed.

"He didn't make you uncomfortable, didn't try to touch you or anything?"

In a single, slow, tortured heartbeat, awareness washed over Lorna. She knew, she empathetically felt, what had happened to Tony. St Peter's. Father Casey. All of it.

"Oh, Tony! Oh dear!"

She reached out a hand to grasp his, but as soon as he felt her touch, he wrenched his arm away and once again turned from his one and only ally and trotted quickly away.

Three days later, Tony's name was called in class. Lorna watched, horrified, as he slowly and deliberately made his way to the door.

For three days Lorna had barely slept. For the first time in her life, the extent of her isolation from the real world forced itself to the front of her mind. There was absolutely no-one she could talk to because she knew no-one. Lorna had been handed to the nuns before she was a week old. She had no clue about any family she might have once had. She thought she and Tony could perhaps run away, but even though money was an abstract concept – she had never held a coin or bank note in her hand any more than she had held an inch or an ounce – she understood that without it, they could not survive outside. A healthy girl, she had never seen a doctor, and a benefit of the repetitive, vegetable-heavy diet in the Home meant she had never seen a dentist either. She had never exchanged words with anyone outside the confines of the Home and the convent where they occasionally were taken for baffling 'retreats' whose purpose remained a mystery to her.

So that morning, she could do nothing but watch as her soulmate walked leadenly out of the classroom.

Half an hour after Tony had left, Sister Mary Joseph strode into Lorna's class, face red and clearly ready to erupt on the slightest provocation.

"Everyone, go to your dormitories immediately. There will be no talking, no whispering. You will go now, and you will stay there until you are summoned. Quickly, now. Go!"

To say that Sister Mary Joseph was unaccustomed to being disobeyed would be a considerable understatement. So, when Lorna stood resolute before her, she was astonished.

"Did you not hear me, Lorna Cruikshank? Go! Now!"

"Where is Tony, where is he?"

The nun was instantly apoplectic.

"Do not DARE to address me in that manner! And do not DARE mention that boy. If I had more time … GO TO YOUR DORMITORY RIGHT NOW, YOU INSOLENT WRETCH!"

The entire class had frozen by this point, appalled and excited in equal measure. The next few minutes were going to be memorable.

Lorna trembled before the nun, who was herself also trembling, but in rage, not fear.

"I WILL NOT! NOT UNTIL YOU TELL ME WHERE TONY IS!"

At that, the enraged nun reached out and grabbed a handful of Lorna's long hair and dragged the girl into the corridor. Seeing that the door to the cleaning supplies closet was slightly ajar, she threw it open with a loud bang and thrust Lorna through the opening and heard her crash into the assorted mops and brooms leaning against the back wall. She slammed the door shut and turned the key, locking Lorna in the unlit closet.

She put her face close to the door and yelled.

"When I have time to deal with you, you'll rue the day you were ever born to that slut of a mother. Just you wait!"

And with that Sister Mary Joseph marched off to evacuate the next classroom.

* * *

"Why didn't you ask for the police, Sister? Someone called 999 and asked for an ambulance, which is just as well or Father Casey might be dead, but why on earth did you not ask for the police as well. Someone, a priest no less, had been stabbed."

The detective had no idea just how bizarre it was for Sister Mary Joseph to be flustered, but flustered she was. For the second time today, someone was challenging her and this time she could not simply command obedience.

Obedience was the over-arching iron rule in Sister Mary Joseph's world. Obedience upwards and downwards; blind, unquestioning obedience. In truth, the nun wasn't much more connected to the real world than young Lorna, and she had been appalled when the detectives had walked in the front door just half an hour after she had called for the ambulance. It never occurred to any of the nuns that as soon as the hospital admitting doctor saw the handle of a rusted screwdriver jutting out of the unconscious priest's abdomen and realised that no-one had in fact communicated with law enforcement, someone would immediately call the local station.

"I, well, I don't know. I, we, we were very occupied with the children, I suppose; it didn't occur to us."

"One of your pupils thrust an old screwdriver into the belly of a priest and it didn't occur to you that we should be called?"

He looked as sceptical as he sounded.

He decided to move on.

"We need to find the boy. Where will he be do you think? It's a long way to a bus stop and miles to Girvan train station so he must still be on foot I would guess."

"He has no money for buses or trains, so yes, he'll be walking, or hiding."

"Are you sure he has no money? Couldn't he have saved some? Even some of his pocket money?"

"Our children have no need of money, so they don't have any."

The detective looked askance at this but decided to move on yet again. He was out of his depth in this alien environment and beginning to feel the cold waters of this unfamiliar swamp seep into his shoes.

"Friends, he must have friends. We need to talk with them; they may have some idea of where he would go."

"He has no friends," Sister Mary Joseph lied.

"But there's Lorna, Lorna Cruikshank, Sister. If anyone knows anything, she'll know. They're tight as anything those two."

The unwelcome interjection had come from Sister Helena, the deputy head, who had not witnessed Lorna's outburst or its consequences.

Initially Detective Inspector John Hughes thought nothing of this exchange. It seemed pretty believable to him that the headteacher might not know one of her charges very well - he doubted his old headmaster would have known much about his own friendships at school. He stood up, eager to move on and get out of this oppressive little room, overcrowded with the two nuns, himself and his Detective Sergeant, Janet Kerr.

"Let's go and get this Lorna. You said the children were all confined to their dormitories? That's handy."

He opened the door and ushered Janet ahead of him into the corridor.

Sister Mary Joseph hurried after him.

"I'll go and get Lorna; you can wait here."

Hughes picked up on the urgency in the nun's voice. He was about to insist on accompanying her but thought there might be a reluctance to allow a man near a girl's dormitory.

"Tell you what, Sister, I'll wait here and have a cigarette, Sergeant Kerr will accompany you."

He nodded to Janet to follow the nun, but Sister Mary Joseph seemed reluctant to move. There was an uncomfortable silence, which even Sister Helena found odd.

"I had occasion to reprimand Lorna Cruikshank. She isn't in her dormitory at this moment."

"Where is she, then?" Hughes asked.

By way of reply, the nun's shoulders dropped, and she replied in a quiet voice.

"She's in here."

And with that, Sister Mary Joseph, followed by Detective Kerr, walked twenty paces or so along the corridor and stopped before a door clearly marked 'Cleaning Materials'. She unlocked the door and, again in an uncharacteristically quiet voice, instructed Lorna, who was sitting cross-legged on the floor.

"Get up and come out here, girl."

In a quick exchange, the detectives had agreed that Sergeant Kerr would take the lead in questioning Lorna, having first dismissed the two nuns, careless of Sister Mary Joseph's protests.

"Hello, Lorna. I'm Detective Kerr, Janet; and this is my boss, Detective Hughes. We have a few questions for you, pet."

However, before any questions could be asked, Lorna butted in.

"Where's Tony? I'm not saying anything until I know where Tony is."

"We don't know where Tony is, Lorna. That's what we want your help with."

Lorna studied the detective's open face for a long time. Eventually she nodded.

"OK."

"Thank you. First, why were you in that closet?"

As Lorna carefully and methodically told her story, starting with Tony's reaction to Father Casey, the detectives quickly grasped the situation. By the time Lorna had finished, 'the very first time I met Tony, years and years ago, I knew there was something about St Peter's, something very bad happened there,' they understood what they were dealing with.

There had long been rumours among police forces of child abuse by Catholic priests. About some ministers too, but mostly about priests. But in the febrile sectarian climate of the West of Scotland, anyone with any political antenna whatsoever knew to steer well clear of the issue. In this case however, there was no avoiding it. The two detectives had absolutely no doubt that everything the young girl was telling them was accurate. She was clearly intelligent and deeply attached to the boy.

"Lorna, we appreciate everything you've told us, and we believe every word of it. We understand now why Tony did what he did, and that is going to make a big difference to how this works out. But he's in a lot of danger. He's out there somewhere, afraid and alone; cold and soon, very hungry. We have to find him, and quickly. Have you any idea where he might be hiding?"

Lorna looked at them both.

"What did he do? Did he hurt Father Casey?"

The police officers looked at each other. This time, Inspector Hughes took the lead.

"You've been very honest with us, Lorna, and you're a clever young woman, so I'm going to be honest with you. It seems that, yes, Tony did hurt the priest. He's OK, he's in hospital, and he's going to be fine. But I won't lie to you, Tony is in trouble. As Janet said, the circumstances mean that, well, people will understand. But we must find him and make sure he's safe. Now, can you help us? Will you help us?"

Tears began to flow silently down Lorna's cheeks as she reluctantly nodded her agreement.

* * *

Lorna stood beside Janet Kerr and silently watched. This was the fourth spot in the grounds that she had led them to. If Tony wasn't here, she really did have no idea where he had gone. But something inside told her he would be here. In truth, this or the old tool shed was always the likeliest hiding place, but she supposed part of her hoped he had got away while she led the police to their other favourite places. But now she watched as Inspector Hughes, bent almost double, led Tony out of the thicket of rhododendrons. Tony's sad eyes met hers, and once again, Lorna began to cry.

* * *

Lorna never got to say goodbye to Tony. He was taken away by uniformed police called in by the Inspector. Before they too left, the detectives went back to the main building, accompanied by Lorna.

Sister Mary Joseph and Sister Helena were summoned into an empty classroom.

Inspector Hughes studied the two nuns, paying particular attention to the older woman.

Gently, he guided Lorna to stand before him, facing forwards, and placed a hand on each of her slim shoulders as he addressed the senior woman.

"I want you to understand that I hold you absolutely responsible for this mess, you and your superiors. You brought this evil man into this environment, despite his history, which *someone* must have known about, in particular regarding the boy. Now, as I understand things, this young girl has to suffer you and this place for another ten months. We'll be checking in on her from time to time, and if we think for one minute that you have done anything to punish or harm this innocent child, we'll make your lives a fucking misery – yours in particular."

The vulgarity exploded into the silent classroom as he pointed straight at Sister Mary Joseph.

"Do I make myself clear? Now get out of my fucking sight. You and your sanctimonious hypocrisy disgust me."

* * *

The silence in the empty restaurant where they were filming following Tony's dispassionate account of his tortured childhood was total. The two members of staff who had been setting tables for lunch had ceased working but they had remained respectfully distant and still as they had listened.

Tony continued, "And that's how I came to be locked up. They called it secure accommodation, but it was, in all but name, a prison for young offenders. The windows were barred, and the exits all locked. We were marched from room to room in silence and were generally treated like criminals."

Tony gave a mirthless laugh. "I have to say, plenty of my fellow inmates really were apprentice criminals. Most of them ended up in real prisons at one time or another. I was one of the few lucky ones."

Lucy kept the camera close in on Tony's face as she asked him her next question.

"Did you ever find out what happened to the priest, Father Casey?"

"Only years later, after I had become … well, after I had the wherewithal to investigate. He died. He was never made to face up to anything. Same with Sister Mary Joseph. She retired a year later and died soon after. Old bitch!" He finished, still with venom in his words.

Unbidden, Tony continued.

"I was only in for two years. When I came out, they gave me fresh clothes and £100 – the money came from a charity. The secure Home was near Stirling, so it took me a few days to get back to Girvan. Sister Bernadette was still there, and I talked to her. Of course, Lorna had left the year before and they had no idea where she was. It's unbelievable. These kids, they turned sixteen and were turfed out, with nothing in most cases. The local parish tried to help, and usually they had somewhere to stay for a week or so and maybe a few pounds to see them on their way. But generally, they were cast out to fend for themselves. Do you know the film, '*Shawshank Redemption*'? Remember the old boy, the librarian, who hangs himself after a few months because he doesn't know how to function in the real world? We were like that."

Lucy allowed the following silence to develop, as the camera caught the emotions play across Tony's face. After a while he blinked and offered her a wan, sad smile.

"I used to wonder about Lorna, all the time. I didn't realise it then, but she was my first true love. Well, after Miss Johnson. My love for Lorna was more like that for a sister than a lover mind you. I just loved her for her, and for her love for me."

His voice broke a little as he continued.

"I missed her so much, for so long. My Lorna. I hated the church more for losing Lorna than for causing me to spend time in that damn prison."

Lucy decided it was time to move things on.

"What did you do when you got out, you must have been lost."

"I wasted a few weeks looking hopelessly for Lorna. I just walked the streets, sleeping rough, in Girvan, then here, in Glasgow, just looking at the faces of every young girl I saw. Pointless, of course. I had no idea where Lorna was. Could have been in Edinburgh, anywhere. Then, I got lucky. I was pretty fit by then, lots of running and weights. I'll say one thing for the secure Home; you got fit or you got beaten up regularly. It didn't take too many beatings before I learned that lesson. I got fit and handy."

Lucy interrupted him.

"Handy?"

He smiled.

"You've had a nice life, Lucy. Handy; I learned to handle myself, to deal out violence in response to violence. There are times and places when the best way to deal with violence is to try to defuse the situation, de-escalate matters. Not in a secure Home for violent young offenders, not for a smaller inmate anyway. I quickly learned to be merciless to bullies, to use everything; hands, teeth, feet, stones, bricks; whatever I could lay my hands on; and to show no mercy short of total capitulation and after dealing out unforgettable pain.

"That was my life lesson from incarceration at an early age – unrestrained brutality has its uses. Although I'm happy to report that I haven't hit anyone since those days. But then again, no-one has tried to hit me.

"Anyway, when I got out, I soon fell into a job labouring in a construction site and never looked back. Once you've worked on a building site and understand how things work, you can always find work anywhere there's a lot of new buildings going up – which is how I wound up in London."

"That's a great place to stop, Tony."

Lucy was uncharacteristically quiet as she packed up her equipment. Tony's story had affected her more than she was willing to let on. What a childhood! And how unlike her own, pampered middle class family background.

They were scheduled to have lunch in the restaurant, The Ubiquitous Chip, owned by an old friend of Tony's. The owner and his wife would be joining them shortly, along with a fellow inmate of Tony's from the secure Home, Stephen, and his lovely wife, Rona. Despite sailing close to the wind on a few occasions, Stephen too had avoided any further brushes with the law and now ran a highly successful fitness centre.

Lucy wasn't ready to make idle conversation.

"I'll just go and powder my nose, Tony. Be back in a minute."

When Lucy returned, Tony introduced her to his friends and over the next two hours the mood was well and truly lifted as the six of them enjoyed a spectacular lunch, aided by several bottles from the Chip's extensive cellar.

When they eventually walked back to their hotel, it seemed only natural for Lucy to follow Tony to his room, where they fell into bed and made love for the rest of the afternoon.

* * *

That evening Thomas made two calls before he called home: to his boss and to Procureur Lenglet. They had both been appalled at his news about the material in the safe. Both men were highly attuned to political nuances, and both understood that this case had just become an even higher profile problem. However they were both impressed with Thomas's approach and understanding of the wider issues, a confidence bolstered when they had a conference call even later that evening which included Juge Françoise Sandral.

When the conference call started, the judge had spoken first.

"It seemed that I got through to the Capitaine before he could reach me. Now I know why I got the busy tone several times; he must have been talking with you two. Anyway, I was calling him to let him know that I had received a call from a partner at Gide Loyrette Nouel. They want to meet me tomorrow on a matter of 'some urgency and delicacy regarding the death of Monsieur Grant' was how he put it. The Capitaine just found out today that Grant visited their Périgueux outpost the day before he died. I will meet with him, of course, in Monpazier, with Capitaine Coman."

* * *

Wednesday, March 9, 2022 – Early morning

Thomas's phone rang at eight o'clock. It was Colonel Digne.

"Good morning, Capitaine. This is just a head's up. The Minister of Culture will be attending the funeral for Grant on Friday. Which means I'll be there, the regional leadership group from Bordeaux will be there, the Departmental team from Périgueux will be there – basically everyone who thinks they're anyone. But don't worry, I know you have your hands full, I've appointing Bounnet as officer-in-charge of security and crowd management. This is just so you know what's happening."

"I appreciate the call, Colonel, but do think this is wise? The forgery issue will come out sooner rather than later – I half expected to hear it was out already when I saw your number on my screen."

"I know, I know, but there's no getting between a politician and a TV camera. I followed up with my warning in writing, because when the shit hits the fan, there'll be fingers pointed all over the place. But the Minister's office insists he has to attend."

Before Thomas had a chance to share his news, his phone rang again.

"Captain, it's Susan. I've just had a text telling me that the British Ambassador is planning to attend the funeral on Friday. I've replied asking for a call with his office later this morning. I'll have to tell him about the forgeries I'm afraid."

Thomas told her about his own call.

"Of course you'll have to tell him, I understand. Let me know how he reacts. Not that it matters too much now, it'll will be a circus anyway."

This morning, he had the team all present once more. Thomas addressed them.

"We can't get too totally focused on the forgery angle, not yet. It may have nothing to do with his murder. Having said that, Baye and Griset, I want you to build a complete picture of Grant's finances. I'll call Bordeaux and have them send someone from Financial Crimes to help but get started on it now. I expect we'll have access to his tax records late this afternoon, and his bank account tomorrow. Yes, Adjudant, what do you wish to say?"

Eloise lowered her hand.

"Has anyone appeared with a will yet? Madame King says he has a lawyer, I think we should speak with him. She, Madame King, is very bitter about something regarding her status. I've been thinking about it since yesterday. Why would she know about French law regarding unmarried partners? How would that have come up in the past? Then I thought, maybe his will. Worth checking out, don't you think, sir?"

"I do, Adjudant, good thinking. Baye, track down this lawyer. Anything else? Detective, why don't you share your ideas with the team after your talk with Lucy Morrison?"

Susan addressed the team in her flawless French.

"Lucy confirmed what I already suspected. Paintings, probably eight or nine, have been taken from the studio, plus, I suspect but do not know for certain, a number, possibly two or three, of Grant's forgeries."

She looked around the table as she continued.

"Lucy was often in the studio, although never alone. She is absolutely certain that at least twelve of the storage slots held paintings the last time she was there, only a few days before the murder. Grant had told her of his policy of having finished canvases ready for Lorenzo Biamonte so his income would be uninterrupted by extended travelling or if he just couldn't finish or even start a new painting. She is adamant that she never had a key to the studio, or knew the code, and I believe her. I don't think Grant would have wanted anyone to have free access to that studio – I'm still surprised he allowed his cleaner to have access, I guess that's a measure of his OCPD. He must have decided it was a worthwhile calculated risk.

"Anyway, we can assume that Grant was a creature of habit. If he held back original works, why not forgeries as well? And there are only three slots in the secret compartment, so a maximum of three missing forgeries to add to the haul. We do have a possible motive for his murder – theft. And there cannot be many people with the opportunity to get into that studio undetected. I've been thinking about that, and I can only think of Caroline King, who was his business partner as well as his romantic partner and so *must* have known there was more money coming in from somewhere and perhaps Camille Pichon, who may have had to get in to model. Although I really can't see Grant trusting her, sex or no sex. The cleaner, of course, and after yesterday, anyone who ever worked for the alarm company."

There was a thoughtful silence after Susan's report, until Kiki had a question,

"Susan, you mentioned OCPD, what is that, is it just the same as OCD?"

"No, Kiki. I called Psych Services in London for advice on Grant. Given what I was able to tell them, they think that a likely diagnosis is Obsessive-Compulsive Personality Disorder, OCPD. People with this condition are generally preoccupied with orderliness, perfectionism and control. They have a need for symmetry, tidiness and exactness – even beyond practicality. They will have rigid rules about cleaning, arranging, scheduling and may insist others conform to their standards, like Grant with his cleaner. And they are often workaholics. This all sounds just like Tony Grant."

Her colleagues, for that is how they saw themselves now, were nodding their heads as she wrapped up.

"Unlike an OCD sufferer, he wouldn't experience distress about his obsessions. He would believe his way is the right way. And he would never seek medical help for his condition. Why would he? It's just how he likes to lead his life, and it helps make him successful.

"Obsessive-Compulsive Disorder patients are troubled with intrusive, unwanted thoughts and repetitive rituals performed to relieve anxiety, like constant handwashing for example. Sufferers of OCD usually recognise that their behaviour is irrational, and hate being trapped by their condition. This does *not* sound like our man.

"And although OCPD may be inherited, it can also be triggered by childhood experiences, where neglect or chaos in early life can lead to order becoming a self-imposed coping strategy. My guy actually volunteered that religious or moral rigidity in upbringing could mean sufferers equate deviation from rules with sinfulness."

"A lot to digest, Detective Howard."

Thomas had been seriously impressed, as much by Susan's work ethic as her insights and how quickly she had absorbed so much background to the case.

He continued, "This morning, Le Roux and I are talking with Jennifer Oakes, she's the one mentioned by Elizabeth MacDonald. But before any of that, Lucy downloaded more video last night, while I was asleep. It was shot in London, apparently. Let's watch it now."

* * *

2001 – London

Eight years of working on construction sites had changed Tony. No longer the diffident boy, he now projected confidence, a swagger even. He was supremely fit, and he always had money in his pocket. He was, if anything, even more fastidious about everything in his life. His after-work clothes were always stylish, spotless and immaculately pressed. The women he took back to his rented rooms were invariably astonished at the cleanliness and minimalist order of everything they saw. He had hospital corners on his sheets. If they hadn't seen him as potential husband material before, they did now.

But nothing was further from Tony's mind. He was beginning to sense that he should be doing more with his life. He had no ties, he was healthy and, although no genius, he knew he had the street smarts to bluff his way at pretty much anything, which, as far as he could see, was all that London required.

For some years he had kept a growing set of scrapbooks where he rediscovered and honed his talent for art. He started using libraries again and visiting art galleries. He decided he should somehow try to find a way to make something of his talent. Maybe he would give it a year or two to discover if he had a viable future doing what he enjoyed more than anything else. And if all else failed, he could always go back to construction, a prospect which bothered him not at all.

* * *

The café was, to put it kindly, unprepossessing. Most of the guys from the building site used the sandwich shop opposite the site entrance. Tony liked to catch a few minutes of respite from the dirt and noise, so three or four days a week he brought his small sketchbook round the corner to this modest café that he had learned was family-run, but that had seen better days – sometime around 1975 perhaps. But the tea was hot, and the sausage and bacon rolls were excellent. So today he was cheerfully ensconced in his preferred spot by the window.

It would have been impossible for Tony not to overhear the passionate conversation going on beside him.

He knew by sight the first speaker, Peter, who Tony thought might be gay. Peter ran the place, working hard every day to keep everyone happy, helped by a varying cast of young women each of whom worked one or two lunchtimes each week, as far as Tony could figure. And presumably someone else, never seen, who was slaving away in the kitchen. But the old man, the grandfather, was new to Tony.

"It won't cost much, Nonnù, I can do a lot myself."

"If you do it yourself, it will take a long time, and if you close for a long time, how do the bills get paid, mmm? If you want it done fast, you'll have to use professionals. And that costs money."

The old man was sympathetic, but he wasn't sure his grandson should be wasting in his life in what had been *his* dream, all those years ago. And he was clear-headed; he could see that his old café was no longer what the young people wanted. The old prints of Napoli on the walls looked exactly what they were, tired old clichés.

"Listen to me, Pietrino. This area is improving, becoming more fashionable, I know that. But that also means this building is worth a lot more money. If we sell, I'll split the money with you, you'll be able to buy a flat, no mortgage, and find something new."

Tony couldn't see the young man reach out to cover his grandfather's liver-spotted hand with his own, but he could hear the love in his voice.

"Thank you, Nonnù, thank you. But you're right, this area is changing, quickly. That new building around the corner, it's going to have galleries and boutiques in the old building on the ground floor, and expensive new offices on the floors above. It'll be finance people; private equity and all that. They'll pay good money for fancy coffees and authentic food. But they want a different look."

The young man didn't want to insult the interior that his grandfather had installed by himself many years ago.

The conversation continued for another few minutes, going nowhere, when Tony decided to get involved. He slid along the vinyl-covered bench until he was alongside Peter.

"Hi. I'm sorry, but I couldn't help overhearing your conversation. My name is Tony. I'm a builder."

He swivelled to face the younger man.

"What is it you want to do?"

Peter was taken aback for a moment, but in an instant the thought occurred to him that he had nothing to lose by engaging with this man, who, he realised, wasn't much older than himself.

"Nothing major. This is an early Victorian building, so I thought to strip off the plywood panelling and plasterwork to reveal bare brick. And I suspect there will be a wood floor under this vinyl. And of course, rip out all the benches to make way for new tables and chairs. And a screen wall extending from the counter to hide the entrance to the kitchen. Then we could remove the kitchen door, which is a pain in the neck all day long."

"You'll have to rewire the whole place when you pull out these walls." Tony responded, giving himself time to think as he looked around.

"One thousand, cash, in instalments. Plus, materials and whatever I have to pay the electrician. Plus," he took a breath, "plus your walls for a year."

Now it was the old man's turn to be surprised.

"The walls? What do you mean?"

"The reason I'm prepared to do this job for essentially nothing, is I'm also an artist. I want to hang my work for sale on your walls. I'll give you a commission on anything we sell. One year, then the walls are all yours. And," he added, speaking to the grandfather now, "I reckon I can do this in a week, two at most, evenings and nights only, and weekends. And I'll rig up a temporary counter near the door, so you can continue your takeaway trade during the day, while the work's going on. So, you'll still get some income throughout."

* * *

The refurbishment was a huge success. Tony hadn't thought it necessary to point out that he could 'borrow' all the equipment he would use from the site, not to mention all the salvaged bricks, wiring and electrical fittings required. His mate Jeff did the electrical work for £200, and grandfather got so excited when he saw the rapid progress being made by Tony working ten hours each night after a full shift, that he paid for some trendy Italian tables and chairs.

Grandfather's respect for Tony took another leap when he saw the quality of the art that Tony hung before their official reopening.

"This is very, very good, Antonio," he announced. "You're going to be famous! You'll see. What's going in that space over there?"

"Ah, that's for the one you'll unveil on Saturday night, at the opening."

The opening crowd was an eclectic mixture. Jeff the electrician had told the guys on the site about Tony's hidden talent and a dozen of them turned up straight from work. Peter had invited all his friends, mostly gay of course, and the entire extended family of cousins, aunts and uncles were in attendance. At Tony's urging, Peter had pasted flyers on lampposts and on the hoarding around the construction site and that attracted quite a few locals, office workers and neighbouring business owners.

Around 9 o'clock, a flustered but very happy Peter found Tony outside on the pavement, mingling with the overflow crowd drinking grandfather's prosecco.

"Oh my God, Tony! It's working, it really is. Everyone loves the new look, and I've sold three of your pictures! Three!"

Peter's eyes were shining with excitement.

"Your mates from the building site? My crowd think I hired them for tonight."

"Sorry?"

"Can you spell Y.M.C.A.?"

Tony exploded with laughter.

"I can't wait to tell them that!"

"If you were gay, I'd kiss you right now!" Peter smiled.

"Sorry, mate," Tony replied with a laugh. "Come on, give me a hug and let's get grandfather. Time to do the unveiling."

When the old man, with help from his grandson, lifted the sheet off the final painting, all the nice words he had planned flew away, never to return. Speechless, he embraced his grandson and then Tony.

In the hours when he hadn't been working since the fateful conversation in the café, Tony had been working on this portrait of the old man. He had surreptitiously snatched a photo on his phone of grandfather sitting at his usual table, his newspaper in front of him, coffee cup midway to his lips. In the panelled background of the old café, Tony had moved a Naples print so that it was visible beside the sitter. He had caught perfectly the man's quiet dignity and sense of being exactly where he should be. Alone among the artworks on display, this one was not for sale.

* * *

Caroline recognised Tony instantly. She crossed the gallery floor.

"You won't remember me, we met a few weeks ago. Briefly."

She held out a hand, "Caroline."

He looked blank for a split second, before swallowing her hand in his. She could feel the hard callouses.

"Of course I remember, the café opening."

"I'm impressed; there were a lot of people there."

The smile in his eyes gave her a feeling she had last experienced when she was seventeen.

"You're not fishing for compliments, I hope? I'm teasing, of course I remember you. You were with a friend, we didn't talk, I was sorry about that."

"Thank you for saying that. What brings you here, sizing up the competition?"

She had said it carelessly, but his answer was very serious.

"I suppose so. Look at these prices." He held up his laminated sheet with numbers and asking prices. "Twenty thousand, thirty thousand, eighty! I would kill for these prices."

"And I thought you were all about the art!"

Now she was teasing.

"You're kidding. Being all about the art is fine when you don't need to think about the money. I do, believe me."

"How are your pieces in the café going?"

"They're going great, far better than we expected. But it's a café, how much would you pay for something on the wall of your favourite coffee bar? If I get 800 for a piece, I'm happy, never mind 80,000! Enough about me. What brings you here? And to my opening?"

"Curiosity, both times. I work at Christies, on their catalogues. Post-war art. It's my job to keep up with what's new."

"So, you're an expert on modern art?"

"No, I *see* a lot of modern art, and I write about it in suitably glowing terms. But an expert? No."

"What did you think of my stuff? And *I'm* not fishing for compliments. I'm taking advantage of an expert,"

He saw her shaking her head, and he continued, more forcefully, "An expert on *valuing*, and that's what I'm asking your opinion on – not if you liked it, but what you think it is worth. On the market."

She shook her head again.

"I write catalogue entries; I'm not the valuer."

"Don't sell yourself short. You've had more experience just observing how this stuff gets valued than 99% of the people here. So come on, your opinion. I'm a big boy; I can take it."

"Well, you asked for it. I thought most of it was derivative. Extremely competent but obviously trying to capture someone else's idea."

She held up her hand to stop his response.

"But I said at the time to Michael, the colleague I was with, one or two pieces were really good. And that portrait the old man unveiled; that was absolutely superb. We would be happy to put that in our catalogue. For serious money," she finished, looking him straight in the eye.

"My turn to say thanks."

"What are you hoping for? Is art a hobby, a sideline, what?"

"I think I'm maybe good enough, but I know enough to understand that having a certain amount of skill isn't nearly enough; art is a product just like any other, and just like fashion or toys or cars, success means having something unique to offer, and I haven't yet figured out what that might be, for me I mean. I'm still all over the place."

"Can I see your work?" she asked.

"You mean you want to see my etchings?" he replied with a smile.

She stared right back at him.

"Yeah, that's right."

The attraction between them was mutual and intense. She spent that night in his Hoxteth bedsit. The next morning was Saturday. They made love again when they awoke and then Caroline took charge.

"Come on then, let me see your stuff, then you can pack a toothbrush; I'm never staying here again, this is a dump. A spotlessly clean, extremely tidy dump, but a dump nonetheless."

"Who the hell are you…"

She silenced him with a finger laid softly on his lips.

"I'm not making a judgment on you, just on this place. Don't get all defensive on me; I'm telling you I want to make love with you again; just not here. Come on, I want to see your work."

It was just as he had told her, all over the place. There were landscapes, portraits, architectural details, still lives, street scenes. Oils, drawings, pastels, watercolours. In fact, pretty much every genre of figurative art she could imagine.

"Nothing abstract?" she asked.

"I don't understand abstract art," he replied. "I tried drips, geometric, colour washes, collage, but I don't get any of it. I went to Tate Britain once; there are some I can admire for their craft – Dali, de Chirico, Lichtenstein, even Warhol, guys like that. But I don't see the point in almost any of it. I mean some things are pretty, but surely that can't be enough?"

As he talked, Caroline continued to look at the work spread over the rumpled bed. She began to pick things out, sifting through the mass of drawings and paintings. Those she discarded made a large untidy pile on the floor. Eventually she was left with eight or nine items.

"Look here, at these."

He came to stand beside her, looking down at her selection of his work. There were two or three drawings, the rest were oils. All were studies of people doing everyday things.

Caroline swept her arm over the bed.

"I think there's something here, something in how you've captured the moment and their personalities."

She turned and looked at him once more.

"Toothbrush or not?"

He smiled. "Toothbrush."

Her place turned out to be a stunning flat in a converted warehouse in Camden Town.

"Wow! No wonder you thought my place was a dump; this is awesome."

"My dad bought this whole building for next to nothing forty years ago, to store furniture, if you can believe it. He had a shop a few blocks away and this place was dirt cheap. I'm slowly fixing it up, but I still have a way to go, as you can see."

The kitchen was clearly the focus of Caroline's apartment life; it took up all of one corner of the enormous space and was full of high-end units and appliances.

A large sectional sofa dominated the area in front of the floor-to-ceiling window, and the brick walls were liberally covered in an eclectic collection of art and posters

"I'm going to take a shower," she announced. "By all means look around, you could make us some coffee if you like, and maybe a sandwich if you're hungry – there's bread in the fridge."

When Caroline re-appeared twenty minutes later, stunning in a white shirt and tight leather trousers, Tony looked bashful.

"I couldn't figure out the coffee machine, did you get it from NASA?"

She smiled.

"From Italy actually. Sit down, I'll get us something in a minute."

"While you're doing that, tell me, what's your big plan?"

"I want to be a consultant, an art consultant."

"What does an art consultant do, for God's sake?"

"Art is a funny thing. No-one is sure what it is exactly. I mean, it's easy if you're talking Rembrandt, or Michelangelo, Caravaggio, those guys. But Pollock, Mondrian – people had to be told these were the real deal. Don't forget, Van Gogh died penniless. Why? Because there was no-one telling the collectors that this was the guy to buy."

Caroline was warming to her pitch, he realised.

"Collectors today, the rich ones I mean, are buying for status, for legacy, for appreciation. They know about futures, about margin calls, P/E ratios. What they mostly don't know is art. They need someone to hold their hand. That could be me. And I love the world, the art world. Sure, there's tons of bullshit, but there are tons of interesting people too. Cool people, great ideas. Since I'm not likely to become a billionaire, I can work for one. Or two, or three," she finished with a smile.

"Well, good to know what you want, I guess."

When they had finished their coffee, Caroline loaded their cups into the dishwasher as she told Tony her plan for the day.

"I'd like to take you back to Tate Modern." She laughed as once again she laid a finger on his lips to quell the protest forming there, "There's an artist on temporary exhibition, I think you should look at him; you might find his work interesting. We can grab something to eat on the way."

When they arrived at the cavernous structure, Caroline guided them to the gallery hosting the Edward Hopper retrospective. She watched carefully as Tony walked slowly past the paintings and occasional drawing, regularly stopping to study something that grabbed his attention. Over two hours elapsed before they exchanged a single word.

Turning to face her, Tony gently took Caroline's arm and led her into the first room they had visited.

"Come over here, I need to show you something."

He stopped before a painting of a woman sitting on the edge of a bed, in her bra and underskirt, sewing a white dress. The woman was facing away from the viewer, with only her back visible. It could have been wedding dress that she was repairing or altering.

"I painted this, a few years ago."

He clarified. "I mean, I painted this idea. My subject was in profile, but the idea was very similar. The girl was wearing the dress and had stopped sewing her hem for a moment as she stared into space. Her face is in shadow, so we can't see her expression very well. She is going to a fancy event, a ball perhaps, and she is contemplating the evening to come. Perhaps she expects a proposal. Perhaps she plans to dump the guy, or sleep with him for the first time. Or maybe it's a first date with the boy next door. You haven't seen it; I gave it away."

He paused and looked around the room.

"Thank you for this, Caroline. Hopper is a genius. I need to think hard about these paintings."

"There's someone else I'd like you see. He's going to be exhibited at Saatchi's soon; we can go see him there."

By the time Saatchi show came around, Tony had moved his few possessions into Caroline's flat. After two weeks, when they had seen each other almost every day, Caroline had suggested that he move in and save his rent money. When he had finally unpacked, he had given her two paintings.

"This one is my favourite, it's a gift. This is my second favourite, this is a loan. When you're fed up having me around, just give me this one back and I'll understand. I won't argue, promise."

Tony's arrival had meant a rearrangement of the space. The area in front of the main window was now his studio, and the sofa and TV were now relegated to the rear half of the room. There was still plenty of room for living, eating and loving.

And with each passing day, the flat became progressively tidier, cleaner and better organised.

* * *

"You're looking very cheery this morning." Caroline observed, helping herself to another slice of toast.

"I'm calling in; I'm taking a couple of days off."

"Oh, yes?"

"I've had an idea, for a painting I mean."

Tony looked at her intently, his eyes very much alive.

"Do you remember the painting I told you about, the girl mending her hem? We were at the Hopper exhibition you took me to."

"You gave it away, didn't you?"

"Yes, but I'm going to do it again, but this time I know what she's thinking, what's actually going on."

He stopped and crossed over to the shiny Italian coffee machine.

"Go on then; what's going on?"

"Can I not tell you? Until it's done? I want your reaction when you see it."

She smiled.

"Very well, but don't take too long!"

That had been Wednesday morning. Tony worked on the painting all day Thursday and Friday as well and begged off their plans for the weekend, leaving Caroline with the prospect of going to a party and an afternoon movie on her own. But she didn't mind. She enjoyed seeing him so totally focussed on his work. On Friday evening when she got home, she quickly noticed that the kitchen was exactly as she had left it, their breakfast dishes the only things in the dishwasher.

"Have you eaten anything?" she asked.

"What? No, nothing. Actually, now you mention it, I'm starving!"

"I'll make us something. But you have to agree to stop for one hour minimum while we eat. Deal?"

"Deal."

She made them a stir-fry and opened a bottle of white wine.

"So, how is it going?"

94

"Not too great this afternoon. I'm having trouble fixing my idea in my head, fixing it well enough to execute. I've a favour to ask; would you mind modelling for me? It'll just be for a few minutes."

"I don't understand. How can me posing for a few minutes help?"

"I'm going to take a photograph of you," he replied.

He could see that she was uneasy.

"Lots of artists worked from photographs. Cézanne, Toulouse-Lautrec, Degas, Manet, Gauguin – they all used photographs, and not just for portraits. I think they may have been dealing with the same problem I have. I start with a clear picture in my head, but as time passes, I need to keep too many things in perfect alignment. It may be the angle of an arm, or the tilt of a head. And without a model in front of me, it's easy to drift slightly off and then suddenly the whole thing is out of kilter."

"Of course, I'll help. But does this mean you'll be painting me, if you know what I mean?"

"No, it won't be anything like you in fact. The woman in the painting is nothing like you. Maybe a similar shape," he smiled, "the shape I like. But she has jet black hair and… Well, truth be told, she isn't realistic at all. She's an idea of a woman; not an ideal, but an idea. She represents a type, I suppose, rather than an actual flesh and blood person."

Next morning, Caroline sensed Tony's urgency and showered as quickly as she could.

"Is there anything in particular you want me to wear?" she asked, standing with a towel wrapped around her.

"Yes, a dress with a full skirt and fitted top, or a skirt and separate top would do just as well. Doesn't matter what colour or fabric. You're mending a hem while still wearing the dress, so it can't be tight, or too short. The top should be as tight as possible – I want to see how your body is moving. I won't be painting it like that, but I need to know what's happening under the clothes."

In a few minutes Caroline emerged from their bedroom wearing a Lycra top over a full frilled cotton skirt.

"That's great, sweetheart, just perfect. Come and sit over here."

He had positioned a dining chair in front of where his easel stood, angled so the light from the window fell across one shoulder.

"Tell you what, never mind how I imagined it; how would you do this? You've just realised that a little section of hem at the front of your dress has come undone. Maybe you snagged it stepping into it. Anyway, how would you position yourself to put in a few stitches before you go out?"

Caroline didn't think about it too much. She settled herself in the chair to find a more comfortable position before reaching down to pick up the hem of her skirt. She examined it, as if studying the problem and then she mimed pushing a needle through the thick fabric.

"Stop! Right there, that's it! Perfect."

Working quickly, Tony picked up his iPad and took five or six photographs.

"Great. You're sitting pretty much exactly as I thought. Now, can you keep your arms and hands exactly where they are, but look away from what you're doing. Look just over my left shoulder."

He swivelled round to see what was behind him.

"The painting of Venice, look at that."

A few more photographs.

"That's it, all done. I told you it would be fast; although you're a natural, by the way."

He pulled another chair over to sit beside her.

"You see, it's just automatic that your arms work in perfect harmony to bring the hem and the needle together just so. And I already got that. But when you looked away, there's a tension now because your body had settled into its sewing shape, but now your neck is slightly tensed, holding your head in a different position. I've not been getting that right. And that space below your arm and breast. See how complicated the shadows are? I would never have been able to imagine that complexity, I don't think."

He was totally animated now, eager to get back to work.

"Thanks, that was really useful. It makes a huge difference, not just observing a scene, but *imagining* it, the whole story I mean. I know everything important that's happened to this woman since she was a child. She likes white wine, but not red. Hates beer. She loves theatre, hates musicals and only listens to classical music and jazz. She reads a lot, but she isn't confident about expressing her opinions about what she's read. She drinks camomile tea. Weirdly, she loves football, supports Arsenal, which is the one subject she is happy to debate fiercely, for as long as it takes to convince you that she is right. Most of all, I know *exactly* what she's thinking at the moment of the painting."

"Wow! Should I be jealous?" Caroline asked with a smile.

Tony missed her attempt at humour.

"She's not real; I mean, she's not based on anyone real. She just ... a person."

"Tony, I was joking!"

"Oh! Well anyway, she's real to me; right now, I mean. And so is this evening ... I mean the evening in the painting."

Caroline stood up and walked around the chair until she stood direct behind him. She wrapped her arms around his shoulders and kissed his neck.

"I think it's all great. I can't wait to see it. Speaking of this evening, you know we're invited to Jeff and Sally's for their party?"

"Yeah, I remember."

She felt his body tense and laughed.

"It's fine, I don't mind going by myself."

Caroline left the dinner party early, but it was still well after eleven when she came home to find Tony still intensely focused on his work.

"Going better?" she asked.

"Much," he replied, without looking away from his canvas.

She came over and kissed his cheek, playfully holding a hand in front of her eyes.

"I'm turning in. Promise you'll wake me when you do come to bed. And I didn't peek. Promise."

Early on Sunday evening, Caroline came home from seeing *The Truman Show*. As soon as she entered the apartment, she knew the painting was finished. Tony had laid the table for dinner, complete with flowers, red and white roses. And he had changed his clothes, no longer in his paint splattered jeans and a t-shirt.

"How was the film?" he asked.

"Who cares about the damn film? Show me the bloody painting!"

Tony led her over to stand before his easel. He had once again covered it with a sheet. Quickly, he lifted the white cloth and revealed his work.

Caroline said nothing for at least five minutes. Then she turned, embraced him, and with her lips touching his ear, she whispered,

"It's wonderful, amazing, really fantastic, Tony. God! I'm so proud of you."

She peeled away slightly so she could look him as she continued.

"Can I tell you what I think?"

"Of course, please."

"She's dressed very carefully; made up beautifully."

She stopped, puzzled; and turned back to the easel.

"I thought she was going to a fancy ball or something?"

"She was before, but no longer."

"Right, but she's still very smartly dressed. She's got ready just like for a date, but she doesn't seem excited. I wonder if mending her hem is a way to delay her departure? Why is she concerned? Or worried, or whatever?"

Tony allowed the silence to grow. He draped his arm across Caroline's shoulder but said nothing. He was intensely curious to hear her final response.

"She's not concerned – she's distracted! That's it! Something else has happened, earlier today maybe. Something important, and now she's not sure she wants to go to wherever it is she's going. But it's too late to back out now."

Caroline smiled at him.

"Listen to me, spouting off. But it's a sign of how good the painting is, how it draws me in. She's very attractive you know, I think I am just a little bit jealous."

He tightened the arm around her shoulders, pulling them closer together.

"You're spot on with the story. She is going to dinner with a man she's been seeing for some time; they're lovers but not living together. She's never felt that he is the one, her forever partner. But they rub along together; he's charming and kind and they enjoy each other's company. This morning, she bumped into someone from her past. They were utterly besotted with each other at college, where he was a year ahead of her. He graduated and went to America, to Stanford Law School. Then, they simply drifted apart; they hadn't been in contact for years; until today. They had a quick lunch in a café. She had heard through the grapevine that he had married years ago, but today she discovered that he is divorced. When he told her this, she realised that she was pleased, excited even. He asked her to have dinner with him that night, but she had to explain that she was already booked. He's going back to the States tomorrow afternoon. Now she's thinking about it all. I'm not sure, but I think that she'll bail out later in the evening and call her old flame and spend the night with him. I think her life is about to change."

Caroline looked at the painting again. She could see the whole tale now.

"Is that his business card on the table?" she pointed.

"Yes, with his cell number of course. She's been looking at it."

"What will you do with this?"

"Sell it, I guess."

"How? I mean, not in the café, surely? This is too good for Peter's place, Tony."

"There are a couple of galleries in the Kings Road who I've been talking to. Maybe I can use this to get in?"

"I know someone, Lorenzo Biamonte. He's a dealer, has a nice Mayfair gallery. He's just inside the top ten I'd guess, but he's a bit hungrier than the really big guys. He's in and out of our office. He's a bit of a snob, to tell you the truth; he likes to tell you how his family was one of the first dealers in London. But he does sell a lot of art and he's very well-connected. I could introduce you, if you like."

* * *

Ten days later, Caroline leaned in to have her cheeks lightly brushed by Lorenzo Biamonte's lips.

"Thank you for seeing us, Lorenzo," she said after the introductions.

"Not at all, my dear. This is the first time in all the years you've known me, so I imagine it will be worthwhile."

"I hope so, but I should tell you first that Tony and I are living together. That isn't why we're here, but I wanted you to know up front."

"Well, thank you for being honest."

He turned to Tony.

"I see you've brought something for me to look at. Good. Let Geoffrey clear this easel, and we'll have a look, shall we?"

Lorenzo's assistant was almost as immaculately dressed as his boss, in a beautifully tailored lightweight suit that screamed class as well as money. For once Tony felt underdressed as he carefully lifted his painting onto the easel.

No one spoke for several minutes until eventually; Lorenzo broke the silence.

"This is very good, Tony, very, very good."

Now he turned to his assistant.

"I'm thinking perhaps David?"

"Or Steve?"

"Mmm, possibly. Let's sit down."

Geoffrey ushered them over to a seating area furnished with antique, but remarkably comfortable, chairs.

"You see, Tony," Lorenzo addressed them like a class in college. "My job is not just to sell art, but to sell it to the right client. Particularly at the outset of a career, it is essential to be taken up by the right people. David Geffen and Steve Martin are two of the most widely respected celebrity collectors in the world, both known for their excellent taste. And I'm thinking Hollywood people, movie people, because your painting is very narrative driven and will appeal to a certain audience in particular. There is so much utter crap out there, it is becoming impossible to separate the garbage from the worthwhile, especially since the art schools began dropping their requirement for drawing. Picasso said that an artist should learn the rules like a pro, so you can break them like an artist. Now they refuse to even acknowledge the existence of rules."

Geoffrey took up the argument.

"Most collectors have no training, no expertise. They fear making the wrong choice and being laughed at behind their back, or even to their face. So, they want reassurance by buying from a respected dealer," he had the grace not to add 'like us', "or buying something by someone in a public collection or collected by someone with an unquestioned reputation for discernment."

Lorenzo changed the subject and the tone by asking Tony some questions.

"Where are you selling your work today?"

Caroline stepped in at this point.

"Tony is just starting out, Lorenzo, he hasn't been launched yet. A friend hangs his works in his bistro, but that's just a casual, friend-to-friend thing. He isn't represented by anyone.

"I see. And how much are you selling your pieces for?"

"A few hundred, maybe a thousand pounds."

"This is essential. If we are going to work together, I need you to go straight to your friend's place, right now and take everything down.

Everything. Do you understand? I would be listing this painting at £40,000. So, you see the problem, I'm sure. When you recover your other items, bring them to me and we'll discuss what happens. But I warn you, I may ask you to hold on to them for a while, perhaps indefinitely."

Tony couldn't help noticing that Lorenzo was talking as if this was a done deal. On the one hand, he was excited, thrilled, but he was also a little ticked that the smooth-talking dealer was taking his agreement for granted.

Lorenzo still wasn't finished. He waved a manicured hand towards the easel with Tony's painting.

"Could you produce a painting this size or larger every month for, say six months? I don't want to flood the market, of course, but neither do I want to generate interest that we can't take advantage of."

"I think we have a few matters to discuss before we get that far, don't you, Lorenzo?"

Lorenzo brushed an invisible speck of dust from his collar.

"Tony, we are here because of my admiration for Caroline. Art is a matter of ..."

"Lorenzo, let's be clear from the very beginning. I don't give a flying fuck about art for art's sake. I'm in this for the money. So yes, I can produce a comparable piece every month until hell freezes over, for the right money. You know the line 'Paris is the only city in the world where starving to death is still considered an art.'? Well, I have absolutely no interest in starving for my art. I want to be rich, and I don't mind you making money alongside me. You can do things I can't, you know people that I don't; like 'Steve' and 'David'. And, by the way, don't ever try to bullshit me with names you *don't* know. So, Lorenzo, Geoffrey, this isn't a budding romance, this is a budding business arrangement. What are the terms, how do you propose to make this work?"

* * *

"Oh my God! I thought I was going to wet myself! Believe me, Lorenzo Biamonte has never been talked to like that, *never!*"

They were walking through Mayfair and Caroline squeezed Tony's arm even tighter. He had never seen her so animated.

She carried on, words tumbling over each other.

"And you know what? I think he quite liked it. The great Lorenzo Biamonte! Beaten down by an unknown artist. I wish he hadn't sworn me to secrecy; this is such a great story. A new artist would *never* get 50% from a Mayfair gallery. And when you told him you would have to give Peter a month to replace your pictures …"

"I'm still coming to terms with 50%, for God's sake, that seems like a fortune to me."

"I know, and it is. But he'll work hard for it, just watch. If he can really sell your art to Geffen or Steve Martin, it's a huge feather in his cap. The New York and LA dealers like to think of those guys as their own. And don't forget, you skipped having to fork out another 10% or 20% for a manager, out of your half."

"You're kidding!"

"No, I'm serious. That's how it works. And if the buyer used a consultant, that's someone else to be paid by somebody. But don't worry," she gave him a pinch and smiled, "I'll take my share in another currency altogether. And I'll even buy us a slap-up meal to celebrate. Come on, let's go crazy, we'll go to Nobu."

* * *

Lucy was still adjusting the lighting. They were in Lorenzo's gallery, but it was late, after nine o'clock and the gallery was closed. Geoffrey was helping, raising and lowering various gallery lights until Lucy was satisfied. It was going to be a fantastic backdrop, and she had persuaded Tony to talk about a couple of his paintings. They had already filmed a segment in Peter's café, a lot bigger now since he had acquired the space next door and knocked down the connecting wall.

Finally, everything was ready and she began filming.

"So, Tony, we've brought the story up to the start of your relationship with Lorenzo Biamonte. How did it go from there?"

"Really well. Caroline was right, as usual. Lorenzo worked his immaculately dressed butt off and we started to sell paintings. Although quite a few months went by before I received any money."

"So, you were still working in the building site?"

"Oh no. Caroline persuaded me to pack it in and work full-time on the art. She paid all the bills for almost four months. I wouldn't be here without Caroline."

By now, Lucy knew that Tony and Caroline were not married and were, in fact, splitting up, but he wouldn't let her use this information, which frustrated the hell out of her, especially as Tony was still being so complimentary about his now former partner.

"And did Steve Martin or David Geffen buy that painting?"

"Not that one, no, but they both bought that first year."

"Steve Martin bought *'Belle Figure'*, didn't he?"

"He did. Steve is an exceptionally generous man. He bought it and then loaned to half-a-dozen public galleries for various exhibitions. It's the painting that really brought me wide attention."

Lucy knew that, at this point, the screen would be filled with Tony's first blockbuster painting, one that had adorned a million postcards, prints, mugs and jigsaws. Two attractive young people were set in a perfect Tuscan landscape. The boy has lifted his girlfriend and spun her around, so her long legs stretched out gracefully, her hair framing both of their heads. It should have been a cliché, but in Tony's hands it had become a symbol of young, carefree love and romance. On close inspection, the viewer could see that the boy was blind. His appreciation of the beauty of the girl and of their shared experience was far more than skin deep. Did he somehow sense the glorious landscape, the soon-to-be-setting sun, the perfection of the moment?

Lucy had discussed the next question with Tony well in advance, so he knew what was coming.

"You know, Tony, most of the critics are really dismissive of your work, in large part because of *'Belle Figure'*. How do you feel about that?"

"You can probably guess. I don't know who said it first, but 'critics are to authors what dogs are to lampposts' works in art as well. Critics are utterly full of shit. I mean, don't get me wrong, a lot of so-called artists are even worse."

He leaned forward in his chair, keen to add force to his words.

"It all went to hell in the sixties. People, like me, with no training and, worse, far worse, with no talent, decided they could create art and sell it. And critics emerged who encouraged them. The blind leading the blind. A new art establishment gradually emerged – a dozen or so gallery owners in New York and London, a handful of curators of big public collections and half a dozen critics with key audiences – the glossy magazines, the New York Times. Then this band of, oh I don't know, say fifty people globally, they and they alone decided what was art and what wasn't; what MoMA, the Tate, the Pompidou Centre would hang and what they wouldn't. And guess what? Anyone producing art that didn't need a truckful of bullshit jargon to interpret it, that no longer counted for shit. A few good people got through, Hockney for example, artists who were just too damn good and too damn popular to be ignored. But they were the exceptions."

He leaned back and took a deep breath.

"Do you ever wonder how the ancient Greeks produced the greatest sculpture we've ever seen? How Renaissance art ever came to be made? How it all existed without critics? Easily. Because real art doesn't need a critic to communicate. The Renaissance popes didn't need *Apollo* or *Frieze* or the *New York Times* to tell them Raphael was a fucking genius – they had *eyes*. As you can probably tell, it drives me crazy. Of course, it doesn't stop people buying my paintings. That drives *them* crazy, I'm happy to say."

He leaned forward once again and stared into the camera.

"Look at the wall paintings in Pompeii. Sure, there a few allegories with gods and frolicking nymphs; but mostly its people eating, still lives, beautiful girls, people having sex. It's beauty, it's life, it's happiness. It isn't a bunch of circles, or dots or … I'll tell you all you need to know about artists and art critics – and this is from the High Priest of modern art, Picasso himself. He said, 'When art critics get together, they talk about Form and Structure and Meaning. When artists get together, they talk about where you can buy cheap turpentine.' We're artists, yes, but we're artisans first."

Lucy signalled the end of that segment.

"That was terrific, Tony. Excellent TV, and I think you made your point. Let's take a minute and let me rearrange things for the next segment. We'll talk about some of your paintings, so you'll be on your feet."

A few minutes later, Lucy was ready to go.

"We're rolling again."

Lucy had mounted the camera on the SteadyCam so she could follow Tony as he stopped before each painting in turn. As discussed, she wouldn't prompt him unless absolutely necessary.

"*Belle Figure* was great for me, but Lorenzo was keen that my next big piece didn't have another romantic theme; he didn't want me to be restricted or, to be honest, to be lazy. This is called '*Over The Top*', although now I wish I had come up with something more original for the title."

The painting, all greys, blacks and browns, was of a World War I trench. The only figure properly defined is a young soldier, one foot on the makeshift wooden step that will lift him above the parapet as his regiment mounts another futile assault.

"He's terrified, of course. I talked with a few soldiers before I did this. They all said the same thing. They do what they do, not because they're heroic, but because they fear humiliation in front of their mates more than they fear the enemy. See that dark patch? He's wet himself. That's how utterly and absolutely terrified he is. And in about twenty seconds, he'll be cut to pieces. That little strip of white? That's the letter they'll find, to his mum. The last letter she'll ever receive. She'll plough on, but her husband, his father, will be dead inside two years of a broken heart. His mother will never forget him; won't ever move house because she can't leave his room behind. She thinks about him every day, but carries on because, well, that's what you do, isn't it? She has courage enough for all of them, you see. Now, I know that none of this is in the painting; but it is for me. I *know* that boy. I know him at school. I know the girl he secretly loves. I know him like I know myself. I believe, I hope, that somehow all of the life I know about this boy and his family, that somehow that knowledge, that intimacy, flows from my brain, though my arm and into the canvas.

"Another celebrity bought this. I won't say who, he sold it again quickly after I went public. You see, he thought it was an anti-war piece and that's why he bought it – it suited his politics. But it isn't anti-war, it's pro-soldier. It's about what soldiers do that we don't want to do, and the price they and their families pay for fighting the fights we won't. But," he smiled as he turned to the camera, "it certainly isn't romantic, is it."

With that, Tony led Lucy and her camera to another painting in the room.

"I'm often asked if standards in the art world have fallen. Certainly, the threshold to be a professional artist in the past was higher. You had to have a high level of skill to be able to paint and have the time and money to make art, or a sponsor who would support you. So, there were far fewer artists. Whereas nowadays, the threshold is lower. I'm with Dorothy Alexander. She was a dance teacher who told her students, 'Technique without art is shallow and doomed. Art without technique is insulting.' But almost no-one believes that anymore.

"What the art world has done, it has been constantly been pushing the boundaries about what art can be. It's expanding its territory. And it's like the Roman Empire: it's got all these troops lined up on the edges, fighting away, and has forgotten what's going on in the middle. It's forgotten that the thing that art set out to create, first and foremost, were objects of beauty, works that inspired. I still think a lot of people go to art galleries to look at beautiful, inspirational things. I don't think that's such a shocking thing to believe."

He stopped beside a painting of people having a picnic in a beautiful landscape.

"That's Skye, the Cuillin Hills. The work is my homage to Manet's *Le Déjeuner sur l'herbe,* in English, *Luncheon on the Grass.* It has inspired dozens of artists: Monet, Picasso, Cézanne and many more. The clue's in the name, *Luncheon in Skye.* It's come down to London for an exhibition, it's on loan. You may remember, this painting caused an uproar. Or maybe you have more important things to remember than a fuss among a bunch of idiots who are so far up themselves?

"It was 2010. By then I was pretty well known, established you could say. But, of course, I had never been hung in any public gallery in the UK. For the Venice Biennale that year, the British Council broke with recent tradition and chose a group of Scottish artists to fill the UK Pavilion, as opposed to a single artist. Well, a bunch of people thought I should be one of them, but of course, I wasn't. Nothing against any of the four artists they chose, but … Anyway, next thing we know, the French selected this painting for their Pavilion, which by chance was themed *'Impressions of Impressionists'* that year, a survey of recent art influenced by the great French Impressionists. Now, this painting fits right in with that theme, but the British media decided it was a deliberate slap in the face of the British selection and went after the Council, big time.

"This painting was also very important in my career. My art dealer, Lorenzo Biamonte had very cleverly arranged to loan it for five years to the Musée d'Orsay in Paris, where the Manet original lives. It was very unusual for a living or a non-French artist to be hung there. It was a very controversial, very contentious decision and it transformed my reputation everywhere except in the UK. The five-year loan was due up when Venice came along, so the French managed to extend their loan for an extra year by selecting it.

"I don't know *what* the French were really up to with the Biennale stunt, but I can't deny I enjoyed all the fuss. Poor Lorenzo, his brilliant strategy ultimately backfired as far as this particular painting is concerned. But it turned out to be maybe the best thing that ever happened to me.

* * *

Kiki broke the silence.

"Interesting, but I'm not sure if any of it helps."

106

Thomas agreed. "No, but if ever an art critic turns up dead, I'll look at artists first. Let's get back to work."

* * *

Wednesday, March 9, 2022 – 10:00 a.m.

Thomas and Kiki met with Jennifer Oakes in her beautifully restored home in the heart of the village. She invited them upstairs to her formal lounge and offered them a coffee, which they politely refused.

Jennifer was an attractive woman. She stood about 1.75m and held herself well; she was very elegantly dressed, and her brunette shoulder-length hair had a wonderful lustre and was naturally wavy. Thomas had a strange feeling of déja vu, which he couldn't shake, even as he opened the conversation.

"Mrs Oakes, we understand that you and the deceased were close friends at one time, but perhaps less so of late. Is that true?"

"Yes, I suppose that is a fair statement. Mr Grant and I were friendly for a while, soon after I arrived in the village. But when my son died, my feelings about Monpazier changed completely and I returned to London. I'm sure it is quite irrational, Captain, but I can't help how I feel."

"May I ask, Mrs Oakes, what happened to your son?"

"You don't know? My son committed suicide, Captain. He took a deliberate drug overdose, in the cemetery, alone, all by himself. Can you imagine? He did it around 3 a.m. on a Monday morning, having called by the doctors' office to leave a note. He knew they'd find it when they opened and would know what to do – and I wouldn't find him. He bought the drugs from someone in the village, and no-one was arrested. I hate this place."

"And yet you are here now."

"Yes, my accountant suggested that I keep the house and let it, it provides me with an income. I spent far too much money restoring the property to get it all back; but there are enough discerning people who like to rent it for two or three weeks each year. I only come here a couple of times a year for two or three days to see that all is well with my property. I'm returning to London next week, for good, I hope. The truth is, Captain, I cannot stand being here any longer than necessary. When Dan died, I took him back to England and stayed away for a year. Now I'm selling this house, accountant be damned. This village killed my son. This picturesque, smug, self-satisfied village killed my only child and you gendarmes did absolutely nothing about it. The drug dealers are still here, nothing has changed."

She drew breath and thought about her next words.

"Some of them, the Brits I mean, like Mrs 'I'm so well integrated' bloody MacDonald, they think the French really care about them, one way or another. That they have true friends among the locals. Bullshit. We're mayflies; here for a brief season then poof! we're gone. We may die here, sure, but only if we have to.

"When their English neighbour brings round a new grandson to be admired, they think, 'what a cute baby'. When their French neighbour brings round *their* new grandson, they look at him and think, 'Maybe my son's daughter will marry this baby one day. After all, they'll both be here, won't they?'

"If you don't understand that difference, you're living in dreamland.

"An English boy is killed by drugs. So what? Why do I give a damn? It isn't like he belongs here; that he's one of us. Of course not. And the gendarmes don't bother their arses. No one cares one way or another. He'd have been gone next year anyway."

"I have children, Mrs Oakes, I cannot imagine your grief, but please indulge me with one last question. Were you at home on Saturday evening?"

"When he was murdered? Do I have an alibi, you mean? No, I don't. I was home. I spent the evening as I spend every evening in this godforsaken place; I sat in my son's bedroom and cried. There were no witnesses."

She continued, "You came here thinking I had an affair with Tony Grant, didn't you? Another of his conquests? I know you talked with that venomous bitch, MacDonald. You're an idiot to believe anything that harridan tells you. If you want to talk to someone who knew Tony Grant in the biblical sense, talk with Gemma Taylor, she'll be quite illuminating, I'm sure.

"And I can see you are confused about something else, Captain, so I'll help you, though I don't know why. Yes, this is the room in *Study in Darkness*, and I am the woman. You would have got there eventually, I'm sure. Even the gendarmes can figure some things out. Just not the important things like, who killed my beautiful son."

"That was harrowing!" exclaimed Kiki as they walked away from Jennifer's house.

"It was, but, losing her son that way, I can't imagine.

* * *

Susan had asked Thomas for the key and alarm code for the studio. She went round and confirmed her initial impression that the small window in the toilet was far too small to pass a painting through, unless the thief rolled it up and left the wooden stretchers behind. There really was no other way in or out of the studio except the alarmed front door.

She was still thinking things through when her phone rang. It was Thomas.

"Gendarme Le Roux and I are going to have lunch in Côté Halles, on the square. Want to join us?"

The three police officers decided to sit outside, in the cool winter sun. They kept their jackets on and ordered their food.

Susan asked, "How did you get on with Madame Oakes?"

Kiki answered for them both.

"Interesting. She's the woman in the painting, you know, the one with the window."

"*Study in Darkness*? Wow, that is interesting!"

Kiki filled Susan in with the rest of the conversation, with Thomas confirming things now and then.

Kiki asked, "What about you, Susan, what have you been up to?"

Thomas couldn't help noticing the informality between his team and Susan. It was slightly unsettling.

"The stolen paintings went out the front door, for sure. The thief had a key, knew the code and knew the paintings were there. It cuts down the number of suspects dramatically."

They talked about Jennifer Oakes until their food arrived, and Susan took a forkful of confit duck.

"God, this is great! And I'm joining the book club this afternoon, to see what they have to tell me." Susan paused for a moment.

"You don't mind, do you, Capitaine? It's just that … well, I don't intimidate them the way you all do."

Thomas was intrigued.

"What do you mean. Is it the guns?"

"Of course, it's the guns – and the uniforms, and the … Well, you're all so formal, all the time. I mean, can you see yourself this afternoon, Kiki, with a bunch of civilians, women, chatting about grandkids, the new hairdresser in Villeréal, complaining about husbands who watch every single Six Nations match? You'd be sitting there, gun strapped to your belt, pepper spray close at hand, impeccable in your uniform, poker up your arse. I'm sorry." She laughed to take the sting out of her comment.

She looked at her colleagues.

"The UK is so different. Civilians, I mean good people, like in this village for the most part, they're not afraid of us. Why would they be? Especially if, like me, you're rarely in uniform. They've nothing to hide; so sure, 'Come along to the book club.' Of course, they're hoping to hear some secrets, and I'll give them some. Harmless BS about you guys, about our terrible bosses, about which of you are single. And in return, they'll tell me their stories, their ideas about the case – 99% rubbish, of course, but maybe 1% useful. Oh, look, there's Eloise."

Without a pause, Susan waved to Eloise walking across the square, indicating that the Adjudant should join them. She took the vacant fourth chair at the table.

"No, no food, thanks, I grabbed a sandwich in Villeréal. I'm just back from there, seeing the Notaire. Not much to report, she isn't Grant's lawyer. She was only employed to help with his house purchase and the lease agreement for the studio, on both occasions because the other party was already using her and Grant saw no need to piss off the locals by getting an expensive Parisien lawyer involved. She understood that Grant had a lawyer in the UK and one in Paris but doesn't have any details. She doesn't know about any French will, but that doesn't really prove anything one way or another, one of the lawyers would know more about that."

The waiter brought the bill, indicating that they had to pay inside. Thomas gave it a quick glance and stood up, holding out a hand, palm up.

"Hand it over, you two, fifteen each please."

While Thomas was inside the restaurant, Susan looked at the two female gendarmes.

"The pétanque group are playing tonight. They're having their own Six Nations. There's only one Welsh player, but she's entering as the Rest of the World. Why don't you come along? It'll be fun and we might learn something.

"I can't," Kiki replied, "I'm babysitting for my sister tonight."

"What about you, Eloise?"

"I've hardly ever played pétanque, Susan, and not for years. I'd be rubbish."

"Doesn't matter. I had *never* played before. And you're French, you're bound to be better than me. But Eloise, go home and change," she finished with a laugh.

Thomas returned and the four of them walked around the corner to the Mairie. The pathologist was coming in at 3 p.m. with the results of the autopsy, and until then there was a lot of outstanding paperwork to be attended to.

Mic was shown in promptly at three and he sat at the long table, flanked by Thomas and Eloise.

"Obvious things first; he died of a massive trauma to the head, sustained by falling from the balcony and hitting his head on the stone floor. And no, Thomas, there were no injuries suggesting he had been hit before his head met the floor. He had not been drinking that evening, although there were some indications that he may have been drinking the previous evening, or conceivably much earlier that day. But he would not have been showing any effects of drink. Or of drugs, none of which were found in his system, nor did he display any indicators of long-term drug use. And there were no bruises or abrasions on his thighs or knees where he would have hit the rail. He was in remarkably good shape in fact. Oh! Apart from being dead that is."

"Very funny, Mic. Anything else? Time of death?"

"Earlier than I first thought, much closer to nine o'clock than midnight, maybe even a little earlier. His last meal was a pizza, an hour or so before he died. No unusual medical history; a few minor breaks, but those healed up years ago – probably twenty years ago at least. Similarly, a few scars. Given his history, the old injuries are consistent with his time on construction sites and maybe a bar fight or two, but whatever it was, it was years ago.

"But, Sherlock, you were right about his fall, it's wrong. The guys in Paris have a cool programme that can simulate a lot of traumas. I think the health and safety people developed it, so we'd stop throwing recruits off ledges and hitting them with metal pipes. Anyway, I asked them about the slipped chair scenario. You got it absolutely right, Thomas. 92 times in 100 the body lands on its back. Even if his torso is twisted somewhat, like he's reaching to the side to straighten the painting, his legs would hit the balustrade with enough force to initiate a flipping motion and, depending on how exactly he was positioned, his head and shoulders would have almost hit the bottom of the rails – he should have been lying much closer to the vertical plane of the balustrade. And he should have bruising on his thighs."

* * *

Late in the afternoon, Judge Sandral arrived at Edward Premier. Thomas had arranged to use a small conference room in the hotel for the meeting with the lawyer from Paris.

While they waited with cups of coffee, Françoise Sandral took the opportunity to grill Thomas about the case, and particularly the forgery issue.

"It's early days, Madame. The victim's partner appears to have a rock-solid alibi. There is a mistress, married; so, there's a jealous husband potentially in the picture. You will not like hearing that he is a retired British Ambassador to France – so another high-profile individual to worry about.

"And there's really no doubt at all that it was murder?"

"None at all."

Thomas told the judge about the conversation with the pathologist. When he was finished, she nodded.

"Sounds like it was crime of opportunity. Someone is with Grant when he climbs on the chair and pushes him over. Is that your theory?"

"Possibly. But at this moment, we can't put anyone in the house after the cleaner left. Grant went to Domme around midday, and he told his cleaner he was planning to watch the rugby alone later in the afternoon. Kick-off was four o'clock so that takes us to around six. Time of death is 8:30–9:30. He'd been using cash a lot in the village, so tracing his movements regarding shops is tricky. We know he ate a pizza in the house – there's an empty box in the recycling and the autopsy gave us confirmation. He had plenty of local friends, any one of whom might have popped on the spur of the moment, but we've yet to find a trace of anyone. Which rather argues against a crime of opportunity."

"How so?"

"Say the murderer arrives for some innocent reason. Sits around chatting, has a coffee or a glass of wine, a beer perhaps. Then the unexpected opportunity arises, and he pushes Grant to his death."

Thomas holds up one finger.

"If someone hated Grant enough to murder him, why is he, or she, making an innocent social call?"

Another finger goes up.

"If the murderer was in the house in all innocence for even half-an-hour before the crime; during that period, he or she is perhaps in the kitchen, maybe the downstairs lounge, maybe uses the toilet, is certainly upstairs. All this time, as they have no criminal intent, they are leaving prints and DNA traces all over the place. Now, we know that everyone has seen CSI, so they know to clean up after the murder. But we know how hard that really is. If you enter with intent, you avoid touching anything unnecessarily, you wear clothes that minimise skin contact with furniture and so on. Eliminating all traces following a casual visit is very difficult indeed."

At that point in the conversation, reception called to announce their visitor.

The Parisien lawyer was just as refined and expensively dressed as they had anticipated. After the introductions, he got straight to business.

"Monsieur Grant called me several weeks ago. He had received certain information that gave him concern for his French assets in the event of his death or a lawsuit. I'm afraid I cannot discuss …"

Judge Sandral interrupted him, "Let me put your mind at rest, Monsieur, we know all about Camille Pichon's announcement that she was expecting your client's baby."

"Very well. He explained the nature of the information as you say, and he understood the position if he died in France – that the child would have an inviolable claim over half of his estate in France and possibly elsewhere in certain circumstances.

"He also explained that, while he was sanguine about the disposal of his house, it was his custom to keep a number of finished paintings here in France and did not want them to form part of his French estate. He had, all by himself as I understood it, devised a scheme to avoid this eventuality.

"Just last Friday, the day before his unfortunate death, Monsieur Grant executed a Bill of Sale in our Périgueux office, selling fifteen unnamed paintings to a Swiss company, owned by a nominee based in the Cayman Isles, and also represented by ourselves. The sale included any work in progress, notebooks, sketches or other creative works of any form whatsoever whether created by Monsieur Grant or purchased by him. In return, €1.5 million was transferred to Monsieur Grant's account in Banque Julius Baer in Geneva. I am here to lay claim to these items and arrange for their safe transport to Switzerland."

It was obvious that neither Thomas nor the judge had had any inkling of this situation. Before they could react, the lawyer continued.

"Perhaps I should explain further. Monsieur Grant sold the paintings, sight unseen, for €100,000 each, considerably less than his proceeds from recent sales. However, he retained the right to buy the paintings back, one a time, for the same price, less a small administrative fee. He gave us to understand that this would in fact happen whenever he wished to send a canvas to his London gallery, for sale. All relevant items would remain in situ, but as long-term loans to Monsieur Grant personally. The loan cannot be assigned."

"Why not simply send the paintings to Switzerland, or London for that matter, to be held until he released them?"

"The very question I asked him, Capitaine. He referred me to Paul Valéry – *'Un ouvrage n'est jamais achevé, … mais abandonné.'* [1] By holding on to the paintings, he could continue to refine them."

"So, the paintings are owned by a Swiss corporation and fall outwith his French estate, to be disposed of in accordance with his will, I presume?"

"Correct, Madame."

"And are you in possession of his will?"

"No, we are not. In fact, I was hoping you could shed some light on that. We are assured that a valid will exists, but we assumed it was here, in Monpazier, among his effects."

The judge looked at Thomas before answering.

"Sadly, no will has come to light; and I have more bad news for you, Monsieur, most of your paintings are missing, presumed stolen by Monsieur Grant's murderer."

* * *

At nine o'clock that evening, Thomas, Susan and Eloise gathered in a corner of the deserted bar of the hotel to watch the latest instalment of the

---

[1] 'A work of art is never truly finished, merely abandoned.'

video material. But first, Thomas wanted a debrief on the book club and the pétanque earlier in the evening.

"Book club was interesting, Capitaine." As always when there were other team members present, Susan spoke in French.

"Only seven members turned up, apparently there are more in the summer months. Anyway, one of them, an Englishwoman called Jan, eats in the brewery three or four times a week with her husband, Ted. According to Jan, Zachary Taylor and Augustin Pichon have been in there together a few times of late. People have commented because they seem such an unlikely couple with nothing in common. Gus really is a piece of work it seems, no-one has a good word to say about him."

"Thanks, Detective," responded Thomas. "What on earth could those two have to discuss, I wonder"

Susan deferred to Eloise to report on the pétanque.

"It was a lot of fun. A French team won of course, although my partners did all the work. Anyway, the interesting gossip concerns a Luc Ribault, a young antiques dealer in the village. He had a few too many in Minou's one night and sounded off about Grant. It seems that Ribault had been carrying a torch for Camille Pichon for years, ever since they were in high school together. So, when he heard about the affair, he was really pissed off. Made all sorts of threats about what he would do if he ever caught Grant alone."

Everyone, Susan included, thought Eloise was done at that point, but she wasn't.

"You know, these expatriates, they're a peculiar bunch of people. Almost none of them are normal."

"What do you mean, not normal?" Thomas asked.

"Well, there are a few, I suppose, who are fairly normal. Former civil servants, accountants, teachers and so on. But … there's one guy, I asked him where he was from. I meant in America, he had an American accent for sure. And sure enough, he told me he was from California; but then he said, 'But, I live in Thailand.' So, I said, 'so are you Thai now?'. 'No,' he answered, 'I'm British now.' I mean what's that all about? He and his partner have a house just a few kilometres away. She's English by the way, but lived in America at some point, but not with the Californian.

"Another couple I met, just the same. The wife was Scottish; I thought she might have known Grant. Turned out she and her English husband mostly live in Spain. I asked her if she had moved there from Scotland. 'No,' she said, 'from Greece.'

"And so it went on. Dubai, London, America, Belgium, Luxembourg, Japan; these people live everywhere and nowhere. What is wrong with them? Why can't they just pick a damn country and stay in it, for God's sake?"

Thomas looked perplexed.

"Don't ask me. OK, Adjudant, check out Ribault, see if you can get an alibi out of him. Let's watch this video."

* * *

2010 – Venice

April would be, Tony decided, a good time to see Venice, if only the circus that was the Biennale wasn't in town. Tony had never visited the city before, and it was living up to every expectation, exceeding them in fact. The buildings, the back canals, the artisan shops and workshops, he found it all captivating. Yes, there were too many tourists and too few locals, but still, what a unique place.

He was in Venice courtesy of the French, who had invited him to yesterday's gala opening. But now he was free, he had escaped the receptions, the viewings, the interminable speeches, in French of course, and he had quickly, and enjoyably, lost himself far from the Grand Canal.

He was sitting happily in a tiny square, sipping a marvellous coffee, when a small group of six British tourists came into the square, led by a woman who was managing to walk backwards as she continued to talk to her charges in a pleasant, and pleasantly muted, Scottish accent which Tony could just about make out. On the very unlikely chance that he might be recognised, Tony buried his head in his book, *The City of Falling Angels*, his introduction to Venice.

He stole a few glances as the tourists arranged themselves along the old stone benches that stood together, almost filling one side of the cosy square. Happily, Tony couldn't hear the guide as she explained whatever she was explaining to her group. After a few minutes, the guide stopped speaking, took orders and disappeared inside the café, re-emerging with a tray of espresso cups and small biscotti.

Tony was still intently keeping his head tilted as he read John Berendt's intriguing memoir when he became aware of a shadow before him, and the Scottish voice asking very, very quietly, "Excuse me, are you?"

She stopped talking as Tony raised his head and a hand flew to her mouth.

Tony slowly stood and faced the woman.

"Lorna?" he asked, hearing the tremor in his own voice.

Lorna mutely nodded her head.

For what seemed an eternity they both stood stock-still, staring at each other, until, at some unspoken signal Lorna reached out a finger to touch the small shock of white on Tony's otherwise jet-black hair. The tension broke and they embraced and clung to each other and shed tears of longing, sorrow, happiness.

"You're Tony Grant, the artist? *Belle Figure?* All those posters? But I don't understand."

"Grant was my mother's name. When I came out of that other place, I just started using it, Tony Gallagher more or less disappeared. I didn't want everyone to know about, you know."

"Of course, of course," she replied, understanding completely. "If you only knew the hours I've wasted, searching for Tony Gallagher. But how could I not see you, your hair, I mean? In pictures, on TV?"

"I've avoided being on TV, for a long time I didn't much like the idea, and up until now anyway, there hasn't been much demand to be frank. And not many photos in the newspapers, they prefer images of my work, which suits me fine. And I, and I, well to be honest, for many years I dyed that bit of my hair black. That priest, Casey, he told me he liked it, said it was 'my mark of distinction'. Then, in the secure Home, I was bullied about it, until I learned to look after myself. And the guys on the building sites teased me as well. Eventually I just thought, 'Fuck it, I'm going to dye it.' So, I did. And then, I don't know, a few years ago it suddenly seemed stupid, I decided I was letting other people define me, in particular that bastard, Casey; so I stopped.

"I'm sorry, I'm rambling. What about you? Where did you go when you left. I looked for you in Girvan, in Glasgow, but then I moved to London and, well, I gave up for years, I'm ashamed to say."

She squeezed the hand that already lay in hers.

"Don't be daft. I went to Aberdeen, of all places. I was dead lucky; I got a job as a nanny to an American family. He was in the oil business. I was with them for years; in Aberdeen for just a year, then in Saudi, the Emirates, Brunei, Texas, all over."

"No wonder I couldn't find you. Later, when I had made a bit of money, I hired an agency, but they couldn't trace you either. Of course," he added bitterly, "the nuns were no bloody use at all. The Home's long closed you know."

"Is it? I don't care. I make it my business to never think of them, ever. I have my life now, and I do this, I have my own wee business, escorting groups of women around Italy. We live in Edinburgh, in a lovely flat in the New Town."

She looked at him oddly, "I'm married, Tony. To a lovely man. We met and got married in Brunei, believe it or not. Andrew was teaching English to school kids. We got married less than three months after we met. We've no kids, but he has sisters and brothers, so there's lots of nieces and nephews, which is great. What about you, married?"

"No, but I have a partner, Caroline. We live together in London, have for ten years now. But not married. And no kids either. Listen, I can see your group are getting fidgety, are you free for dinner tonight? Can they fend for themselves? Tell you what, I can probably get them invited to something, a showing or a reception. They'd like that wouldn't they? And I can have you to myself."

* * *

In less than an hour, less than half-an-hour, their bond was fully repaired. It wouldn't be exactly the same of course, they were older now and had other ties, to other people. They wouldn't be the only other person who mattered ever again. But, in all the ways that counted, they were soulmates still, just as they had been when there really was no-one else in all the world who mattered.

"I don't know why we never got married. There was a time I thought we might, or maybe that we should. We get on well, there's love, or at least a great deal of affection between us. We rarely row, except … well, there's something about artists, and musicians, I think. Women are, what, drawn to us? Intrigued? Maybe we're a challenge? Whatever. It's hard to say no when it's on offer, even when I should. But I never make promises, never raise expectations – quite the opposite, in fact. Anyway, Caroline more or less tolerates me on that score. And she has been absolutely key to my career, I know that. Even now, I take her advice on business matters. And she's achieving her own goals. As my profile rose, so we got to know more and more of the people who make the art world turn, even if some of them secretly despised me and my art. She's a consultant now, telling millionaires and billionaires who and what to buy, who the next big thing will be. So…" he tailed off.

"Is Caroline happy with the situation?"

"As far as I can tell, yes. I mean with no kids, there would be nothing to hold her if she wasn't, right? We used to talk about getting married, having a family; but that was long ago. And really, we are happy with each other. We respect each other. We share things – successes and failures, life's ups and downs. What about you? What does Andrew do?"

Lorna's face brightened immediately.

"He's a teacher, history is his subject, but occasionally also English. He wrote a book two years ago," she added proudly, "About the English Civil War and its impact on Scotland. It was very well received. He's not much of a traveller, though, Brunei was his one big adventure, so he's happy to let me do my thing with the business. I love it. But we do have a narrowboat, in Norfolk. We spend a lot of time there, in the summer months. I avoid taking groups away in the summer, too busy everywhere, and too expensive. My life isn't as glamorous as yours, Tony, not by a long shot. I still can't believe you're Tony Grant! I love your work; I'm not just saying that."

Lorna looked down at her hands, shy now.

"We have a print of yours, in the lounge. The one in Skye."

"*Luncheon in Skye*," Tony reminded her, with a smile.

"That's it, that's the one! I love it so much. Sometimes, I, we I mean, Andrew and I, we imagine ourselves in that scene, in Skye. We've never actually been to Skye, but still, your picture takes us there. It's such a happy image. I think the woman on the left has just learned she's pregnant and is about to share the news with her friends. My God, listen to me, telling you what I think's happening in *your* painting!"

"Don't be daft! That's exactly what I want to happen! I want you to be there, so you have to know what's going on, or at least wonder. Would you like to know what I thought was happening?"

"Yes, please!"

"Well, you're quite right, it is the woman on the left who is keeping a secret. She's been told that she's being promoted at work. She's nervous about saying anything in case her friends think she's boasting. She's the first of the four of them to make any progress in their careers – as you can see, they're all quite young. But she will tell them in a minute or two and they'll be happy for her. They aren't two couples, just four friends. Eventually she and the guy on her left will get married, he's already smitten with her, but he has kept it hidden until now. But the way he reacts to the news tells the other girl how he feels and that makes her a little wistful, because their friendship group will change, and she's not sure how."

"You know all that? Goodness!"

"Oh, I know a lot more than that about my people, about all my people."

They only left the restaurant because the waiter asked them to go, well after midnight.

It seemed only natural for Lorna to link her arms through his as they walked along the canals towards her hotel. Suddenly, Tony stopped, realising where they were.

"Can we just go down here a minute; there may be a guard on duty."

With that baffling comment, he led them through a little tunnel to emerge in a grand square, with a brilliantly lit palazzo filling the far side. Sure enough, the doors were locked, but a guard appeared when Tony banged on the door. By great good fortune there was a huge poster in the lobby area. This was the home of the French Pavilion, and the poster prominently featured the six artists represented in the exhibit, including Tony. By a series of gesticulations, Tony eventually made the guard realise that he was, in fact, one of the artists, and he opened a side door to let them in.

Tony turned to Lorna.

"It's too bad you're leaving first thing in the morning, but you might like to see this."

He hadn't mentioned his participation in the Biennale, so Lorna was already thrilled and excited as the guard led them to the grand room on the upper floor and switched on the lights.

"There it is, your painting, *Luncheon in Skye.*"

When Lorna had drunk her fill of examining the original painting she turned to him.

"I'm so glad to have found you, that we found each other. Thank goodness you stopped dyeing your hair, that white flash is what made me wonder if it was you. I love your painting, Tony, and I've always loved you. We mustn't lose each other again."

"Don't worry, we won't."

Six months later, when the Biennale was finally over, Lorenzo was devastated when Tony told him that *Luncheon in Skye* was already on its way to its new owner, in Edinburgh. And there would be no commission.

* * *

"How did you feel, getting back in touch with Lorna after all those years?"

"I'm sorry, Lucy, but Lorna is a private person, I have no right to discuss our friendship with the world at large. Let's just say, it was wonderful to see her again and we've seen each other many, many times since. Her husband, Andrew, is a charming and a very erudite man, a fantastic bloke to talk to. I only wish we had teachers like him when I was a kid."

* * *

As soon as the video finished, Thomas turned to Eloise, "First thing tomorrow, get onto Financial Crimes and have them look for bank accounts belonging to Anthony Gallagher. It would be easy enough for him to resurrect that name if he needed to."

* * *

"Hi honey, how are you?"

"I'm good; how about you; you sound tired, Thomas."

"Not too tired. The case has become complicated. I'm becoming nostalgic for a simple random stabbing of a total stranger."

"How is Monpazier?"

"It's really lovely. We should come for a weekend in the summer; it's only a couple of hours away. You'd love it. And my hotel is superb. If this case drags on, I'm going to suggest you and the kids come for a couple of days. Although something tells me this is going to wrap up soon, one way or another."

"Well, it'll be good to get you home, the kids miss you, and so do I. I saw Elisabeth Bounnet today. She's really upset. Claude got his next assignment yesterday; they're going to La Courneuve and she's beside herself about the terrible schools. It's so brutal, the system takes no account of children and the disruption these moves create to their education."

"I'll be seeing Claude tomorrow. He's in charge of the funeral for my victim on Friday."

"They're sending someone from here! Why?"

"His name was Tony Grant; he's a famous artist. We've got ministers from Paris, the British ambassador, celebrity collectors, all sorts. Claude's staying here, in my hotel, tomorrow night."

"Well, be nice to him, he's getting nothing but grief at home."

2010 – Venice

* * *

Thursday, March 10, 2022 – Morning

For almost seven hundred years, through war, revolution and pestilence, Monpazier has held a market every Thursday morning. In the summertime, market stalls spill out north from the square along both main streets, offering food and crafts, clothes, soaps in every colour and scent, a huge variety of cheeses, dried sausages, olives and tapenades, local wines and liqueurs and yet more cheeses, and, bizarrely, mattresses. Throngs of people from neighbouring villages, from the innumerable campsites hidden among the surrounding forests and from every rented villa for many kilometres came to stock up, enjoy the sights and sounds, catch up with friends and buy lunch in one of Monpazier's many restaurants.

However now, in the first half of March, the market was just shaking off its winter doldrums. The stalls still encircled the square, and a few had even been pushed into the centre. At this time of the year everyone in the square was a full-time resident of Monpazier or one of the surrounding hamlets, so no-one could walk more than a few metres without encountering a friend or an acquaintance. A five-minute trip to buy some vegetables turned into an hour or more over a coffee or a hot chocolate in the café, the tabac or the boulangerie.

Susan had taken a minor detour to have a look at what was on offer. Her favourite stall was the long, illuminated wet fish stall offering a dazzling variety of raw and prepared fish and seafood, and the front portion of what must have been a truly gigantic tuna, its baleful dead eyes scrutinizing her as she absorbed the sights and smells.

Sadly, none of the produce on display was for her today and she pressed on to the Mairie. She and Thomas were scheduled to sit down with Lorna Hamilton this afternoon – she had flown in on Tony Grant's jet the previous night.

But meanwhile they had other fish to fry.

* * *

Thomas was all smiles as he spoke.

"Thanks for agreeing to come in, Gus, we have a couple of issues to clear up. As you can probably imagine, we're interviewing anyone who could possibly help us understand what happened to Tony Grant.

"Now, as we're obviously gendarmes, even though we're not in a Gendarmerie, I have to remind you that, if at any time you think you should have a lawyer to help you, you only have to ask. Understood?"

Gus nodded his assent.

"Excellent. Now the first question is really simple. I called round your house the other afternoon and had a good chat with your sister, but she said you were in Bergerac on business. Is that right?"

"That's right, I was."

"And what business would that be, Gus? You don't seem to have a job, not as far as the Employment Centre are concerned."

He watched Gus's thought processes flit across his face as he pondered his answer.

"It was family business, actually. I was seeing our lawyer."

"About?"

Thomas allowed the silence to go on, and on, and on, knowing that sooner or later, Gus would be compelled to fill it.

"Well, if you must know, about the Englishman's money and the baby, Camille's baby."

"Ah, and what did the lawyer tell you?"

"She, I mean it, I mean the baby, will get it, at least half and maybe much more."

"Well, that's exciting. Did you let Camille know this news?"

"Of course I did. It'll be hers, won't it? I mean the baby's just going to be a baby."

"Thanks for clearing that up for us, Gus. Now, our other question. Apparently, you've been seeing quite a lot of Ambassador Taylor recently. We can't help wondering what you two have been discussing."

"They've been very nice to Camille, him and Madame Taylor, very nice indeed."

"So we understand, Gus. But that doesn't explain why you two keep getting together, does it? Are you chatting about ante-natal classes? Late-night feeds? Favourite brands of nappy? You see my problem, Gus, I can't *imagine* what you two find to talk about. Paris St-Germain's chances of ever winning the Champions League perhaps?"

126

"Yeah, all those things. You know what, I think I'm done. I think I'd like to leave now. Or talk to a lawyer."

"OK, Gus, off you go. I expect we'll want to have another chat, or maybe we'll ask the Ambassador."

Thomas stood up as he spoke once more.

"Anyway, don't worry about it. By the way, Gus; did the lawyer ask you to tell Camille about DNA testing?"

"Why the hell would she need a DNA test? She was working that night, nowhere near the Englishman's place`—why would she need a DNA test?"

"Not Camille; the baby. You don't think the court will just hand over the money without checking that the baby is really Grant's, do you? And Gus, Monsieur Grant wasn't English, he was very Scottish indeed."

Gus had an extremely worried look on his face as he stood to leave.

At that moment, Thomas's phone rang and as he answered, he put out a hand to signal to Gus to wait. He listened for several long moments then turned to Gus once again.

"Actually, Gus, I just received some new information. I'd like you to stay here for a while. So, call your lawyer and have him come here so you and he can talk. I don't have anywhere to lock you up right now, but Gendarme Baye here will keep you company. I'll talk to you again this afternoon."

* * *

While Thomas was interviewing Gus, Kiki Le Roux and Susan were in an interview room in the Gendarmerie at Beaumont with Gemma Taylor. Susan had been an interested observer as Kiki showed her quickly around the building, explaining the various offices. They had decided to send two Beaumont gendarmes to pick Gemma up and bring her by car. They wanted the young woman to be intimidated.

Kiki led the interrogation.

"Madame Taylor, you are here because you were not truthful when Capitaine Coman and I interviewed you at your home in Monpazier. At this point we are still treating you as a witness and not as a suspect, but I must warn you that if we are not satisfied with your responses this morning, you may be formally charged. Do you understand, and do you want to have a lawyer present at this time?"

Susan and Kiki were both struck by the fact that Gemma looked far less intimidated than they had expected. She was certainly a little nervous but seemed fully in control of her emotions.

"I don't need a lawyer, and I will tell you the truth, especially as you probably know that I had been having an affair with Tony."

Kiki nodded.

"Thank you for being straightforward. Now please help us understand the nature of your relationship with the victim and why we should not treat you as a suspect."

"Very well."

Gemma sat forward in her chair and interlaced her fingers on the Formica-topped table.

"I'm not super-clever, but clever enough to get good A-Levels in English and French, and my father is a civil servant in London, so he knew how I should go about getting a secretarial job in the Embassy in Paris.

"Initially, I was what they call a floater, working for whatever person or group needed help. After six months or so, I was assigned to the Ambassador as maternity cover. He liked me and I liked him. I liked him because he was a gentleman. I knew I was attractive to men, guys in the embassy hit on me all the time. But Zachary's behaviour towards me was impeccable. We worked late into the night sometimes; sometimes I'd travel with him for meetings, or factory visits or whatever, and never once did he make me feel even a little bit uncomfortable."

She paused to gather her thoughts.

"You need to understand that in those days, Zachary didn't drink much at all. Of course, he attended a zillion lunches and dinners, and we are in France, so there was always wine, but he would sip and sip and make sure he never had more than one glass at lunchtime and only two or three at dinner.

"Anyway, then his wife died. He was devoted to her, and she was lovely. Of course, we all knew her, and liked her. She took me aside once and said, 'I know my husband likes you my dear, and I know he'll always behave; but you are very beautiful and if you are having trouble with any of the married men in the Embassy, you must let me know immediately, do you hear? I'll take care of them. I'll leave you to deal with the single ones yourself.'

"A year, almost to the day after Evelyn died, Zachary and I were married. It was a disaster, for both of us. Is there any chance I could have a coffee?"

Kiki nodded and disappeared out the door.

"Shall I continue, or should we wait?" she asked Susan.

"Best if we wait. You're doing fine, it's usually easier to just tell the truth sometimes, even if it can be painful."

"You've no idea how much I know that; I've been living a lie every day for years."

Kiki returned with three coffees, but no biscuits, Susan noted with regret. Some English customs aren't so bad.

Gemma nodded her thanks, took a long sip and continued.

"He thought he needed a wife. He was 64, he was desperate for one final posting, to Washington, had been manoeuvring for it for years. But, well, after Evelyn died, his drinking started to become a problem. You see, even after Zachary began pursuing me, we never slept together. I thought it was charming, old-school, and, to be honest, a pleasant change. But it meant he was alone at the end of every day, and he began to drink. People started to notice and, frankly, when he married a 22-year-old, and one who looks like me, well, he became a laughingstock."

"You said the marriage was a disaster for you too, Gemma. Why was that?"

"He couldn't have sex with me. I mean, even after we were married. Guilt. Disloyalty to Evelyn's memory, maybe. And," she paused again before sighing, "And fear that he couldn't please me, that he was too old, that I was too young and … anyway.

"And then there was the family. I was so naïve, I had no idea. All I knew was I would be going from crappy junior staff quarters on the outskirts, to living in one of the most beautiful homes in Paris. I didn't realise that Zachary came from old money, as did Evelyn. To announce the engagement, he brought his four children and their spouses to the family home in Wiltshire, and we flew over. I was desperately trying to deal with the fact that he had this huge home in England, not to mention four children, three of whom were older than me, when I was dropped in the middle of it all.

"The thought of old money hadn't occurred to me because neither Zachary nor Evelyn ever made any reference to it or treated any of the staff with anything but easy, friendly courtesy. But their children, nightmares, all of them. They had all been in boarding school, Eton for the boys, Cheltenham Ladies for the girls."

Gemma looked at Susan, "Perhaps you could explain all this to you your colleague later."

"Four complete and utter snobs. They took one look at me and heard my accent; Pinner, by the way, and instantly decided I had seduced their father. If only they knew; chance would be a fine thing. They made no attempt to hide their contempt for me and their disgust with their father. They refused to attend the wedding, so we were married before two witnesses, no one else, not even my Mum. Zachary re-wrote his will and cut them all off without a penny, them and their kids. I'll inherit everything. Of course, I plan to investigate the grandkids and see of any can be salvaged, and if so, share it with them. But his kids can go to hell."

"So, is that why you don't just leave him?" asked Kiki, "His will?"

"No! How can you be so dense! I've cost that man his career, his last ambition, his family, his friends, his pride. He can't even go back to live in his family home; he's seen through the eyes of his children, the reaction the neighbours would have at the sight of me. How can I abandon him after all of that? He doesn't deserve any of that. He's not a bad man, he's just overwhelmed by too many sudden changes: in his status, in his bed, in his life. And most of all, he misses Evelyn every minute of every day. When he's sober, which is most of the time, he tries to make sure I don't know that. But when he's drunk, he can't help it."

"I apologise." Kiki said, "But then, why Grant?"

"Because he was charming, fascinating, sympathetic, strong. Because sometimes I want to slap Zachary in the face and tell him to pull it together, for God's sake, before it's too late for all of us. Because I make mistakes. Because I'm a woman."

Susan wanted to ask a question.

"Gemma, you and your husband seem to have befriended Camille Pichon and her brother Augustin. This seems somewhat unusual. Can you explain?"

"Huh! That was Zachary. We heard that Camille was pregnant, and that Tony was the father. I think Zachary wanted to make me face up to the fact that I was just another of Tony's long list of conquests, and here was the latest, an even younger and prettier model, paying the price. We had dinner with them once, that's all."

"But Zachary has been seen with Augustin several times since. Didn't you know?"

Gemma's hand flew to her mouth.

"Oh no," she whispered. "You think that Zachary and Gus. You think they killed Tony! No! No! Zachary would never do such a thing. He just wouldn't. He said to me once, 'If I was thirty years younger, I'd straighten him out.' He meant Tony, of course. But, God this is so embarrassing! I've seen Tony, I've learned a little about his life, I've seen his body. He was fit, hard, tough. I know Gus is much younger, but honestly, in a fair fight, or even a dirty fight, Tony would have beaten him senseless, never mind a forty-something civil servant like Zachary. And anyway, I won't believe that Zachary tried to kill Tony, or have Gus kill him, if that's what you're thinking. And even if he had, Gus would have needed a gun or an accomplice to do the job."

* * *

The team were scheduled to sit down together at 12:30 to have a sandwich and watch the last video segment, but it was 12:45 before Eloise and André arrived, a little out of breath, having jogged up from the lower car park.

"Sorry, Capitaine, market day, parking's a nightmare. And we were already late, tracking down Luc Ribault took a while."

Eloise composed herself and flipped open her notebook to check a date before giving her report.

"There isn't a great deal to report, in fact. Luc did make threats against the victim. I think he saw himself as some kind of knight in shining armour defending Camille's reputation against a predatory Brit. He knew Camille had been modelling for Grant and then some of regulars in Minous began teasing him about artists and their models. He was already riled up by that, when word began to get out that Camille was pregnant. On Friday, almost three weeks ago, Luc had had too much to drink when he heard about the baby, and that was the first time he let off steam about Grant. He threatened to beat him up as soon as he saw him. He repeated the threat several times over the following week.

"But Capitaine, having finally spoken with him, I think Luc's a blowhard. As far as anyone can tell, Camille never gave him a second look when they were at school, she went for the rugby players apparently. I when I say she went for them, I mean she *really* went for them. Camille has, shall we say, a chequered history with many of the young men in this area. Anyway, we warned him about making threats; I think he was terrified when Grant turned up dead. He knew we'd be speaking to him, but, as I say, he's not a suspect. Would you agree, Gendarme?"

André Lefèvre nodded. "Absolutely not, he doesn't have it in him. Luc is more likely to be holding the shining knight's horse than leading the fight."

"So we'll scratch Luc, at least for the moment. We need to figure out who had or could get hold of the code for the studio alarm. Yes, Susan?"

"We know that Loulou Brouzet had the alarm code. What about her son, or a friend or relative; I bet a lot of these village families are related. Or maybe she just wrote it down and carried it in her purse – all kind of people may have seen it then, shopkeepers, stall holders, restaurant staff."

Thomas nodded.

"Adjudant, take another run at Madame Brouzet and her connections. Establish whether in fact she did write down the code; and check out her son. And we need to absolutely nail down Caroline King's alibi – she certainly had keys to both the house and the studio, she knew the alarm code, she knew about the forgeries, and she must have been royally pissed when she learned Camille's news, whatever she says.

"Baye, get onto the highway people. See if you can track King's car that day. Gendarme Le Roux, how did you get on with Gemma Taylor?"

Kiki gave a concise, accurate resumé of the interview in Beaumont.

She concluded, "No matter how long I've been in this job, I'll never get over how surprising people's lives can be. But the fact is, she didn't know about her husband and Gus Pichon, so he was hiding that from her. She did however alibi her husband, she swore up and down that he was with her on the night of the murder, and I am inclined to believe her, as does Sargeant Howard. And we know that Grant wasn't killed in fair fight or indeed any kind of fight, he was simply pushed to his death. So, Gus must be in the frame. Whether Zachary Taylor was paying him or just egging him on so his sister would get the baby's inheritance, one way or another, he had motive."

"But how do we place him in the house?" asked Thomas. "And why would Grant invite him upstairs even if Gus did call by?"

Eloise Brunel chipped in, "Say Camille arrived at the studio unexpectedly one day and walked straight in, while Grant was there, so no alarm to deactivate, and saw him working on a forgery, would she understand the implications? I doubt it very much; she doesn't strike me as an art expert. So, she can't tell her brother about the forgeries, so we're back to a coincidence – Gus kills Grant while someone else robs the studio. Or, Camille is much smarter than we think and somehow knew

132

about the code, did in fact know about the forgeries and the secret storage, knew how to get her brother into the house and orchestrated the whole business. Neither alternative seems credible."

"Good summary, Brunel. Let's eat these sandwiches and watch this video – the last one. This was shot just two days before Tony Grant was killed. Maybe we'll get the key piece of the puzzle there, or this afternoon."

* * *

2013 – Monpazier

It was purely by chance that Tony and Caroline found themselves in the village that would become Tony's home. The Venice Biennale selection had raised Tony's profile in France even higher, and now a gallery in Bordeaux was mounting a major retrospective of his work. The young curator had worked ceaselessly to persuade more than twenty collectors to lend him pieces, and Lorenzo had promised to almost empty his gallery of Tony's paintings and to send him six new works, never seen before.

The timing couldn't have been better, for both of them. Tony had been working around the clock and Caroline felt that she was spending the best years of her life in airport lounges. They agreed it would be an excellent plan to drive to Bordeaux, taking a week to get there.

"I'll do all the bookings for us, it'll be fun choosing hotels just because they look lovely and not for their broadband speed."

"Go for it, sweetheart. Just point me to where I have to go. Unless you want to do the driving as well?" He finished hopefully.

"We'll share, promise."

Caroline had been as good as her word. And she made sure that they didn't have to drive too far on any day of the trip. They had two nights in Reims, in a small boutique hotel with a huge bath in the middle of the bedroom. They shared a bottle of champagne in the bath and that night they made love, slowly, properly, for the first time in many months. Then two nights in Amboise, where they visited the chateau where Leonardo spend his final years. One more night in Limoges before they checked into the beautiful Hôtel Edward 1er in the medieval village of Monpazier.

As they sat in the bar before dinner, Caroline read from a brochure she had picked up from reception.

"Monpazier was founded in 1285 by the local representative of King Edward 1st of England, who was also the Duke of Gascony. It is a *bastide*, which means a fortified village, originally completely walled, with seven fortified archway entrances, of which three survive. It is the best-preserved bastide in France and officially one of the Most Beautiful Villages of France. And here endeth the lesson."

Dinner was superb and they finished half of the second bottle of wine before making their way upstairs to make love once again. Tony had seldom felt so utterly relaxed.

Tony was entirely captivated by the village the following day, which happened to be a Thursday, market day.

"Look at these people, Caroline. That woman, playing the accordion. She's a stallholder. Why is she playing the accordion? And that old man, buying cheese, with the walking stick and the dogs. My God, there are a hundred, a thousand stories here. And the square! At first you think it's all neatly planned, and of course it was, but there are round arches, pointed arches, double arches, square arches – mmm, a square arch isn't actually an arch, is it. But what stories these stones could tell!"

Indeed, the village was spectacular, the streets a rigid grid, with no more than three or four buildings from the 20th century. And everywhere, mysteries and stories. Carved stones on walls where they had no business being. The outline of windows, long since blocked up and half overlapped by a more recent opening, itself remodelled long ago. Narrow lanes to explore, and even narrower gaps to be explored only by cats. And there were lots of cats.

Inevitably, there was an estate agent with a large window. And there was a house for sale, on the square, and the price? Less than a Chelsea garage. Before Caroline could get her head around it, they had visited the house, and Tony had agreed to buy it.

"Are you sure, Tony? You don't know the place. What's it like in winter? Who are your neighbours? Why not rent somewhere first?"

"This is it, Caroline. I could spend the rest of my life painting this place, these people. If I only get two or three paintings, it'll be worthwhile. And I have a feeling there will be two or three *hundred*."

* * *

Caroline had already called to say she was on her way; she'd been chatting with a neighbour and lost track. She'd be there in five minutes. He ordered a Scotch. He loved this room; in the intervening years it had become his favourite spot in the village. He was on the top floor of the Restaurant du Chapître in Monpazier. Higher than any other spot in the village, with the exception of the church steeple, it was an eyrie looking across the medieval roofline and with a spectacular view of the old parish church. Every time

135

he ate here, he saw another detail he had overlooked. A misaligned wall, carved stones out of place, a tiny, secret courtyard, visible only from this vantage point. And the food was excellent.

His gaze swept around until he suddenly focused on a window of the handsome building across the street, what the French called a *maison du maître*. His attention had been caught by the sight of a woman in a brightly lit room a floor below. Her windows had internal plantation shutters, angled to allow the light to come in but to screen out prying eyes. She hadn't considered the top floor of the restaurant, obviously. The woman had her back to him as she stood, slumped, knuckles white on the back of a sofa; head hanging down, defeated; her long glossy brunette hair obscuring her profile. Tony sensed that without the support of the furniture, the woman would collapse to her knees. She was wearing a classic little black dress, but it was unzipped; he couldn't tell if she had been putting it on or taking it off. She wasn't wearing a bra, and he was mesmerised by the long sensual sweep of her back, and the deep shadow between her hunched shoulder blades.

Quickly, he took out his phone and snatched the image, fixing it forever. When he looked up again to check the fine details, he caught the merest glimpse as the figure disappeared from view through an unseen door into an adjacent, unlit, room.

He took in more details of the illuminated room, expensively furnished with tasteful modern pieces, dominated by a large landscape that he thought might be of somewhere in Italy – Tuscany or Umbria. He already knew that this scene would be his next painting – and that it would be very good.

He had owned the house in Monpazier for five years now, and he was still in love with the village. Although his commercial paintings were still about captured dramatic moments, he spent many happy hours wandering the village with his sketchbook, capturing small details of buildings, or a beautiful window, or some particularly complex or mystifying stonework.

The houses were so old, some six or seven hundred years old, that many walls had fallen down and been rebuilt, roofs had collapsed, and the opportunity taken to add a floor. Some apparent buildings were actually just shells with no roof and no floor, awaiting someone with enough money to create something wonderful. By and large the French weren't interested in these restorations, the local French anyway. They had a more pragmatic, less romantic view of their village, where many of their families had lived for untold generations. They wanted double-glazing, central heating, square walls, low ceilings that meant low heating bills.

The beautiful square, pride of the *bastide*, had a few gaps in the arcades where building facades had fallen or been torn down. Their walls and windows, doorways and decorative stonework had been reclaimed and reused, usually with no logic whatsoever. It made for an endlessly fascinating source of investigations for a curious artist.

His favourite aspect of the village, however, was not the picturesque square, but the *carreyrous* behind each of the main streets, which were laid out in a perfect grid. He learned that the principal streets of the village were wide enough to allow two carts to pass each other, while the cross streets would have permitted just a single cart to travel to or from the market and the *carreyrous* could accommodate a man leading a horse. There were firebreaks between many houses, and these narrow gaps provided a secure, private transit network for Monpazier's many felines.

The *carreyrous* retained a mysterious, secret quality which Tony loved, and they afforded occasional glimpses inside some of the modest homes. Within a year, he knew every inch of them and had sketched many of the buildings.

It was during an early exploration that he found the building that would become his studio.

Tony had become friendly with the post lady and happened to be wandering along the street that formed the northern boundary of the village as she was on her rounds.

"Good morning," he greeted her. "Tell me, who lives in this house, I love these huge windows, but I never see anyone coming or going."

"Madame Toussaint lived here, but she died, oh thirty years ago. It's been empty ever since. It is very simple inside. No hot water for example, and just two rooms. People today want something else, better. And, of course, no sunshine and no terrace."

"Who owns it?" Asked Tony.

"I don't know, Monsieur Tony, ask in the Mairie, they'll tell you."

He decided to waste no time and walked down to the Mairie.

"That building belongs to Monsieur Grudier, would you like his telephone number?

It took three or four weeks to track down Monsieur Grudier and negotiate a deal. The old man wasn't interested in selling but was happy to agree a small monthly rent. He would contribute nothing to fixing up the place, although he generously gave Tony permission to spend as much of his own money as he wanted restoring the building.

Tony now had a French studio, and within a few weeks he had it arranged just as he wanted. The walls were painted pristine white, and the floor was concrete, polished to a deep lustre. A local carpenter built him a very special storage unit where he could keep finished canvases.

For one reason or another, almost two months elapsed before he was able to start work on the painting of the mystery woman in the illuminated room. As usual, he would be making significant changes to the composition. He did not want the precise location or indeed identity of the woman to be identifiable, and so he adopted a dramatic device. The lit window was set brilliantly against an almost entirely black background with only the merest hint of a building around the window. He had decided on a large landscape format. The illuminated window was set off to the right of the painting and on the far left a single dramatic streetlight emerged from the gloom to cast a radiant glow onto an uneven wet cobbled street. If the viewer looked closely, they could just discern gold letters reflected in a dark puddle in the gutter. They were part of the ornate calligraphy lettering on an elaborate storefront: *'ompes Fenèbr'*. Other than the setting, he changed little of the room itself; the woman was the same, the sofa the same and the painting in the background was altered just enough to suggest England or France rather than Italy.

A curious viewer may have figured out that the unseen storefront would have actually said: *Pompes Fenèbres* – Funeral Parlour.

Tony worked on the painting more or less continuously for two weeks until he was satisfied that he had captured the scene as well as he could. When he stood back to take in the finished work, he was very satisfied. This would be one of his best works.

In his wanderings around the village, Tony had been keeping an eye out for the woman from the room. By making a few discreet enquiries, he discovered that she was a newish arrival, from England, but no one seemed to know anything about her. As far as anyone could tell, there was only herself and her adult son living in the house, no sign of a husband.

And then, just as he finished the painting, he had the chance to chat with Carole, an Irish woman who was married to an antique dealer in the village. He spotted her in the Écureuil café and joined her for a coffee. She was able to fill him in.

"She's English, from London. Her name is Jennifer, and she's divorced. She's come to Monpazier because she thinks it will be a better environment for her and her son, which is a slightly odd thing to say, because her son is in his early twenties, I would say. Anyway, she's very nice, and looking forward to settling into the village. At the moment, she's still running backwards and forwards bringing personal items from her house in London. I'm going to have a dinner party next month, I'll be inviting her, and I'll invite you and Caroline, you can meet her then."

Throughout the five years that Tony had lived in Monpazier, Caroline had remained a resident of London.

"My business is there, I pay my taxes there, I really don't want to relocate to France. I understand why you want to get away from London, and I'll spend as much time with you here as I possibly can but, at least for the next few years, I want to stay there."

In fact, Caroline did spend a significant part of her year in Monpazier with Tony. She would probably have spent even more time if the village had been closer to a major long-haul airport. As it was, she was continually flying back-and-forth from London or Paris to New York or the Middle East or Hong Kong, where most of her clients were based. Monpazier meant an additional leg to her journey, even if she generally made in it the Cessna.

Of course, she had seen the painting of the women in the room and was just as intrigued as Tony to meet the subject.

"Are you going to tell her that you've painted her?"

"That depends," said Tony, "we'll just have to see what she's like. Of course I would rather tell her, I wouldn't want it to come as an unpleasant surprise. Maybe I'll give her one of my finished sketches of Monpazier. I could have it framed. What do you think?"

"Good idea," reply Caroline, "I'm sure she'd like that."

Parties at Carole and Olivier's were always entertaining. They invariably managed to collect an eclectic bunch of people, and, as it was summertime, they had been able to invite over a dozen people and set up the table outside. With a galaxy of flickering candles and twinkling lights around the garden it was a magical setting.

As people arrived, Carole made the necessary introductions, and soon enough she brought Jennifer over to be introduced to Tony and Caroline. The three of them chatted for a while, and Tony and Caroline discovered that, as Carole had promised, Jennifer was a very engaging woman.

"Carole tells us you are here with your son," said Caroline, "he's not here tonight?"

"No," replied Jennifer, "he doesn't come out much, he's rather solitary. I may as well tell you, because I'm sure people will wonder, and gossip, which I hate. My son, Daniel, has had some problems. He got in with the wrong crowd at university and started using drugs, a lot. I brought him here to get him as far away as possible from his so-called friends and from the temptations of London. Anyway, enough of all that. I gather you're the rather famous artist, Tony. I must say, I do like your work."

Tony looked at Caroline who gave him a discreet nod.

"Well, it's funny you should say that", Tony said with a nervous laugh. "I really hope you don't mind, but you are already in one of my pieces, my latest in fact."

Jennifer was startled.

"How can that be? I don't understand."

"Why don't you come to my studio tomorrow, and I'll show you. It's much easier to show you than to try to explain."

He gave her directions to his studio.

"Well, I'm intrigued. And I'll certainly call by tomorrow morning."

With Caroline on her way to Dubai, via London, Tony was alone when Jennifer knocked on the studio door. He invited her into the large room, with its double height window.

"I always imagined an artist's studio would be a total clutter, with canvases and paints and whatnot all over the place. This is like an operating theatre." Jennifer was smiling as she spoke.

"I like clean and tidy. Not very atmospheric I'm afraid. Look, I'll show you the painting now, and Jennifer, you don't have to like it. Really, just say what you think, or say nothing, I won't be offended either way."

With that, Tony lifted the sheet from the painting on the easel. It was two metres long and one metre high, so it made a huge impact. He watched Jennifer's face as emotions washed over her. First shock, then recognition and then, to his horror; despair, a flood of tears and her face crumpling before she could cover her distress.

Tony rushed to her side, snatching up a tissue as he did.

"Oh God, Jennifer. I didn't mean to upset you like this. Please forgive me..."

She raised an open palm to stop him, and in a moment recovered herself. She dabbed her eyes and looked at the superb painting once again.

She spoke unprompted.

"It was the terrible end of a dreadful day. I just reached the end of my tether. My ex-husband had called that afternoon to tell me he was remarrying, which shouldn't have bothered me, but it did. And the selfish bastard had forgotten it was Dan's birthday, his 21st, for God's sake. How does a father forget his son's 21st? I was dressed up because I was taking Dan to Edward Premier for a special birthday dinner. He had changed into his suit; he looked so handsome – and then I saw his eyes. He'd been using, I could tell straight away. I've no idea how he got drugs in Monpazier, for Christ's sake. I mean look at the place, how on earth did he get drugs here? I've got the car keys, and I didn't think he had met anyone here, never mind a dealer. I think he's been clean since, but ..."

Her voice tailed off. Tony was still silent as he let her compose herself. Finally, he went over to his storage unit and picked up the small package lying on top.

"This is for you, a gift, a thank you for, well not for posing exactly, but being my inspiration for this," he waved at the easel.

"You didn't have to; but thank you."

Jennifer held out a hand and their fingers touched as he gave her the framed sketch. For a second their eyes locked until Jennifer quickly looked away.

"Can I open it now?"

"Of course."

She carefully unwrapped the heavy white paper and unveiled an exquisite pastel. Tony had portrayed one of the tiny niches found on the outside walls of some of the village houses. Inside was an ancient stone Madonna and Child.

"You are so talented. This is divine and this," again she turned to the painting, her painting as she now thought of it, "this is unbelievable. It's so, so dramatic! You've captured just how I was feeling. How did you see this anyway?"

"From top floor of the Chapître – you need to be more aware of that restaurant. Even though you're above street level, so is the restaurant – and it's much taller than your house."

"You're right, of course. I won't make that mistake again. But I *hate* net curtains, swore I'd never have them. May I ask, what will happen to this painting? I mean, have you sold it?"

"Not yet, but that's the plan. My dealer hasn't seen it yet, just a photo. It's being sent to London next week. It's possible it might go on show in a public gallery. There's a rumour that Edinburgh might just crack and hang it in a temporary exhibition. We'll see. But one way or another, it will be sold sooner or later. Probably to an American – they're my biggest fans it seems. Or my biggest fans with money anyway," he finished with a smile.

"I wouldn't dream of asking normally, but since it is a portrayal of me … how much will it cost, do you think?"

"Don't worry, I'm not bashful about the money, that's why I do what I do. This is a big painting and quite dramatic, as you say. And a beautiful woman is always popular."

He looked her straight in the eye.

"I really think this is exceptional, even if I say so myself. I felt something special from the moment I saw you and at each stage of the work. I think this could be the first of my paintings to sell for a million dollars. How does that sound?"

"My God, my God! A million dollars! To think of it!"

"Meanwhile, on a more prosaic note, I'm going round the corner to the brewery for a burger, would you like to join me?"

"I would, but I better get back to Dan. He's worse than hopeless in the kitchen. He'd starve if I didn't make him something. Next time? And Tony, thanks. For my painting, and my pastel, it will have pride of place. And I'm sorry for my, well, you know."

"Don't apologise. It's your life; I'm only stealing a moment from it."

* * *

During her filming, Lucy had asked about *'Study in Darkness'*, the name Lorenzo had insisted upon for Jennifer's painting. He told her its story, holding back anything that would identify where the scene was, but implying probably Paris or maybe Bordeaux, and he was fairly sure he hadn't given a clue who the woman was.

"The lady knows who she is, she gave the painting her blessing years ago. She's never gone public with her identity, so neither will I. Anyway, she could be any of us. At various times we all got through moments when everything seems just too much. But we get through it. Or most of us do. Turn off the camera please, Lucy.

"Lucy, this is the one segment I need to see before your final edit."

"That wasn't our deal, Tony. I told you; we don't do that."

"If I explain why, will you agree? If not, we're done. No more footage, no more interviews. This isn't about me, Lucy, someone else could get badly hurt if I've said the wrong thing by mistake. I don't want any chance of that. Do you understand?"

"You're not giving me much of a choice, Tony. I thought, after …"

"Lucy, sweetheart, don't confuse sex with something else. We're having good time, it's fun, it suits us both. But we're professionals. Act like it."

"Screw you, Tony Grant. OK, you can see the footage. Now why?"

He explained how Jennifer came to be in the state she was, and the problems with her son. Without mentioning any names, he made Lucy understand that the connection with the woman in the painting wasn't just about a photograph.

"We were pretty friendly for quite a while. Lunches, a few dinners."

He saw the look on Lucy's face.

"No, not that! We flirted a bit, but as time went by, she and Caroline developed a close friendship, especially after… after Daniel, her son, committed suicide."

"Oh my God! How terrible! What happened?"

"He just couldn't get free from his habit. Eventually he just couldn't carry on, I guess. I only talked with the boy once. His mother sent him to me; apparently, he had some thoughts of being some kind of artist – collages as I recall. I couldn't do anything for him; the boy had no talent whatsoever. I explained how brutal the art world was and that he was well out of it. He'd watched some things online, thought anyone could make money at it. Two months later, he was dead. His mother, damn it, her name is Jennifer, but don't mention her name *ever*, do you hear? Jennifer went back to London immediately. She still has the house here, rents it out. I rarely see her, and we don't talk. She and Caroline are still thick as thieves and see each other often in London."

"So Monpazier didn't take with her?"

"Monpazier is strange in some ways. From Easter to autumn, it's nonstop – events, exhibitions, music festivals – good ones, and visitors. Winter is very different. Dinner parties mostly, but otherwise quiet. And January and February are bleak – rubbish weather and a lot of places are shut. I usually leave, for London or Spain or the States. I'd be somewhere warm now if it wasn't for you lot.

"So why do you stay here? Apart from the summers?"

Tony thought for a while.

"One day early on, I was walking through the village, heading to my studio. For some reason, I looked in the side window of one of the antique shops. The owner and his wife also run the most important event of the year, a classical and jazz festival in some the amazing venues in the area. Anyway, I noticed that under the perfectly normal shop window there was a large, worn, but easily recognisable stone salamander. It was obvious to me that the stone was once on top of the entrance to a grand home, or more likely above its massive fireplace.

"So, I did some research. Turns out that the salamander was the emblem adopted by Francis I, King of France in the sixteenth century and the final patron of Leonardo da Vinci. His salamander is carved in stone in world-famous chateaux like Blois, Chambord, Fontainebleau. And under a bloody window of a modest shop and home in Monpazier!

"Just think what this means. Someone important to the king who cared for Leonardo da Vinci in his final days owned a house in, or near, this village. This someone died, or fell out of favour, or whatever, and 500 years later, I'm looking at this stone randomly reused under a village shop window. If this kind of stuff doesn't grab you, you might as well be dead."

"I'm going to get you to repeat all that on camera, but can we get back to Jennifer? Why do you think she left?"

"I imagine it all got a bit too depressing for her after what happened. Anyway, now do you see why I want to make sure I don't accidentally give a clue as to who the mystery woman is? The last thing Jennifer wants or needs is a pack of journalists on her doorstep asking what was wrong that night."

"You're right, and I'm sorry, for my outburst. It's a terrible story, and absolutely, that poor woman doesn't need any aggro from us. I think we're done, unless there's anything you want to add before New York?"

"Why don't we take a walk around the village, with the camera? You can intercut with some of my drawings and sketches if you want. It would make a nice change of pace. And the village is very photogenic. We can visit the salamander."

"What a great idea! You should be in this business, Tony."

"Oh, but I am, sweetheart. It's just that my images don't move."

* * *

Lucy Morrison had already explained to Thomas that this was the last video footage. It had been filmed exactly a week ago, last Thursday, two days before Tony Grant was killed. She had delivered the thumb drive to the hotel herself that morning, finding Thomas and André Lefèvre at breakfast.

Thomas thought the young woman looked pale, as if the recent events had impacted her more than most.

"I thought you might have left by now, Madame Morrison."

"I wish I could," she replied, "but my boss wants me to get some footage of the funeral. The bastard is quite excited; he thinks our programme will get a much bigger audience now. People can be so … I don't know, drawn to tragedy I suppose. Morbid interest."

"Anyway," she sighed, "that's the job. I don't suppose I could persuade you to give an interview, Captain? Discuss the case on film?"

Thomas gave a gentle laugh.

"Not a chance, Lucy. But, and you didn't hear this from me, understood? I'd try Madame le maire if I were you. I understand she has ambitions for higher office, maybe even an MP's seat. Politicians seem to be drawn to cameras like moths to a flame – even if the result is the same. And Lucy, I didn't say it before, but my condolences. I know you must have liked him."

"Thanks, Captain, I appreciate that. I'll try the mayor."

* * *

Thursday, March 10, 2022 – Afternoon

Kiki was first to speak when the video finished.

"That was much more interesting. I wonder why the relationship with Jennifer Oakes went sour. And this friendship between her and Caroline King, what's with that? And why did Jennifer not mention it yesterday?"

Thomas was clearly thinking hard about the information in the video.

"I agree, I think this is important somehow. We need to get to the bottom of this. Who could shed light on Jennifer's friendships with Grant and with Madame King?"

Susan had a suggestion.

"How about Jennifer's ex-husband? She was pretty bitter about him, but he could have some ideas, at least give some names of her close UK friends. I'd need to come up with a way to approach him that doesn't suggest Jennifer is a suspect."

Thomas agreed.

"I'm sure you'll come up with something, and it certainly can't hurt."

He changed the subject.

"Baye and Griset will be ready to give us a sense of the victim's finances later this afternoon. So, let's be back here by say 1700 to hear their report."

* * *

Once again, Thomas had arranged to borrow the small conference room in the hotel for their interview with Lorna Hamilton, Cruikshank as was all those years ago. They also decided that Susan would lead the interview to keep it as informal as possible.

"First of all, Mrs Hamilton, our deepest condolences for your loss. We have watched extended interviews with Mr Grant, and we have some idea of how very close you two were. He was incredibly fond of you."

"Thank you, and Lorna will do just fine. And you don't need to choose your words carefully; Tony loved me, and I loved him. We loved each other since we were two lost and broken children who found each other.

146

Then we lost each other again. Other than my wedding day, finding Tony in Venice was the happiest day of my life."

"Very well, Lorna, I'll be straight with you. Did you have any idea Tony was forging paintings?"

Lorna smiled at the two police officers opposite her.

"I've thought very hard about how I would answer that question, thought very hard indeed. It requires me to tell you a rather long story, so please bear with me.

"It was April when Tony and I bumped into each other in Venice. In May he came to Edinburgh and met my husband, Andrew. It was lovely. The two of them got on so well; they'd go off on long walks together. And on every walk, Tony wore his scarf, the scarf I knitted for his fourteenth birthday. Somehow, through all the ups and downs, he had kept hold of his terrible brown scarf. And he got to see again, framed and hanging on my wall, faded, creased and folded a million times, the drawing he did for me, of the statue in the grounds of the Home."

Lorna paused for a moment, lost in her memories. After a moment, she smiled and continued.

"Anyway, before he left, Tony asked what we were doing for a holiday that year. I reminded him that I had already told him about our wee narrowboat in Norfolk, so he asked if we would like to have another holiday, just for a week maybe, on a bigger boat, in the Mediterranean. Well, Andrew isn't much for planes and airports and all the hanging around you have to do, and Tony knew this. He reassured Andrew, 'You won't have to worry about queues at security, or customs, or waiting for your bags, Andrew, I promise.'

"Well, Andrew loves me," Lorna took out a tissue and dabbed her eyes.

"I'm very lucky, aren't I, to have two wonderful men love me so much. Andrew knew how much I wanted us to spend time together, so he said yes.

"Well, in October it was, the autumn mid-term break from Andrew's school. It was the most amazing thing ever, honestly. A big black limousine turned up at our house, with a chauffeur who insisted on carrying our cases from our front door. He drove us to the airport, right onto the tarmac mind, and stopped in front of a private jet. A man was waiting to check our passports and that was that! We never even saw our bags until they were in our room! We sat down and a lovely man called Gerald appeared with glasses of champagne and asked if we were ready to leave. The whole experience was a dream. We flew to Nice and a helicopter, a helicopter!

brought us to Monte Carlo where we were taken on board this absolutely gorgeous yacht, with about ten smart young people who would be at our beck and call the whole week, and Tony standing there with a huge grin on his face. 'Welcome aboard sir, madam!' he said.

"I won't bore you with everything we did, but it was magical. That first night we were taken to a place called Chateau Eza for dinner on a private terrace looking over the Mediterranean. We went to ... Never mind, you're not interested in all of that.

"I was on at Tony about how much this was all costing. I mean, I knew his paintings sold for a lot of money, but this was ridiculous. And then he said that he had arranged for money to be paid into my account every month. Well, I just couldn't accept that at all, and I pestered and pestered until one night he sat Andrew and I down. 'I'm going for a drink with the captain; we have some details to sort out. I'd like you two to watch something while I'm away. It's a DVD of a BBC documentary I saw seven or eight years ago. Now, after you watch it, you'll have questions, I'm sure. But I want you to agree you will never, ever ask me those questions, that you'll never refer to the programme again, and you'll never ask me about money again. You just have to trust me on this. And you have to let me share what makes me happy.'

"Well, we watched the DVD. It was about a man, I forget his name, who spent his life tracking down paintings stolen from Jews in Germany before and during the war. A lot of the paintings were now in museums and the rest in private collections. It was obvious that many of the people who had them knew, or at least suspected, where the paintings had come from, but they didn't care. Even when this man confronted them, they just brushed him off. The man was interviewed of course, and he said that these people were no better than the Nazis who had stolen the paintings in the first place. And then, near the end, the man told the story of a painting he had recovered that turned out to be a forgery. Neither the latest owner, nor the original Jewish owner may have known it was a forgery, he couldn't be sure one way or another, but he felt that the time he had spent on that particular case had been a waste."

Lorna paused and looked at the officers.

"Could I have a drink of water, please?"

Thomas hurried to the phone and asked reception to bring some water and glasses. While they waited, Susan prompted Lorna.

"So, you think maybe Tony was telling you what he was doing, without actually telling you?"

"If he was selling forgeries of paintings that were supposed to have been stolen from Jewish families to people who didn't ask any questions, that would be quite clever, wouldn't it? I mean, they were never going to get an expert opinion and, as I know because I own *Luncheon on Skye*, people, nice people, are always wanting to borrow paintings for one exhibition or another. Well, if you really knew your painting had been stolen, you wouldn't do that, would you, lend it I mean? So, no one who would maybe know better, would ever get to see the painting. It took Andrew and I a while to work all this out, you understand and, of course, it is only a theory."

Lorna smiled, "But Tony was a *very* clever man."

"Were there other cruises? Other holidays?"

"Oh goodness, yes. With Andrew's brothers and sisters and their kids; all the nephews and nieces have had at least one or two holidays on one of these lovely yachts. Of course, Tony's jet is only big enough for six people, so the rest have to fly with EasyJet, but we've had the best holidays you can imagine. The Riviera, Majorca, the Greek Islands twice, the Virgin Islands. We had Christmas in the Caribbean one year. And Tony loved those holidays too, and Caroline when she came. They're like Andrew and me, no kids of their own, so we get to borrow other people's now and then."

"And the jet?"

"The jet! Can you imagine, two kids from Sister Mary Joseph's Home, flying to a David Bowie concert in Prague, in a jet that one of them owns! 'I know it's a bit pathetic, Lorna', he said to me once, 'but I just love having this plane. I don't want a Rolls-Royce, or a Ferrari, or even a Patek Philippe watch. But when I think of all those bastards who told me I was thick, that I would never amount to anything. This is my revenge, I suppose.'

"We flew to concerts and once, really, he phoned and said I had to get dressed up and get Andrew into a suit and take a taxi to the airport, right away. He and Caroline picked us up in the plane to go to Copenhagen. A restaurant there had been voted the best restaurant in the world, so we went. It was dreadful! So-called foraged food. '£300 each for a plate of fucking weeds and nettles!' he called it. 'We didn't know we were 'foraging' when we ate wild raspberries in the grounds of the Home, did we, Lorna?' We laughed ourselves silly! Oh, the fun we've had!"

Lorna sat back in her chair, finished. Except for one more thought.

"But I'd trade every day of all of it to have him back."

* * *

While Lorna was talking, Eloise was sitting down in the modest home of Louise Brouzet.

"Thank you once again for seeing me, Madame. We are still working to create a full picture of Monsieur Grant and his life here in Monpazier. Apart from yourself, did Monsieur Grant employ anyone else to assist around his house or studio?"

"Yes and no. Which is to say, he left everything to me, and I had my son, Philippe do anything I could not manage myself."

"Is Philippe here? I'd love to talk with him too."

"Of course, I'll go and get him."

In a few minutes, Loulou reappeared, shepherding her large, ungainly son ahead of her. Eloise formed the instant impression that Philippe would still be living with his mother many years in the future.

Obviously already primed by his mother, Philippe started talking before Eloise said a word.

"I do lots of jobs for Monsieur Grant. It is so sad that he has gone to heaven. Mama and I will pray for him at his special Mass tomorrow. Yes, I do lots of things to help."

"Like hanging his paintings?" Eloise prompted.

"Exactly! And I found these very clever lights for the paintings as well. They have magnets, you see. The tube with the lights sticks onto the arm. And they come on at the same time, every evening, for six hours. Every week, I would go with Mama and take down some tubes and replace them with ones I have recharged at home. This way, there are no wires. It really is very clever. Monsieur Grant was delighted. He gave me a little extra that week. He said I was very clever to have found the special lamps. 'How could I manage without you, Philippe?' He said that, out loud."

The not-so-very-young man was still proud of the famous artist's compliment.

"And the normal lightbulbs, when they stopped working?"

"Yes, of course, I would change those as well. The lights in the lounge are very high, because of the height of the balcony of course. And the studio lights also, very high. I had to buy an enormous ladder, which Monsieur Grant paid Mama for, of course. I also can clean the windows with the ladder. I wonder if the new person will need someone to change his lights?"

A sudden thought struck Philippe.

"Mama, what will happen now? To you? To us? What of the new person doesn't need us? What will we do?"

He was becoming distressed. His mother soothed him with a few gentle stokes of his arm.

"Don't worry, cheri, it will be fine. Don't worry. There are always people who need help, especially the English. We'll be fine; just leave it to Mama."

By this point, Eloise was just about certain that this helpful, but limited soul was not murderer material. She turned her attention back to Loulou.

"Madame Brouzet, we believe that someone, other than Monsieur Grant and yourself, someone entered the studio on the day of the murder. Now, I want you to be reassured that there is no implication in my next question. Many of us need to write things down that we are told not to, like PINs for example. Did you ever have to write down the code for the alarm in Monsieur Grant's studio? Perhaps in the beginning of your work for him?"

"Never. Monsieur Grant asked me to choose the code; it is the birthday of my mother, together with my age when I met my late husband, fifteen. No-one alive now knows this information."

"And you never gave the code to someone else, to Philippe for example, or someone who cleaned when you were on holiday, or sick or indisposed?"

"Never. Philippe always accompanied me to the studio, always. And we took our holidays when Monsieur Grant was himself away, which was often enough. And, unlike young people today, people like me are *never* indisposed; we work, we work through challenges, we do not take to our beds for every minor ailment. Monsieur Tony trusted me with his studio and with his home and I would have never let him regret that trust. Never!"

* * *

Thomas and Susan were alone in the spacious council room in the Mairie. Everyone else was out chasing down one idea or detail or another and Caroline King was due to arrive in a few minutes.

"It is a pain," Thomas was saying, "normal people, citizens who are not habitual criminals, are intimidated when they are brought into the Gendarmerie for questioning. It must be the same in England I imagine?"

"Of course. This is far too comfortable and bland. But slightly better than the hotel I suppose."

"Slightly," Thomas agreed. "I don't mind admitting that I'm struggling with this case. I'm beginning to think that maybe my first thought was correct – that the murder had nothing to do with the forgeries. But I just struggle with the coincidences that would imply. Grant gets murdered and on the same day, his studio is burgled, and by someone who knows about, or figures out, the secret section with the forgeries and just casually takes them as well. That's all just ridiculous."

"I agree, but who else knows the alarm code, apart from King and the cleaner? I wonder how Eloise is getting on there. What about the alarm company?"

"Bordeaux checked them out. They have been in business for decades, without a hint of scandal. And, to be frank, they protect a lot of valuable things a damn sight easier to convert to cash than a bunch of paintings. This would not be the robbery of choice for a corrupt employee."

"What about someone we haven't heard of yet? A customer who somehow discovered that he had been sold a forgery, and tracked Grant down for example? Maybe the husband of another of Grant's mistresses, perhaps from years ago?"

"You have put your finger on my biggest fear. If either of those scenarios is correct, it will be a nightmare to identify the guilty party with no physical evidence. And as of right now, we have none."

At that moment, a knock on the door announced that Caroline had arrived. Susan went to admit her.

Thomas stood and shook her hand.

"I am delighted to meet you, Miss King. And may I add my own condolences. Thank you for coming in to talk with us. As I'm sure you know, I am Captain Thomas Coman and this is Detective Sargeant Howard from the Metropolitan Police who is assisting us with the tragic case."

Caroline nodded at these initial comments but said nothing.

Thomas continued.

"First things first. Miss King, as you would expect, we have checked Mr Grant's house for fingerprints. Because people like yourself and Madame Brouzet have been all over the house over an extended period, we need samples of your fingerprints for purposes of elimination. Do you mind?"

"Of course not, I understand completely."

Thomas went through the process of taking a full set of fingerprints before handing Caroline a small cloth impregnated with spirit to remove the traces of ink on her fingers. When they were finished, he thanked her and moved on to his questions.

"Miss King, I hope you understand that I have to ask some very personal and perhaps painful questions?"

Caroline nodded and Thomas proceeded. He opened with a seemingly trivial question

"Miss King, we've been told that Mr Grant, and yourself when you are in France, are regulars at several of the restaurants in the village, for lunch and dinner. Chapître, Côté Halles, Privilège, Bistro 2, all count you as regulars, as do the brewery, the café and the wine bar. But for the past month or so, Mr Grant hasn't been seen at any of your usual haunts. Why is that?"

"There's a simple explanation, Captain, neither Tony nor I believe in being vaccinated."

"Miss King, are you quite well?" Thomas was genuinely concerned; Caroline had turned as white as a sheet. He looked at Susan who was equally worried.

"I'll get some water. Caroline, do you need a doctor? Are you on medications?"

"No, I'm … " Caroline stammered, "I just, somehow it just hit me, he's gone. Talking about the restaurants, our lives together. I haven't really had time to come to terms with separating, and now he's dead. So many years together, so many memories. I'll be fine, really, I feel better already. Thank you, a glass of water would be lovely."

"Would you prefer to wait before we continue to talk, Miss King?"

"No, I'm fine, but thank you."

She took a few long sips of water and visibly pulled herself together before carrying on.

"You asked about the restaurants. Since the end of January, we haven't been able to go into those places as our old passes are no longer valid. More French rigidity, I'm afraid. I was out of the country for the first couple of weeks, but poor Tony must have been beside himself – the man could barely boil an egg."

"Well, that explains that. Are you quite certain you are ready to carry on?"

Caroline nodded.

Thomas continued. "Very well. Now a more intrusive question, I'm afraid. It appears that the victim had relationships with several other women. Were you aware of this, and how did you feel about it?"

Caroline did not pause before confidently answering Thomas's question.

"Tony was a handsome, fascinating man, and women found him quite irresistible. I must confess it was me who initiated our relationship all those years ago. He generally did not have long-running affairs, but he employed a series of young, beautiful models and they invariably fell for him, and he invariably took advantage of their availability. Of course, I didn't like it, but I surprised myself by how little it bothered me.

"For some reason, and I've never fully understood this myself, neither Tony nor I wanted to make the final commitment to each other – I don't just mean marriage, but we kept two houses, two lives, two existences. I had a few dalliances myself over the years, but like Tony's, nothing that impacted our relationship."

"And how would you describe that relationship?"

"We were good together; we were good *for* each other. We helped each other. If there wasn't a grand, life-altering passion, there was respect, affection, admiration. I look at my friends in conventional marriages and I often think I have the best of it. We didn't grow to resent each other, be bored by each other, be overwhelmed by the everyday grind of children, housework, 9-to-5 jobs. I was his entrée into a fulfilling life in art, and he was mine. If I helped get Tony launched, he helped let me achieve my ambitions."

"So why leave him?"

"He became careless of other people and their lives. Gemma Taylor is married, and they behaved as if her husband was deaf, dumb and blind as well as too often drunk. It became embarrassing. And Camille? She's nothing but a wilful child. What was he thinking? Eventually what was merely embarrassing becomes ... I don't know, something more soul-destroying. I had had enough. So, I gave him back his painting, and I left."

"And yet you were still here, as recently as last week. Why?"

"Bad timing. I made my mind up, then I disappeared to Hong Kong and London on business. Then I came here to talk with Tony, and he

154

promptly went off to Glasgow with Lucy – another temptation surrendered to, by the way. I finally packed the last of my stuff and left Tony a list of my paintings, he promised to have them boxed up and sent to London, but…"

Caroline began to cry, softly, and Thomas had no doubt whatsoever that her sorrow was real. He gave her time to collect herself before turning to his other main question.

"OK, Miss King, let's move on to another area. In the videos recorded for the documentary, Thomas is very complimentary about you and he acknowledges how much he relied on you for guidance on business matters. With that in mind, would you please give me a better understanding of how much money Mr Grant was making each year from his forged paintings?"

There was a long silence while Caroline looked coolly at Thomas.

"That was very well done, Captain. You just slid that in there, didn't you?"

She smiled and continued, in a completely different tone from her earlier responses. Susan realised that she was now speaking as if reading from a script, which she was, a memorised script unspooling in her head.

"All artists seek inspiration from those who have gone before. Tony started his journey by first copying paintings and then by mimicking the style of other artists. He was good at it. But he didn't want to confuse the market by selling these other derivative works alongside those in his own, unique style. There are many steps between derivative works and forgeries, Captain. Anyway, he didn't sell these pieces through Lorenzo, and he thought it best to keep the details from me. He banked the proceeds, whatever they were, in a separate account that I had no access to, and he kept any expenses completely separate from the bank accounts I managed. I'm afraid I can't shed any further light on the matter, Captain."

"You never wondered where the money came from to keep a private jet, or to donate one and a half million pounds to charity every year?"

Caroline looked genuinely shocked.

"A million and a half! I had no idea…" She pulled herself up.

"As I said, I cannot shed any further light on these matters, Captain. I'm sorry."

Thomas, aided on occasion by Susan, persisted for some time, but it was clear that Caroline had rehearsed her answer and was determined not to embellish or develop it one iota, especially after her slip in reaction to the scale of the charitable donations. She did add a denial of having any idea about the secret compartments in the studio storage unit but acknowledged knowing the alarm code and having gone into the studio alone to arrange shipping of a painting on numerous occasions.

Eventually, Thomas had no choice but to let her go, with a final question, "You mentioned something about giving Mr Grant his painting back. What did you mean by that?"

"That's a slightly long story, Captain; but I'm happy to explain."

Caroline recounted the story of how she and Tony met, and his loaned painting to be returned as a signal that the relationship was at an end.

As soon as Caroline closed the door behind her, Thomas let out a sigh of frustration.

"Tony Grant was indeed a clever man. Both the women he cared about were let in on his secret, but in each case in a way that allowed them to avoid being tainted by his crimes, at least legally. There would be no point in going after them as conspirators, or even beneficiaries – any decent lawyer would help them dodge charges."

Susan agreed. "But she knew all right, although not perhaps everything. I think the charity money surprised her. And her explanation of the split with Grant didn't sound quite kosher to me. There's more to that to uncover. Although, I have to say, she seems truly upset about his death – that turn she had would be impossible to fake."

"I agree, but so much seems to point to her. She ticks every box, except that her alibi makes it impossible for her to be in two places at once."

Thomas stood and looked at his watch.

"I better let Gus go for now, he's been stewing all afternoon. He can come back in the morning. Actually, we're looking at Gus as a potential patsy for Zachary Taylor, but what about Caroline King? I don't mean Gus,"

"But perhaps she used someone else!" Susan interrupted. "That could be it, Capitaine! She has the motive: sex and money, the usual. She has the key, knows the alarm code, she may easily have lied about the secret compartments; is it possible that Grant kept the safe combination from her? Otherwise she'd know about the donations. She is certainly smart enough to find someone to do the job. But I can't picture the murder itself. Grant should be shot or stabbed."

Thomas nodded.

"I agree. A hired killer would be much too cautious to risk tangling with Grant in a struggle – a gun or knife or a drug would be the way to go. But the crime scene doesn't support any of those options."

* * *

Pierre Griset opened the financial presentation. As they didn't have a projector, he had printed out a sheet for each of them, which he now began to review.

"I'll start with the legal side of things. Bear in mind, I'm showing you 2024. Grant's legal income has been rising steadily each year as his paintings have fetched higher and higher prices. Since he moved to France in 2015, the price of his paintings has roughly doubled; so now they average three-quarters of a million euros each, ranging from 300 thousand to almost 1.5 million."

"Now," he continued, "his gallery takes exactly half, and taxes take a big bite out of what's left. He gives half a million a year to charities, this is just the legal stuff remember, and he spends another 1.2 million on everything else – a lot of it on fantastically expensive hotels and restaurants around the world. Wherever he goes, he stays in the most expensive suites, eats in three-star restaurants.

"So, as you can see, in 2024, Grant received about 1.3 million euros more than he spent. We can't see any evidence of share dealing and he seems to own only two properties – Monpazier and the London flat, which he co-owns with his partner, Madame King. The rest is sitting in his bank. His balance in Crédit Agricole was a little over five million euros."

"Was?" asked Thomas.

"On Friday, just before the close of business, 4.5 million euros were transferred to Grant's own account in Switzerland."

"Really! 4.5 million, just before he is killed. But to his own bank account? Is there any more information on the transfer?"

"Nothing. It wasn't so very unusual. In January he transferred over 40 million, leaving almost nothing in his accounts here. But there was a large deposit recently, from his London dealer, Lorenzo Biamonte."

Thomas wondered out loud, "Why would he have his London dealer send money to France, only to immediately send most of it to Switzerland?"

Pierre finished and his partner, Christophe Baye, took over.

"Like Pierre, I'm going to give you averages, although Grant's income from his forgeries has been more or less steady almost from the start.

"Grant earns an average of approximately €300,000 from each forgery. He pays only 20% commission to his unknown agent or dealer and, of course, there are no taxes to worry about, lucky bastard!"

Christophe joined in the laughter for a moment before carrying on.

"He gives about €1.5 million of this money to charity each year. It sounds unbelievable, but we've verified most of the French donations already. It costs almost a million to run his jet and we now know that the other big mystery purchase is chartering a yacht every year for his cruise with Lorna Hamilton and her family.

"He gets through a fair amount of cash throughout the year, about €50,000 in 2024. We haven't found any correspondence with the Swiss bank yet, and I'm guessing it will be weeks if not months before we prize any information out of them, so we have no idea how much is sitting there."

"Basically," he summarised, "Grant did the forgeries so he could own a private jet, take his old friend and her family on a fabulous holiday every year, tip like a madman – and give various children's charities €1,500,000 a year. It's illegal and it's terrible and I can't help admiring him just a bit!"

Eloise chipped in, "And look at who he sold his forgeries to, creeps that thought they were buying paintings stolen from innocent Jews. It's hard to see who the victims were in Grant's crimes."

Thomas replied, "Well, fortunately, we don't have to worry about that, the Art Crimes people have that bag of worms. We just have to find out who killed the man. If it turns out to have been a disgruntled customer or a jealous husband, we're in deep trouble – I wouldn't know where to start."

Eloise wasn't finished however, "Capitaine, we have another mystery. It occurred to me that Grant must have shipped his forgeries to GPM, whoever they are, and he didn't just pop them in the post. I asked Gendarme Lefèvre to do some digging."

She nodded to her colleague, who took up the story.

"Years ago, Madame King set up an account with a French company called Convelio. They are specialists in shipping artworks round the world. They confirmed that they regularly collect canvases from Grant's studio and ship them, usually to Biamonte in London, but occasionally to a different address. The last order they processed was to send a painting to a Miss Amy Johnson, in Scotland. I have the address. I've sent the shipping records from Convelio to the accounting person in Biamonte's gallery and asked her to confirm all the deliveries. She'll get back to me by Monday at the latest. I also asked Convelio to contact their competitors and ask if any of them are also picking up canvases here. Someone must be collecting the forgeries – it would be useful to know where they go."

"Excellent work, you two." Thomas responded.

All day, between interviews, the entire team, and especially Susan, had been ribbing Thomas about that evening's Six Nations match between Wales and France.

"Who will you be supporting, Capitaine? And remember, I can probably find your mother's phone number and call her with your answer. So come on, Wales or France?"

"Yes, Capitaine," Pierre added, "we all want to know. France or Wales?"

But Thomas refused to give anything but a diplomat's answer, "Whoever plays best, deserves to win."

Now Susan, Thomas and André were walking back to the hotel when Susan had another idea.

"Why don't you two get into your civvies and we'll watch the match in the brewery. It'll be packed tonight and a lot of fun."

"We can't, Susan," André explained. "Even out of uniform, they know we're Gendarmerie, and that's a problem."

"Why?"

Thomas replied.

"Ever since the Minister made his announcement that all the restrictions would be lifted on Monday, people have been more and more ignoring them already – not wearing masks, not checking passes, and we'd have to insist … Oh my God! That's it!"

Without explaining his outburst, in English, Thomas grabbed his phone and keyed in a number.

"Kiki, it's Thomas Coman, sorry to call you at home."

Susan was intrigued by Thomas's outburst and amused by his sudden informality; he must be really excited, she thought.

"Kiki, I need you to drive to Bordeaux first thing in the morning. By the time you get there, I'll have had someone text you the address of the owner of the restaurant Caroline King ate in that night."

He explained what he wanted her to do.

"Tell you what, you two come up to my suite; we'll order food from room service, open a bottle and watch the match together. I'll enjoy watching you argue over the game."

* * *

Friday, March 11, 2022

On the day of the funeral the sun rose on a perfect Dordogne spring morning, sunny and crisp, with the promise of real warmth for the first time in the year. The team had abandoned any thoughts of looking out for out-of-place mourners at the funeral – there were hundreds of attendees. The ancient church was crammed to the door and speakers had been rigged up so the villagers could listen in as they stood outside.

After some confusion, caused largely by a surplus of officious functionaries from different jurisdictions, each vying to be seen to be in charge of proceedings, everyone was seated, with Caroline sitting alone on the front lefthand pew. However, just before the service began, a large group arrived, corralled by Lorna. Two competing civil servants were for once united in barring this untidy gang from entering.

"Who are you?" one demanded.

"Mr and Mrs Hamilton." Lorna replied.

The officials examined their lists and became instantly obsequious.

"Ah yes! Madame Hamilton, Monsieur; please be seated next to Madame King, in the front row."

"Come on everyone, you heard the gentleman."

But the bureaucrats imposed themselves once more.

"I am sorry, Madame, but who are these other people?"

"Do you really want all their names? Are you sure? These are my brothers- and sisters-in-law and the others are my nieces and nephews. And this gentleman," Lorne gently grasped the hand of a bemused, elderly-looking man and eased him forward, "this is Mr Joseph Gallagher, the father of the deceased. In other words, son, aside from Caroline, we are the only people in this building with a *right* to be here!"

Suddenly Lorna's voice changed from its habitual soft lilt and became a granite burr.

"And you will cease causing a fuss and escort us to our seats, immediately!"

She turned to the other suit and gave him his marching orders.

"You, go ahead and tell those people behind Caroline to move along or move out. Now!"

As soon as Caroline had called with the dreadful news, Lorna had set about finding Tony's father, if indeed he was still alive. After half a day of fruitless internet searches using the sketchy information she had about Tony's mother and father, she had a brainwave and called back the BBC reporter who had earlier called her to ask, politely, for background on Tony. Their history was regularly rehashed every time she loaned 'Luncheon on Skye' to an exhibition, so she was on every reporter's call list.

She asked the journalist, a woman called Anne, for help in tracking down a Joseph Gallagher, labourer, who would now be aged around 64 or 66, last known address Townhead, Glasgow. Miraculously, thanks to the resources and contacts of the BBC, Anne found Joe in under four hours and passed his phone number to Lorna to break the news, with a promised exclusive interview to come the next day.

Lorna called the number, which was answered immediately.

"Mr Gallagher, you don't know me, but I was a great friend of your son, Tony. I'm afraid I have some sad news, Mr Gallagher."

And then Lorna displayed once again the empathy and generosity of spirit that had attracted the young Tony all those years ago. Sensing that Joe was having trouble grasping the improbable course of his son's life, none of which he had the slightest clue about, Lorna arranged to take the train to Glasgow the following day. She had spent a couple of hours in the 1960s era council flat that Joe had been moved into when his second wife left him after only four years. Then she took him into town, to Marks and Spencer, and bought him a suit, shirt and tie and new socks and shoes and explained that she and Andrew would pick him up in a few days to take him to Glasgow Airport where Gerald would be waiting in Tony's jet to bring them to the funeral.

It was mention of the jet that finally brought home to Joe the remarkable scale of his son's achievements and, amidst all the regret and self-abasement that he would feel, there was also the stirrings of the pride that would bring him comfort in his remaining years. Years which, thanks to Lorna and Andrew, would have a few more creature comforts and, much more importantly, some human warmth.

Although the funeral had quickly escaped out of the control of Madame le maire, she had been able to relay Caroline's request that the music should include *'Amazing Grace'*, played by a piper from Toulouse, who also played *'Flower of Scotland'* as the mourners filed out at the end of the ceremony.

In the Mairie, Thomas could hear faint echoes of the bagpiper's final tune as he sat opposite Gus and his Bergerac lawyer, who had returned for their postponed interview. The lawyer spoke first.

"Capitaine, my client has a statement to make. I've explained to him that, if he cooperates fully, you will make a recommendation for leniency as no harm was, in fact caused by my client."

"If what you say is true, I will certainly consider my recommendation very carefully."

The lawyer nodded to Gus, who looked down at the sheet of paper in front of him.

"The Ambassador and his wife befriended Camille and I after they heard about Camille's pregnancy. After a while the Ambassador took me for a drink in the brewery and told me about Grant's affair with his wife and how angry he was. Then he said that Grant had used his wife and Camille and didn't care about the trouble he caused. We met several times and finally he explained that he wanted me to set fire to Grant's studio – at night you understand when there would be no one there. No one would get hurt, just Grant's painting. He gave me €500, with another €1500 to come after. But I never got round to it before Grant died. That's it."

"As your lawyer well knows, you committed a crime when you took the €500, but," he held up his hand to forestall their protests, "as you have confessed and saved us a lot of time, I'll recommend leniency, but for the last time. I'll also recommend that if we ever have trouble from you again, Gus, for anything at all, they throw the book at you. Understand? And stay well away from Monsieur Taylor, I'll be having a word with him later."

Meanwhile, Susan was on the phone to Jennifer's ex-husband. Her cover was that she was confirming that Jennifer met Tony well after their divorce and that he, the ex, could not, therefore, be a suspect. Amazingly, the man became flustered and bought the flimsy pretence. Susan was then able to ask him about the tragedy of their son's death and its effect on Jennifer.

Thomas had asked Lucy for Lorenzo Biamonte's contact details and had used them to set up a meeting in the Mairie after the funeral.

"Thank you for being available on such short notice, Mr Biamonte, there are a few things I hope you can clear up. I am Captain Coman, in charge of the investigation. I thought your assistant, Mr Montague would be with you?"

"Poor Geoffrey is still distraught about Tony's death. He said he couldn't bear to attend the funeral. I closed the gallery yesterday and today, as a mark of respect, which means Geoffrey can have a few days to hopefully pull through this awful business."

"Very well, perhaps to begin, you could tell me about the Tony Grant you knew – what he was like, how you worked together, things like that."

Lorenzo held up a hand.

"Anything, anything that might help you find out what happened. Tony was my favourite client; straightforward, hardworking, willing to listen, good with clients; he was just excellent!"

To the surprise of both men, tears began to trickle down Lorenzo's cheeks. He wiped them with an immaculately folded square whipped from his breast pocket.

"I've never actually used one of these before," he smiled, clearly unembarrassed.

"Tony was the smartest artist I ever knew. He learned very fast. He understood that art is a business, and he wanted to succeed in that business. He was a sponge for information; on pricing, on exhibitions, on talking with clients, on everything.

"And he knew that he must not saturate the market. Even when," Lorenzo smiled wistfully, "even when I wanted him to produce more paintings. 'Ten, maybe twelve a year, Lorenzo. I'm in this for the long haul, and I'm still young, old man. I want to be selling pieces long after you're retired. So, one a month, maximum. Fewer when we're successful.' I remember the day he told me that, right at the beginning of our relationship.

"I knew he always held some paintings back; in fact, he admitted to me that he always had a dozen or so more or less finished pieces in the studio. As he completed a new work, he'd chose one out of his inventory and send it to me for sale, replacing it in his private stock. 'What if I'm ill, or maybe I just want a break? I'll still need the money, won't I?' he explained to me.

"Trust me, Captain, no other artist I represent has ever thought so deeply about the business.

"So clever! I'm going to miss him terribly. And what a hard worker! He told me once, 'Listen, Lorenzo, art is bullshit. You want hard work? Work on a building site for five years. Carry hod after fucking hod of bricks up five flights of scaffolding in the pissing rain, or sleet, or snow for eight solid hours – then tell me that what you and I do is hard work.' I think that's why he didn't care about the critics, who were brutal, by the way."

Lorenzo paused, wondering if he had said enough; but no, he wanted to tell one more story.

"Quite early, I thought I would try to fix things with the critics and the public galleries, even just a bit. In all my years, I've never seen anyone treated the way they treated Tony. They hated him, really. It wasn't just that they didn't like his work; they hated him, they especially hated his enormous success. Anyway, I arranged a lunch in a private room in my club. Half-a-dozen critics – the big magazines, the BBC, The Times; and curators from Tate Modern, the National, Manchester, Edinburgh.

"It all went fine at first. The conversation was about politics, America, sport, the usual inane matters. Then the waiters cleared everything away, and we were left alone with coffee and wine.

"Immediately, Tony stood up and looked around the table. 'You're probably expecting a plea from me for a truce, for a justification for my art and why you should look at it anew perhaps. But have you ever wondered,' he asked them, 'how Michelangelo, Raphael, Rembrandt, how they ever produced anything worthwhile without critics to guide them? Or, an even bigger mystery, how anyone knew how fucking great they were, with no critics to tell them? You see, I think there have always been people who wanted to produce great art, or music, or literature, but realised that they just couldn't, just didn't have the talent. And they became frustrated – bitter and angry. And then, a couple of hundred or so years ago, one of those bitter and angry guys realised that he *did* have a talent after all – he could find endless ways of saying shitty things about others who *could* do it; of being destructive, but in creative ways, and, and this is the good bit, he could get *paid* for this talent – by becoming a critic.

"So, I'd like to thank Lorenzo here for organising this little get together so I can tell you to your faces that I think you're bunch of worthless, talentless pricks. That you have no idea of the depth of my contempt for each and every one of you. That I could give a flying fuck about what you say about me or hang or don't hang in your galleries that my taxes help pay for. That you're parasites sucking on the tits of people who actually have talent. So, you carry on doing what you do, and I'll carry on making things that bring people happiness and even a little joy, *and* that make me rich. And when, a week after each of you miserable, pathetic bastards die, and you and everything you have ever written are instantly forgotten; my paintings will *still* be bringing people happiness and joy. Feel free to quote me on any of this, by the way.'

"Well, you could have heard a pin drop. I was appalled, of course, but what could I do? One by one they left, not saying a word. I'm glad I got to be there!"

"Mr Biamonte, a question about your financial arrangements with Mr Grant. You recently deposited €5 million in Mr Grant's French bank, but he very quickly moved it to Switzerland. Can you help me understand? Why did he not ask you to send the money directly to Geneva?"

"He did. A month or so ago, he asked me to send all his future earnings to his account with Julius Baer. My bank, Barclays, made a mistake and ignored my new instruction, sending the money to the account he had been using since he moved to France. Tony didn't explain why he made the change, and I never saw him to ask. It didn't seem like something to discuss on the phone."

* * *

Saturday, March 12, 2022

On Friday night, Thomas was up until one in the morning, editing the daily report. He was excited, sure that the case was about to break. Earlier, when he called Charlie, he was able to tell her he was very confident he'd be home the following day, Sunday at the latest. Before he went to bed, he sent a text to the team, calling them to the Mairie by nine on Saturday morning. Well, the whole team except Kiki La Roux, who he thought deserved a break.

The day did not disappoint.

The first development was from Christophe Baye.

"Here are the photographs from the motorway cameras on the day of the murder. There are lots more, I picked out these, these are the clearest."

He brought the images up on his laptop. It showed Caroline's car with a rather indistinct image of the driver.

"That's her, that's Caroline King for sure," Eloise exclaimed.

Thomas looked closely at his Adjudant.

"How can you be sure? It isn't a very clear image."

"The hat, that's the Ralph Lauren baseball cap, you can see the sparkly gold RL logo. She was wearing it when she got off the plane. I remember thinking how cool she looked. It isn't an easy look to pull off, but she looked fabulous – cap, blazer, striped man's shirt, great slacks and killer heels. She looked amazing, and that's her hat. There can't be many of them around."

"We'll come back to that. Gendarme Griset, what do you have for us?"

"Madame King's fingerprints were found on one of the snooker cues in the victim's house."

"Any other prints on the cue?"

"None, or on any of the other cues. Loulou Brouzet did her job well."

"Excellent!" exclaimed Thomas, with a wide smile on his face. "Excellent! Now," he continued, "you'll notice that Gendarme Le Roux is missing. I told her to take it easy and come in a little later if she wished, she didn't get home until after 2 a.m. It turned out that the restaurant in Bordeaux was closed – the owner and her family were celebrating her daughter Geneviève's birthday with a family weekend in Arcachon. Le Roux didn't track her down there until almost eleven last night. She called me on her way back. I won't tell you what she learned just yet, but sit anywhere you want, within earshot of me, and you'll find out in a minute or two. We have a visitor this morning. Sargeant Howard, you sit beside me."

No sooner had everyone sat down than there was a knock on the door and Madame le maire ushered Jennifer Oakes into the room and left, closing the door behind her.

"Mrs Oakes, please sit there. Mrs Oakes, may I call you Jennifer? A nice name, Jennifer, if I may say. More common I think in England than France."

With that strange introduction, Thomas pretended to look at notes in an empty folder.

"You are in a great deal of trouble, Jennifer. I will be charging you with the French equivalents of conspiring to commit premeditated murder, aiding and abetting a premeditated murder, lying to police and no doubt many other charges relating to COVID regulations, impersonation and so on."

As the blood drained from Jennifer's face, Thomas made his pitch.

"I know you did these things and I know why and I will have the final piece of evidence on Monday, when the Department of Health sends me the record of the various times and places where you checked in with your COVID pass, including at Restaurant Gironde in Bordeaux at about nine o'clock last Saturday evening, when you should have been grieving your son and when Caroline King was driving away from Monpazier, having murdered her husband."

In the shocked silence that followed, Thomas addressed Jennifer for the final time.

"I'm telling you all this because I'm giving you a final chance to confess, before it's too late. I have a tiny shred of sympathy for you, Jennifer, so take advantage of that while you can."

* * *

When Jennifer was finished with her confession, she was quietly taken into custody by the two gendarmes Thomas had requested from Bergerac.

Thomas asked everyone to wait in the Mairie until he returned with, he promised, the whole story.

Two more Bergerac gendarmes, accompanied Thomas to arrest Caroline King.

They found her in the hotel lounge, reading that month's *Frieze* magazine.

"Hello."

"Good day, Madame King."

"Oh, I think we're way beyond the Madame King stage, don't you, Thomas?"

"You know we arrested Jennifer Oakes then?"

"It's a small village; news travels fast. What was it?"

"I suspect you know, Caroline." Thomas replied, lowering himself into a chair beside her.

"The damn restaurant! Right?" She saw him nod his agreement.

"I should have changed my plan. The restaurant wasn't really needed anyway, she could have taken a sandwich back to her hotel room; but no, I just had to over-elaborate, didn't I? Idiot! Was there anything else?"

"The snooker cue. It had been wiped clean that morning. Yours were the only prints."

"Ah! Loulou; ever methodical. And I should never have taken the forged paintings – that must have really narrowed down your list of suspects. Well, I don't feel so bad now. Loulou – what a woman; what a cleaner! I warned him, you know, about Camille. She tricked him."

"How so?" asked Thomas.

"In London, he never kept a model for more than a month or two. They'd all be on the pill, of course, and London has an endless supply of long-legged girls with perfect tits called Tiffany, or Amber, or Crystal."

She laughed mirthlessly, "I mean the girls, not their tits; although, you never know with these girls, maybe they gave their breasts names – Tweedledum and Tweedledee, Thelma and Louise. They were brainless, for the most part. They had no inner life, so sitting still for two hours? No, thank you. They'd offer Tony sex out of boredom. And there were so many of them. Neverending. Monpazier, not so much.

"He'd always hated it when they got needy, clingy; and he'd drop them. But here? What were his options? It used to be very different, you know. He'd get them in, give them what they had to wear, pose them, take a dozen or so photographs and they were on their way home in under an hour. But it got to be too easy, a drug, I suppose.

"I told him, after he'd been banging Camille for six months or so. 'She'll get pregnant, just watch. If she doesn't work it out, her scheming brother will.' But he wouldn't listen."

She stood up and smoothed her skirt.

"I could have done that, you know, tricked him into being a father. But I didn't, I couldn't. Oh, I thought about it, years and years ago, but …"

"Sit down, Caroline. There's no rush, let's have a coffee; I want to know more. And it may be a while before you have another really nice coffee."

* * *

Thomas once again invited his team to sit together, this time including Kiki Le Roux who had arrived, having missed the earlier excitement.

"Here is how it happened, and just as important, *why* it happened.

"Caroline King resented Grant's affairs much more than she pretended. But she was absolutely distraught when she heard about Camille's baby. When she and Grant first lived together, she desperately wanted a child. He kept putting her off until, by the time he moved here, she was forty-one and she felt that her time had passed. Then, when she began experiencing symptoms of her menopause, she began to feel that she was getting old and to resent even more Grant's continuing affairs with young women. She saw a future where she would lose her role, her status, and would be humiliated by an endless series of Grant's mistresses.

"Learning that Grant was to become a father with Camille's child tipped her over the edge, especially after she had warned him that this would happen. All the accumulated resentment now spilled over, and she decided to seek a new life while she was still attractive. She knew that legally she was entitled to nothing if she simply left Grant; they weren't married after all, or even in a civil partnership. She would be dependent on Grant's charity to settle some money on her. And anyway, she wanted to punish him for the endless humiliations and for denying her a child all those years ago. She decided to murder him.

"Grant told her years ago that he had provided for her in his will, alongside other beneficiaries. She found out that French law would give half of all of his French estate to the child, no matter what any British will said. She faced losing a hell of a lot of money in the French bank, and half the value of the finished paintings. She had no idea about Grant's move to transfer ownership of his paintings to the Swiss company."

Thomas paused for a moment before making his next comment.

"I don't know how you all feel; but having watched the video material and seen the way he talked about her, I suspect that Grant would have been extremely generous in a settlement. We'll never know, I suppose.

"She decided to kill Grant, steal the paintings and get them to England where they would be outwith his French estate. By the way, Caroline had no idea about the safe. She did, of course, know about the secret compartment for the forged paintings, but not about the other section. At least she had a better excuse than I did, she was only overlooking a portion of the empty space; I missed most of it! And, as his business partner, for his legitimate business anyway, she had access to the Crédit Agricole account. It was Caroline who moved the money on Friday, not to steal it exactly, but to get it out of France before Grant's death.

"She also knew, because they had become close friends, what Susan discovered yesterday from Jennifer Oakes's ex-husband: that Jennifer blamed Grant for her son's suicide. Her son's account of their one meeting was that Grant had brushed him off, telling him that he had no talent and not to waste his time. When the young man killed himself, she became fixated on somehow getting her revenge, but she lacked the killer instinct, so her emotions just festered for years. When Caroline told her that she was leaving Grant, Jennifer confessed her true feelings about him and Caroline recruited her to her scheme.

"The two women are somewhat similar in height and weight and, while both are elegant and attractive, neither has particularly distinctive features. Some time ago, they went shopping together and bought identical Ralph Lauren outfits. When Brunel and Lefèvre first saw Caroline, her clothes, and particularly her hat, imprinted themselves on them. This was a very clever touch. If we had been given a description, or saw a fuzzy motorway image, we would be swayed by the hat and believed the substitution.

"It was Jennifer who drove to Bordeaux in Caroline's car, using the motorway; Jennifer who paid the tolls, was captured by the cameras, went shopping for a new handbag and checked into a small hotel chosen because it had no night porter. All day, Jennifer used Caroline's debit card and PIN to pay for everything – including dinner in a restaurant."

Thomas paused for dramatic effect.

"Where she unthinkingly showed her *own* health pass. Remember, Caroline told us that both she and Grant were vaccine refuseniks, which didn't matter too much until the latest restrictions came in, requiring vaccinations to obtain the health pass for restaurants and bars. And, by the way, that's why Grant suddenly started shopping – he couldn't eat out. And why he kept inviting his friends round for snooker or to watch the rugby matches – he couldn't go to the brewery. And that's also why Caroline had a panic attack when we were interviewing her, Susan. As she told us about not being able to go into restaurants, she suddenly realised the problem with the Bordeaux story. She recognised her mistake, but it was too late to do anything about it. At the time, we simply thought she was emotional about Grant's death. I think she started planning this whole thing the instant she learned about Camille's baby, and she could eat in restaurants then.

"It was her incredibly bad luck that the restaurant owner has a daughter called Geneviève or she might not have registered the fact that the name on the debit card didn't match the name on the health pass, but she did – she had wondered if Jennifer was the English version of her daughter's name. At the time, she didn't think too much about the mismatch and since the debit card payment processed without a hitch, she let it go until Le Roux tracked her down last night.

"While her alibi was being created, Caroline went to see Grant. She led the way upstairs to the balcony. Then she suggested a last drink for old time's sake before they parted for good and she asked for a bottle of the 2010 Angelus, her favourite, knowing that Grant would have to go down to the cellar to get the bottle. As soon as he went downstairs, she picked up a snooker cue and used it to push the painting out of alignment, knowing that Grant's OCPD would force him to straighten it out. She put the cue back in its rack and sat in one of the club chairs beside the coffee table, making sure that Grant was in the chair directly facing the offending picture. Grant came back with the opened bottle of wine and two glasses and sure enough, as soon as he sat down, he saw the skewed picture, brought over a chair and went to straighten it out. And she pushed him to his death.

"She picked up the chair, sat on it and pushed herself backwards, scratching the floor – another clever touch. She wiped the chair and kicked it over again.

"She sat back in her club chair, sipped a glass of wine until she calmed down, and to kill some time. Then she wiped down her chair, went downstairs to wash her glass and pour away the rest of the superb wine, put both glasses back where they belonged and took the empty bottle with her. She didn't have to worry too much about incidental fingerprints, given how much time she spent in the house. The snooker cue was a special case, and despite all her meticulous planning, she forgot about Madame Brouzet, who had carefully wiped any old fingerprints off the cue that morning.

"Anyway, she let herself out the back door and used the *carreyrous* to cross the village to the studio, dropping the empty wine bottle in the village recycling bin on the way. She let herself in with her own key and disabled the alarm. She picked out the nine paintings she wanted, and, of course knowing all about the forgeries and the hidden key, she removed the those as well.

"Now came the riskiest part of her getaway. Jennifer had already parked her car on the other side of the street. Caroline had to move the pictures across the street to the car and hope that no-one was coming out of the brewery or Bistro 2 while she was doing this. She got lucky it seems. She reset the alarm, then drove on Route Nationale, avoiding tolls and cameras, to meet Jennifer.

"Meanwhile, Jennifer finished her meal and drove to the rendezvous, also using the RN. The conspirators met up, Jennifer gave Caroline back her debit card, the hotel key and the code for the night entry lock, before getting back in her own car to drive home. Caroline drove her car to Bordeaux, dropping the paintings off en route, in a small 24-hour self-storage unit she had rented in Bordeaux, intending to return in a month or so and somehow spirit them out of the country and the clutches of Camille Pichon and her baby. That done, she drove to the hotel, let herself in, slept, badly one hopes, and flew to London the next morning, complete with her new handbag, chosen by Jennifer, of course.

They all pondered Thomas's story until André had a question.

"Capitaine, you told Jennifer that her story would fall apart on Monday when we got her records from the Ministry of Health, but there are no records kept of people being scanned into restaurants."

"Ah, yes. Thank Sargeant Howard for that. She pointed out that being English, Jennifer would assume that her details were being recorded, they call it 'Track and Trace' in England apparently. I lied. And she fell for it."

* * *

Monday, March 14, 2022

On Monday morning, it seemed that Thomas's phone in his Bordeaux office would never stop ringing.

The first call was from Susan, on her way to the airport for her flight home.

"I just called to say goodbye and thank you, Captain. I appreciate that you allowed me to become part of the team when you could easily have frozen me out. It has been a real education."

"Not at all, it's me who should be thanking you, you were a huge help and a true colleague. And maybe there are times when we could be a little less formal with each other, Susan."

She laughed. "Say goodbye to the rest of the guys for me. And you never know, maybe we'll get to work together again one day. Oh! One more thing. The night of the match, I saw into your bedroom. I saw your Welsh rugby shirt lying on the bed. But don't worry, Thomas, your secret's safe with me. Probably. Bye!"

The next calls were congratulations, from Procureur Lenglet and Juge Sandral. Then he received a rather wistful call from a still upset Lucy Morrison, now back in London.

"It's going to be awesome for my career, we've already had requests to license the programme from all over the world, and it isn't out of editing yet! But still..."

She paused before continuing. "He was such an interesting man, don't you think, Captain? Not perfect, but fascinating. And what a life!"

"I agree completely, Lucy. He didn't deserve what happened. Hold on a minute, I'll be right back."

Thomas crossed his office to close his door before returning to his chair and picking up the phone again.

"Are you still there? Good. What I'm about to tell you is completely off the record. You can use it, but not a hint about where you got the information. It will all become public in due course, but it would be a shame if your film, and Tony Grant's story, didn't have a proper ending."

And with that, Thomas told Lucy about the nature of Tony's forgeries, who he sold them to, and where most of the money ended up.

"Oh my God! He was donating millions of pounds to children's charities every year? And stealing money from rich hypocrites who thought they were buying paintings stolen by the Nazis? Oh my God, this is so great! Captain, there were rumours that you brought in an art expert. Can I use him? I mean, on screen. The programme won't go out for weeks, at least a month. Will everything be in the open by then?"

"Oh yes. I'll text you the professor's details. Tell Tony's story properly, Lucy."

"Oh, I will, I will. And Captain, thank you, truly." She blew him a noisy kiss down the phone.

Thomas laughed as he put down the receiver. Lucy's voice was already regaining the enthusiasm he had heard on the videos.

For the fifth or sixth time he turned back to his final report which had to be finished that day. He wanted to give due prominence to the role that Eloise Brunel had played in their efforts. However, he hadn't made much more progress when the phone rang yet again.

"Thomas, it's me again. You're not going to believe this."

"Believe what, Susan?"

"I'm at the airport; I just received a call from London. Biamonte called. His assistant, Geoffrey, has disappeared. Geoffrey Percival Montague, GPM! Geoffrey was Grant's secret dealer for the forgeries. He took off on Thursday, as soon as Biamonte left for the funeral. UK emigration have him on a flight to the Maldives, but the authorities there claim to have no record of his arrival. Maybe he has two passports, maybe someone was paid to look the other way, or to forget to record his arrival. I doubt we'll ever know. There's no extradition treaty; and anyway, he could have flown on to somewhere else by now."

Thomas sat back in his chair. Of course, he thought, it wouldn't be difficult for Geoffrey to make sure he was in charge of taking delivery of the forgeries; perhaps they were timed for when Lorenzo was away on business. And Geoffrey would have the contacts and the credibility with buyers. Clever.

Thomas had just decided to find an empty office to borrow when the phone's urgent ring demanded his attention yet again.

"Coman!" he snapped.

The person on the other end said nothing for a moment, then a soft, uncertain, Scottish voice asked in atrocious French, "Is that Capitano Coman? Of France police?"

Thomas replied in English, trying to rein in his exasperation. "Yes, this is Captain Coman, how can I help you?"

"Oh, thank goodness! My name is Alistair MacKenzie, of Edinburgh, Scotland. You see, Captain, every year my wife and I go hill walking in the Isles, that's the Western Isles; Skye, Uist, Harris and so on. We had a wonderful time on Mull last year and we thought to return again, and indeed…"

"Mr MacKenzie, I am sorry to interrupt, but I am *extremely* busy at this moment. Can you *please* tell me why you called."

"I am sorry, Captain, people tell me I do wander, verbally that is, as well as…"

"MR MACKENZIE!"

"Sorry! I am the lawyer for Anthony Gallagher, also known as Tony Grant. I only read of his death yesterday, upon my return. It's called 'digital detox' I'm told. We had no computers, and our phones were turned off. There were so many messages! Including from the Procurator Fiscal herself, instructing me to phone you. That was on Friday I believe. I am so very sorry, Captain."

"Well, you have my full attention now, Mr MacKenzie, what can you tell me about Mr Grant, or Mr Gallagher, if you prefer."

"Oh, I have no preference, Captain. A man may call himself whatsoever he pleases, as long as it is not with intent to deceive or defraud. There I go again! I have the Last Will and Testament of Mr Gallagher, as redrafted in 2011. I am also in receipt of a Special Delivery letter, signed for in my recent absence by my neighbour, Mr Seaton, a very nice man. It is a letter from Mr Gallagher, although on this occasion signed as Tony Grant, no matter. The letter contains details of a company recently established by my client for the purpose of taking ownership of certain works of art, together with instructions on replacing the beneficial owner, in the event of his death or incapacity.

"The letter also asked me to add certain codicils to his will, for his signature on his next visit to Edinburgh."

"I see, Mr MacKenzie. And can you tell me who the beneficiaries of the will are?"

"Certainly, as you are a duly constituted police authority and given the nature of your investigations. I will paraphrase in order to be brief. There are certain bequests to individuals and organisations:

Miss Caroline King gets Anthony's share in their joint property in London. A Madame Brouzet of Monpazier receives 100,000 euros net of tax, with the money going to her son in the event she predeceases Anthony. Miss King becomes Anthony's artistic executor and is paid £200,000 per annum for that role. Madame le maire of Monpazier gets €100,000 to distribute to organisations dedicated to the artistic, cultural and sporting life of the village and its inhabitants.

And finally, Bière de la Bastide and Chez Minou of Monpazier are each to receive €500 to finance drinks on the first anniversary of Anthony's death."

Mr Mackenzie paused, and Thomas thought he may have had a drink of water before he continued.

"The remainer of the estate, including all future income, is bequeathed in four equal portions:

One, to Miss Caroline King during her lifetime.

Two, to Mrs Lorna Hamilton, née Cruikshank during her lifetime or that of her husband, Mr Andrew Hamilton.

Three, to a schedule of charities appended to the Testament.

Four, Anthony wished to establish the Maggie Gallagher Art Scholarship, which finance a young artist for one year and provide him or her with exclusive use of Mr Gallagher's studio in Monpazier during that year. There is also a provision providing for the costs and maintenance of the studio in perpetuity.

The Testament also provides that, in the event of Miss King or Mrs Hamilton pre-deceasing Mr Gallagher, their portion will be divided equally between the surviving heirs.

Now, Captain, if I may anticipate your next question, Miss King's portion of the estate will be held in escrow, pending the outcome of her trial. If she is found guilty, it will be as if she did, indeed, pre-decease Mr Gallagher, and her portion will pass to the other heirs. In Scotland, and indeed in most jurisdictions, a murderer may not benefit from the estate of their victim. The matter of her artistic executorship is much more complex and will have to be resolved by a judge."

"And the new codicil?"

"Of course, he never did sign it, but a court may well find that his instruction is sufficient to indicate Mr Gallagher's intent and instruct me to execute it. I will, in any event, bring it to the attention of his heirs. In my experience, people are often surprisingly honourable in these situations."

"And the codicil?"

"Oh dear, there I go again. The codicil relates solely to Mr Gallagher's French estate and the possible birth of a baby. A copy of the codicil was to be provided to Miss Camille Pichon of Monpazier as soon as it was executed. It is my intention to send her a copy today, if you would be so kind as to supply me with an address.

"In lengthy legalese, the document sets out two options.

Option A: On the birth of the child a DNA test is undertaken to establish the child's paternity.

If Anthony is not the father, the child gets nothing.

If Mr Gallagher is the father, the child will inherit 50% of the French estate. The remaining 50% plus up to €1 million will be used by Gide Loyrette Nouel, lawyers, to ensure that every euro of the inheritance is spent wholly, necessarily and exclusively for the direct benefit of the child until it reaches majority. Gide Loyrette Nouel are instructed to use any means necessary to ensure compliance, including use of private investigators. Failure to comply will result in legal action to have the child removed from Miss Pichon's guardianship.

Option B: Miss Pichon agrees, within seven days of receipt of the Codicil, to become and remain a responsible guardian of the child, meaning among other things, no more smoking or drinking until the child is one year old, then no smoking at home until the child is eighteen and no drug use ever. Again, Gide Loyrette Nouel will be instructed to use any means necessary to enure compliance. Furthermore, Miss Pichon will accept that Mrs Lorna Hamilton will be appointed as a co-guardian of the child. Mrs Hamilton will make further funds available at her sole discretion for the educational or other needs of the child and will settle €1 million on the child if and when Mrs Hamilton deems appropriate, on a date after the child reaches majority. Under this option however, the remaining 50% of the French estate will be paid to Miss Pichon over eighteen years for her personal use. No DNA test of the baby will be required.

"In simple terms, Captain, if she agrees to behave, Camille will receive an income for eighteen years for herself; and the child will be extremely well provided for, all irrespective of the true identity of the father. Alternatively, she will have no access whatsoever to the money for her personal benefit and she will be hounded night and day to ensure her complete compliance with the requirements of responsible motherhood. And there is also the possibility that neither she nor the child receive anything."

* * *

Thomas was in a pensive mood as he carried an armful of papers into an empty office along the corridor. If only Tony had told Caroline about the Swiss company and the will. If only he had been more attuned to the vulnerability of Daniel Oakes. But he reflected, as his Welsh grandmother had often said, 'If ifs and ands were pots and pans, there'd be no work for tinkers' hands.'

'What the hell does that actually mean?' he wondered as he settled down to work.

Author Notes

Monpazier has been home to the author and his wife for fifteen years. It is a beautiful and remarkable village with more than its fair share of restaurants, bars, cafés, interesting and practical shops and ateliers of talented practitioners of various arts and crafts. Visit monpazier.fr for more information.

The superb building housing the Restaurant Chapître is, in real life, an excellent boulangerie and café. The handsome house opposite, portrayed as Jennifer's home, is a real building. However, the author has no knowledge whatsoever of its interior or its real-life inhabitants. The descriptions of Tony's house and his studio are entirely fictitious. The other places mentioned are real, including the salamander.

The cover was designed by my brother, Stephen McPhee, of Glasgow, Scotland. Together with his wife, Rona, he makes a brief cameo appearance in these pages.

The Hawksbys, Carole and Olivier and Jan and Ted are real people, friends of the author. The pétanque group really exists, but Monpazier's mayor is a charming man and not a helpful, but ambitious, lady. All other named characters are entirely fictitious and bear no resemblance to real people, alive or dead.

Regular inaccurate references to Thomas's mother and to Tony as being English are not mistakes, simply a reflection of reality.

I took small liberties with the schedule for 2022's rugby Six Nations and big ones with BA and Ryanair flight schedules.

The Venice Biennale hosts major national exhibitions in permanent pavilions some way from Piazza San Marco. In 2013 France was represented by Anri Sala, Albanian-born but resident for some years in France.

I accelerated the speed at which the gendarmes could obtain access to financial records and decelerated the speed of Monpazier's internet service.

The forged painting on page 59 and its catalogue entry were originated by ChatGPT, which was also used for research into French police structures and procedures, plausible forged artists and relevant charities. No narrative text was produced, edited or otherwise influenced by ChatGPT or any other AI program.

Monpazier
July 2025

Information on the author's other works follows.

All are available from Amazon:

France: https://tinyurl.com/BMPFrance

UK: https://tinyurl.com/BMPUnitedKingdom

USA: https://tinyurl.com/BMPUSA

BUNCO

Painting a portrait of idyllic American suburbia before shifting gear to a gripping chase from Long Island to the seductive streets of Barcelona, *Bunco* is a story of resilience, justice and second chances – with a delicious final twist.

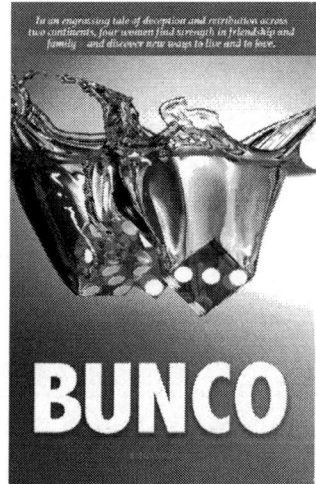

A captivating story, beautifully written, ... I could almost taste the food and the cava. Truly enjoyable in every way. ...very hard to put this one down! *Amazon 5 star review*

... About a third of the way through the book, the storyline takes an unexpected twist and I could not put the book down. I have not visited Barcelona, but it is now on my bucket list. ... *Amazon 5 star*

A great first novel ... I particularly loved the section on Barcelona, which again showed great attention to detail by the author, who created a wonderful sense of atmosphere – and menace. By the end, I couldn't put this novel down ...! *Amazon 5 star*

... A fast-moving story fuelled by lies, lust, money and shocking crimes cleverly balanced with friendship, trust and love. The narrative captures character, time and place with skill and credibility. A gripping read with a nasty twist in the tail. *Amazon 5 star*

EMPRESS

When a deep-sea salvage team breaks into the bullion room of a sunken luxury liner, instead of a fortune in wartime gold they find a mysterious corpse, forever floating in a sealed tomb.

Inspired by a real-life mystery, **Empress** is the story of a legendary ship and two generations of a family whose fate is intimately bound up with her.

The saga travels from a shipyard on the River Clyde, to tropical seas where the rich and famous cruise in dazzling opulence, and to the perilous waters of the Atlantic Ocean during World War II. The dramatic conclusion is set against the glamorous backdrop of the Cannes Film Festival in the sixties.

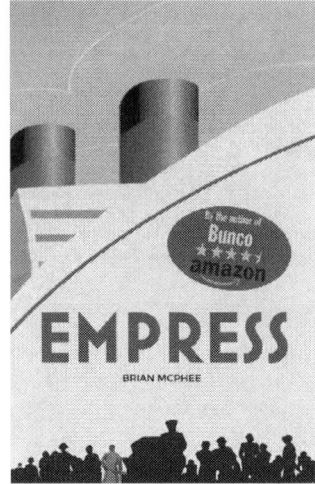

I have just finished reading Empress and the time is ten past four in the morning. It's a gripping read, and I thoroughly enjoyed it. *Amazon 5 star*

...The transition from the gritty realism of an impoverished and depression scarred Glasgow to a Hollywood lifestyle for the family at the centre of the story is as emotionally satisfying as it is extraordinary.... *Amazon 5 star*

Thoroughly enjoyed this. Something to please everyone... history, family saga, romance, and a thriller all rolled into one. I couldn't put it down! *Amazon 5 star*

An intriguing story which I enjoyed very much. The descriptions of working-class life in Glasgow then are particularly accurate. *Amazon 4 star*

ALL VISIBLE THINGS

An accidental discovery reveals an epic tale of romance and deception echoing down the centuries.

When a young researcher stumbles across the diary of an assistant to Leonardo da Vinci, we are immediately immersed in the dramas, personalities and intrigues surrounding the greatest genius in history.

We meet the inspiration behind some of Leonardo's greatest paintings; uncover the secret of Mona Lisa's smile and observe as a fateful deception leads to unforeseen consequences that continue to reverberate 500 years later. And we are witness to one of history's greatest love stories. The fascinating diary entries are interwoven with a dramatised account of the discovery of this remarkable document - and the even more astonishing aftermath.

...A fantastic read.... *Love Reading*

... A thoroughly well-written and enjoyable book with plenty of insight into Renaissance life and art. *Amazon 4 star*

... I felt as though I was living in the period. The juxtaposition between the ancient and modern periods was very well handled and the writing painted such a realistic picture of life in the time of Leonardo da Vinci... *Amazon 5 star*

I just loved this book from start to finish...An incredibly good read. *Love Reading*

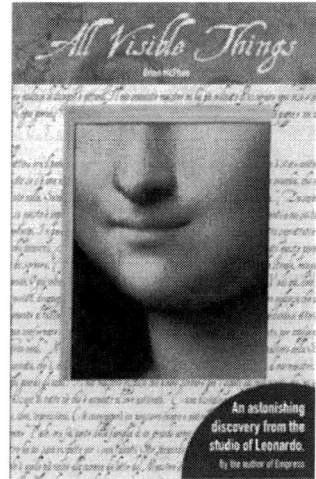

THE DANCE WE DANCED

*"No matter what, nobody
can take away the dances
you've already had."*

Gabriel García Márquez

Epiphanies, revelations – heightened
moments when we are intensely connected
to the world, and all of its endless
possibilities.

Mike Burton had such an experience, flying
his Hurricane during World War II.

But, is that it? Is that all there is? Is the rest of his life destined to be an
anti-climax? Or can he rediscover his lust for life with the woman he
loves?

From the author of *Empress* and *All Visible Things*, **The Dance We
Danced** is an engrossing tale of an epic twentieth-century life richly lived.

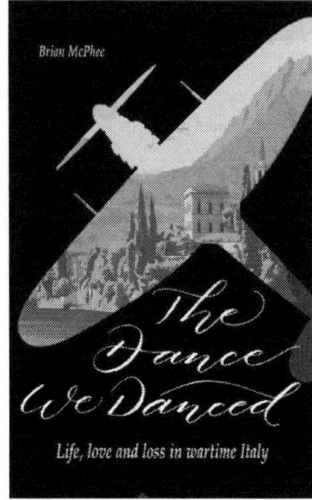

A COLD DISH & OTHER TALES
(Short Stories)

The 8:03

George is frantic to be on time for the 8:03. What can be so important that he comes close to a total breakdown when it seems he'll be late? And who is sending early morning text messages to his gorgeous young wife?

The Girl He Left Behind

Young love blossoms between an unlikely pair of star cross'd lovers during World War I. In this tale, that might even be true, individual lives play out against a background of epic struggles.

18B

What happens when you force total strangers to invade each other's personal space – and then subject them to all manner of stress? Normally, nothing much; we do it every time we fly in a plane. Sometimes, however, strange things do happen.

A Cold Dish

This tale confirms that, while revenge is indeed a dish best enjoyed cold, there can be lots of heat in its preparation.

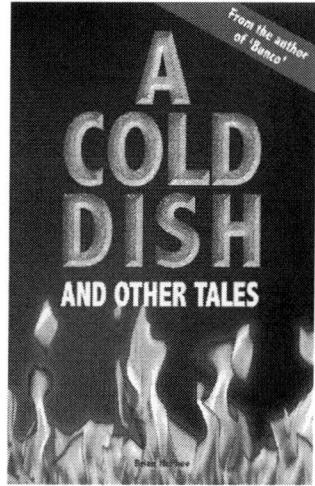

WORDS FOR THE WISE
(Quotations for Students)

'You should attempt to give the perception that you are intelligent. You don't actually have to be intelligent, if you can just create the perception. This can usually be accomplished by a reference to Kafka, even if you have never read any of his ... or her, works.'

Bob Newhart

Words For The Wise

Almost 900 useful, funny, unusual, thought-provoking, **QUOTATIONS For STUDENTS**

Edited by Brian McPhee

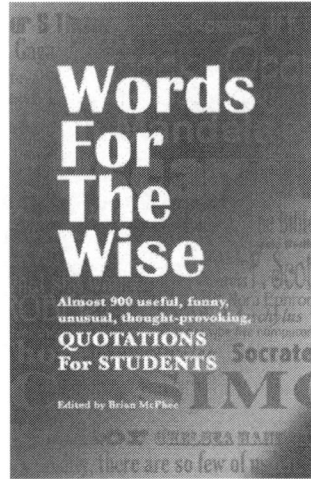

Just one of nearly 900 quotations by around 500 authors in **Words For The Wise**, each selected specifically for college and university students.

In our age of information overload, this slim volume is the perfect gift for students facing term papers, essays and other assignments, but with too little time to spend searching for that elusive quote to enliven and add spark to their efforts.

If you have ever found yourself struggling to remember the perfect quote for the occasion, this book is for you.

THE 50 WEALTHIEST PEOPLE OF ALL TIME

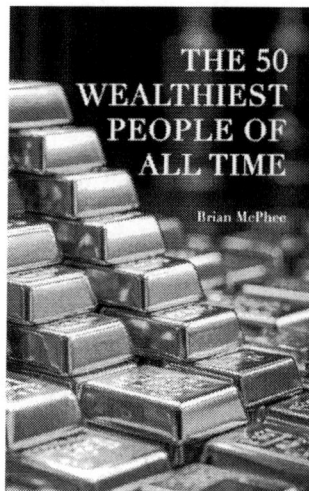

Who were the richest individuals in history — and how did they build fortunes that reshaped the world?

The 50 Wealthiest People of All Time is a bold, compelling journey through centuries of ambition, innovation, conquest, and extraordinary wealth. From ancient emperors to modern entrepreneurs, each detailed profile explores not just how these figures amassed their fortunes, but how they used – and sometimes abused – their power and influence.

This richly detailed volume doesn't stop with the top 50. It also unveils lists of royalty with unimaginable riches, criminals who turned corruption into empire, athletes and artists who broke the mould, and dynasties whose influence stretched across generations.

Clear, engaging, and packed with fascinating facts, *The 50 Wealthiest People of All Time* offers readers a sweeping look at money, power and legacy – and the individuals who stood at the centre of it all. Perfect for history lovers, business enthusiasts and anyone curious about how wealth has shaped human civilization.

A must-have addition to any personal library — and a brilliant gift for anyone who's ever wondered: just how rich is "richest of all time"?

100 AMAZING LIVES

Queens and emperors. Explorers and pirates. Writers, warriors, visionaries and revolutionaries.

Across two beautifully illustrated volumes, *100 Amazing Lives* introduces readers to remarkable men and women who shaped history through ambition, courage, compassion – and sometimes sheer daring. From Hatshepsut and Cleopatra to Peter the Great and Sojourner Truth, these are the true stories of people who refused to accept the world as it was and helped to forge something new.

Spanning from ancient Egypt to today, this collection offers an inspiring and refreshingly balanced portrait of history, highlighting extraordinary women and men from every background. Designed for curious young minds aged 10 to 15, these accessible mini-biographies encourage further exploration and a lifelong love of learning.

Perfect for thoughtful readers — and an ideal gift from parents and grandparents looking to spark imagination and ambition.

VOLUME I: FROM THE PHARAOHS TO SHAKESPEARE

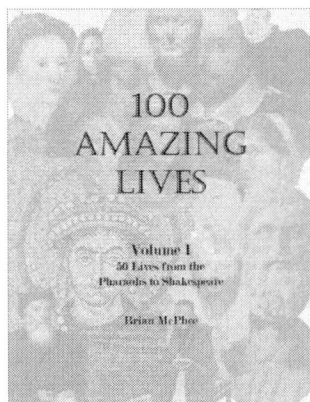

100 AMAZING LIVES

Volume I
50 Lives from the
Pharaohs to Shakespeare

Brian McPhee

Meet the trailblazers who made history long before Shakespeare put pen to paper. In Volume I discover fearless queens like Hatshepsut and Zenobia, wise philosophers like Confucius and Marcus Aurelius, daring adventurers like Marco Polo, and legendary leaders like Cleopatra.

Clear, lively writing and rich illustrations bring each story vividly to life, offering young readers a window into the dreams and struggles of extraordinary individuals who changed the course of human history. A perfect start for readers aged 10 to 15 with a hunger for true stories of adventure, wisdom and boldness.

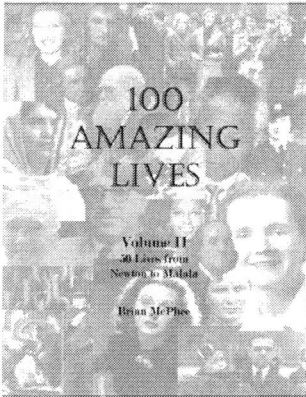

VOLUME II: FROM NEWTON TO MALALA

From the spark of scientific discovery to revolutions and global exploration, Volume II tells the stories of the remarkable people who shaped the modern age. Encounter thinkers like Isaac Newton, fighters for freedom like Giuseppe Garibaldi and Sojourner Truth, adventurers like Gertrude Bell, and even fearsome women pirates like Zheng Yi Sao.

These fascinating mini-biographies highlight courage, resilience, and the restless desire to challenge limits – told in a clear, engaging style and beautifully illustrated to captivate young readers aged 10 to 15.

Part of the 'Books to Inspire Young People' series

AN AMAZING ABC OF PEOPLE, PLACES & HISTORY THAT MAKE GREAT BRITAIN GREAT

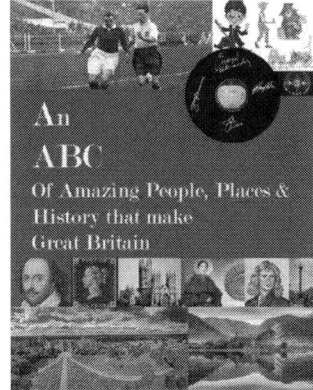

An ABC Of Amazing People, Places & History that make Great Britain

A celebration of the people, places, ideas, events and inventions that put the Great in Great Britain.

Discover the UK's astonishing legacy from Harry Potter to Shakespeare; penicillin to public health; Charles Darwin, Isaac Newton and Adam Smith.

At a time when patriotism is often misunderstood or maligned, this inspiring and lively book arms British teenagers with the facts, figures and stories that show why their country has made a greater contribution to human development than any other since Ancient Greece — and continues to shape the world today.

Whether it's welcoming foreign ideas or inventing new ones, Britain's legacy is a remarkable inheritance to embrace, celebrate and be inspired by.

As the introduction says: *"That this nation would produce Newton, Darwin, Shakespeare, the Beatles, Paddington Bear, football, penicillin and the Industrial Revolution would be beyond belief — if it wasn't true!"*

This book will inspire sceptical young Britons with quirky and compelling evidence of their unique inheritance of truly astounding achievements.

Perfect for teenagers – and for parents and grandparents who want to pass on pride based on realism, not myth.

Part of the 'Books to Inspire Young People' series

THE AMAZING WORLDS OF MYTH AND IMAGINATION

Step into a breathtaking journey through the greatest myths, legends and stories ever told. ***The Amazing Worlds of Myth and Imagination*** is a beautifully illustrated, full-colour celebration of human creativity – from the ancient gods of Egypt, Greece, and Rome to the mighty heroes of Norse sagas and the timeless adventures of Troy, the Odyssey, and the Epic of Gilgamesh.

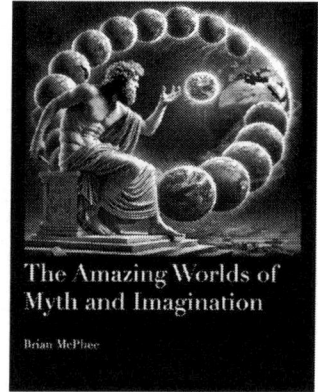

The Amazing Worlds of Myth and Imagination

Brian McPhee

This lavish large-format book brings the past to life, retelling legendary tales in a vivid, accessible style perfect for young adults with a thirst for knowledge. Explore the mysteries of King Arthur and the Round Table, then travel forward to the magical worlds crafted by modern masters such as Tolkien, C.S. Lewis, J.K. Rowling, Philip Pullman, and Frank Herbert.

Carefully curated and visually stunning, ***The Amazing Worlds of Myth and Imagination*** invites readers to discover how ancient myths continue to shape the stories we love today. Ideal for intelligent, curious young minds — and a perfect gift for parents, grandparents, and anyone who believes in the power of imagination.

Part of the 'Books to Inspire Young People' series

Printed in Great Britain
by Amazon

1087243a-4d48-4095-bee6-3b87c8262ea0R02